NOR
STAR

We All Need Something To Light The Way

ETHAN DAY

Praise for
NORTHERN STAR

"The book combines humor and sadness just as life does - but what really stands out for me are the characters. This is the kind of book that you can read again and again."
Reviews by Amos Lassen

★★★★★

"*Northern Star* was a great read that I highly recommend. I loved this book. It's sexy, charming and funny."
5 Stars from Live Your Life Buy the Book Reviews

★★★★★

"Overall, an outstanding book. The reader is allowed to feel the emotions of all of the characters instead of simply being told what they are feeling. Not many authors can pull that off but Ethan Day does it brilliantly."
5 Stars from On Top Down Under Book Reviews

NORTHERN STAR

We All Need Something To Light The Way

ETHAN DAY

WILDE CITY PRESS

WILDE CITY PRESS
www.wildecity.com

Northern Star © 2013 Ethan Day
Published in the US and Australia by Wilde City Press 2013

All rights reserved. No part of this book may be reproduced or transmitted in any form or by any means, electronic or mechanical, including photocopying, recording, or by any information storage and retrieval system, without permission in writing from the publisher. This book is a work of fiction. Names, characters, places, situations and incidents are the product of the author's imaginations or are used fictitiously. Any resemblance to actual events, locales, or persons, living or dead, is purely coincidental.

This book is licensed to the original purchaser only. Duplication or distribution via any means is illegal and a violation of International Copyright Law, subject to criminal prosecution and upon conviction, fines and/or imprisonment. This eBook cannot be legally loaned or given to others. No part of this eBook can be shared or reproduced without the express permission of the publisher.

Published by Wilde City Press

ISBN: 978-1-925031-56-0

Cover Art © 2013 Wilde City Press

DEDICATION

For anyone who's ever believed themselves undeserving of love and happiness.

Special thanks to Kris Jacen, Jambrea Jo Jones, Hank Edwards, JP Bowie & Jason Huffman-Black for being my Northern Star during the writing and editing of this book.

CHAPTER ONE ~ December

Staring at the screen on his phone, Deacon Miller periodically tapped it with his thumb each time the back light began the process of going dark in an attempt to save the life of his battery. His email was open and the words were staring back at him in stark black and white, yet he could also hear them playing over and over on a loop inside his head—the voice of his boyfriend for the past year and a half cutting into his chest like a hatchet.

I can't be with you anymore, Deacon, you're boring. There's no passion here, the sex has gotten really lame, and if I'm being totally honest, I'm not sure I ever even loved you. Either way, I'm pretty sure I don't particularly like you, at least not anymore.

Hollow—that was how it felt, like he'd been gutted. His insides had been ripped out and tossed aside like waste.

Placing his phone down on the bar, Deacon picked up the rocks glass, sucking down the rest of his Sapphire and tonic before signaling the bartender that he'd be having another. On the emotional scale of totally-horrific-life-lessons-learned, he was currently sitting somewhere between desperation and completely numb. He didn't intend to stop sucking down booze until he was safely situated completely on the numb side.

Alcohol had never really been his go-to solution for disappointment or disillusionment, having grown up with a raging alcoholic for a mother, but Seth's email had been particularly harsh. Some train wrecks were simply too horrible to stare down without a filter, and on this night, Deacon had buckled under the pressure and gin had become the filter of choice.

He'd always known deep down what a prick Seth could be—completely conceited and selfish. When they'd first met, his attraction to the man had actually embarrassed him. How could he have ever been into someone who had such a capacity for cruelty? What did that say about him?

Of course, Deacon had never been good when it came to paying attention to warning signs.

Winding Road Ahead? Curves keep life interesting, right?

Road Narrows!?! I'll go on a diet!

Dead End!!! Too little…too late.

He'd always been a bit of a 'village idiot' when it came to men. It didn't help matters that Seth had a rakish charm, which made the awful things he sometimes said seem like a slightly destructive form of foreplay. Seth had always tested the boundaries to see how far he could push before breaking them, and loving him had felt dangerous as a result.

Living life on the edge.

Glancing back down at his phone, Deacon read the words once again, and another wave of emptiness came over him. "I'd consider us…shattered."

"On your tab?" The bartender asked, setting down the freshly made cocktail.

"Yup," Deacon said, smiling slightly when his lips made a faint popping sound, like a cork being violently liberated from a wine bottle.

He did his best to ignore the judgmental expression on the bartender's face. Glancing down at the name tag, he shook his head, disgusted anyone named Clifford would be casting stones. The pious pity of Cliffy wasn't what Deacon needed at the moment, and he said as much with the dirty look he offered as a thank you for the drink.

They both turned, hearing a loud group of twenty-something's come stumbling into the hotel bar. They were all visibly wasted, and from what he could make out from their rather gregarious bitching, they'd each been bumped from their flight as a result of their intoxication.

More rejected casualties, redirected to purgatory via this airport adjacent, cheesy-ass hotel bar that hadn't been updated since the early nineties.

The burgundy and blue commercial grade fabric was rough

to the touch, as if designed to ensure you didn't make yourself comfortable. That combined with the brass railings that ran along the bar and atop the booths located along the far wall, all the mirrors and glassware dangling from above, the entire room screamed Loser-ville.

"And I am right at home with my fellow loser-residents," he muttered.

Deacon could practically smell the sweaty desperation of yester-year that hung in the air like the scent of stale smoke, from what had no doubt been the scene of many a one-night hookup over the years. Chewing on a chunk of ice, he took a moment to glance around the room at the rest of the poor schlubs.

Two gray-haired business men types were huddled at the far end of the bar. One was a bit of a chunk but had an abundance of snow on the roof. His business-bud was more fit but had little roof left at all. The lights above the bar reflected off the top of the shiny bald-headed portion of his receding hairline, and it dawned on Deacon that perhaps no man was allowed to have it all.

"Fat man, tall man, big dick, small, ain't nobody gonna have it all," he mumbled, snickering to himself.

He was certainly beginning to feel less pain thanks to the alcohol.

Perusing the rest of the room, attendance was pretty sparse. There were only a few other random couples and a handful of singles like himself of various ages and sexes nursing cocktails. All making an attempt to avoid the solitude of a lonely hotel room on the eve of Christmas Eve.

They all looked as tragic as he felt, save the older guy who just walked in. He was kinda hot. Deacon watched the man shake the snow off his coat before hanging it on a peg just inside the entrance. He smiled warmly at Deacon as he made a beeline for the bar, taking a seat on the stool next to him.

"Guess I shoulda asked," the guy said, waving at the bartender. "Was anyone sitting here?"

"Nope," Deacon said. "Seat's all yours, pal."

Mr. Smiley was hunky, in that hetero, somebody's-father kinda way. Late thirties, he guessed. Very athletic looking, the drool-worthy type you'd expect to find coaching his son's little league team.

Deacon imagined all the other mommies spent more time watching the coach than they did their kiddies—probably a few of the daddies too, for that matter.

For some reason, that thought made him chuckle.

His new neighbor was dressed more casually in jeans, a black thin cotton sweater and a pair of well-worn leather snow boots.

Very butch.

The sweater looked new, but the man was slightly weathered in the best sense of the word with a bit of gray speckled throughout his sideburns. His face had the slightest hint of stubble, which suited the masculine jawline and chin dimple.

Salesman, Deacon figured, already turned off by that thought. Of course, if he promised not to speak, Deacon would definitely be willing to work the bod.

Smiley's light brown hair was well manicured, longer on top and combed back with enough product to keep everything in its place. Deacon had just begun to imagine what he looked like naked when Mr. Smiley gave him a sideways glance and began to grin once more.

Deacon turned away, unsure if he was embarrassed or if he'd had too many cocktails to care. He was aware that he should've been, though, staring at a total stranger for that length of time, as if he'd actually been considering the possibility.

The stir of activity between his legs was evidence that he had been.

Why not? Nothing like random sex with a stranger to make a boy feel better about himself. *Not like I'm in a relationship anymore.*

He cringed through the sharp pain in his chest and sucked down the rest of his drink, once again, signaling the barkeep with the clinking sound of ice against glass as he gently shook it.

Again with Clifford's judgey sigh?

The rat bastard.

Get a different job if you can't handle the sight of intoxication in process. He glanced over at Smiley to see the man was staring at the television hanging on the wall behind the bar. A basketball game was on, but the volume was muted so it didn't interfere with the nauseating vocals-with-jazz being piped in through the sound system.

Like that wouldn't be enough to require one or two extra cocktails.

The current selection was some bastardized-rapage of a Carpenters' tune, Top of the World, he thought, which seemed a little insensitive considering his current situation—having been dumped and all.

Probably Clifford's doing—the little weasel had it out for him.

Deacon sneered, glancing up at the speaker in the ceiling above his head.

The crappy song choice aside, they'd apparently hired the horrifically off-key singers featured on *Dancing with the Stars,* adding insult to injury. What asshole gave those tone-deaf fuckers a recording contract?

Stupid show.

Seth never missed an episode. Perhaps that was the silver lining to the knowledge Deacon was apparently an un-passionate, cold-dead-fish-fuck in the sack? He'd never have to sit through another episode of *DWTS*.

In an attempt to be a little stealthier, Deacon took to further examining Mr. Smiley utilizing the mirror behind the bar.

Definitely a hot dad type. A real man, no doubt. Bet *he* doesn't watch totally gay reality television. Of course he unfortunately probably fucks like a straight man too—just shoves it on in and starts pounding away. Deacon hated that.

He sure was sexy, though, like the older male models featured in the back of his mother's JC Penney catalog, which Deacon used to jack off to as a teenager—the ones posing in their Jockeys.

He smiled at the memory while attempting to ignore the wood growing in his trousers.

The guy's probably married.

Clifford reluctantly placed Deacon's fourth cocktail onto the bar.

"Tab it," Deacon said, not giving Clifford the opportunity to recommend any other alternatives. "I'm staying in the hotel, dude. Not driving, so tab it."

Clifford held up his hands like he was shocked by the insinuation that he gave a good goddamn either way, which made Deacon wonder if he hadn't been imagining the whole thing. Perhaps he was mildly sensitive at the moment? The knockdown, drag-out with his mother followed by having been ruthlessly dumped by his boyfriend via email had caused a mental breakdown, and as a result, he'd been forced to invent someone who cared about his well-being?

That was a particularly sad and wretched thought. Poor Cliffy's getting the raw end of that imaginary deal.

Need to try thinking about something else.

Deacon glanced back into the mirror behind the bar, deciding his new neighbor on the stool to his left would do in a pinch.

Mirror, mirror on the wall, should I fuck Smiley in a bathroom stall?

He grinned to himself, deciding one thing was certain. Deacon was seldom wrong when it came to sniffing out the gay, regardless of the married-het vibe the man exuded. That meant Mr. Smiley was either bi or a gay man who'd gotten married back in the day and now trolled bars looking for cock while on business trips.

It was a particular breed of gay that Deacon didn't like thinking about—the self-loathers. They depressed him. Fortunately, thanks to Seth, he was already depressed, so fuck it if he gave a shit at this point.

Taking in his own reflection in an attempt to ascertain his physical state, he smirked, deciding while he might not be the hottest piece of ass out there, he was indeed attractive in that cloned-gay-way. Deacon wasn't overtly fem, or at least he didn't think so, but he had the look—over-primped and manscaped down to the nearest centimeter. Too tan, despite the fact it was the dead of winter and he wasn't visiting from Florida or southern California.

All he was missing was some glitter.

With well-gelled, dark hair and sharp blue eyes, he was borderline pretty, but Deacon spent enough time in the gym to keep his body tight. He'd been a fat kid and teased to the point he was now overly sensitive about his waistline as a result. It had become an unhealthy obsession.

Deacon utilized the mirror to glance back over at Smiley only to discover he was being watched. He wondered how Seth would feel if he took Mr. Faux-het up to his room and cold-dead-fish fucked him.

That'd learn him.

His attention was diverted back to the loud lot now laughing hysterically at their friend who was so drunk she'd limply slipped out of the booth and onto the floor underneath their table. He couldn't imagine how they'd managed to find their gate in the first place, but that, no doubt, made not being allowed to board even more upsetting.

Deacon had been bumped from his flight too. Though in his case, it had been self-inflicted. By the time they began announcing his flight was overbooked, he'd been staring at his Dear John email for a good forty minutes in disbelief. When they asked for volunteers to opt for a later flight, Seth's evil words finally sank in…he no longer had anyone to rush home to. Then his later flight got cancelled due to the blizzard.

This had been his first trip home to Detroit since he'd left six years before.

If you could call it home.

His mother, Patricia, was pretty bad off, facing real jail time after her third DUI in too many years. Patty's latest piece of shit trailer-trash boyfriend had run off to boot, leaving he and his half-sister, Ashley, to deal with the fallout. It was difficult to feel bad for his mother considering the last time he'd seen her, Patty had told him she'd rather have a dead son than a gay one.

Yeah, a real sweetheart, proof that some people shouldn't be allowed to breed.

Were it not for Ashley, pleading for him to come home for Christmas in the first place, Deacon wouldn't have bothered. He'd lasted a day and a half and was now departing two days before Christmas due to the incessant fighting.

Patty drank so much and so often that Deacon was never sure what was the booze and what was truly Patty, and though he decided to blame the booze for her general evilness, he'd made the decision to leave Detroit years before and had never looked back…until now.

So he'd gone from family drama to boyfriend drama and now found himself all alone in the world once again. The fact Seth had sent an email should have been Deacon's first clue that something was up, the man was addicted to texting. Perhaps Seth decided a breakup message of *I hate you* was too harsh for a text?

From where Deacon sat, fewer words could've been utilized.

The apartment they'd shared back in Chicago was Seth's, and he'd sweetly mentioned that he'd be on a cruise over the next week and could Deacon please have all his shit moved out by the time he got back.

Nice to know Seth was worried enough about his well-being to give him so much time to find a new place to live. The entire day had pretty much sucked ass, and he'd been in a daze since getting out of bed that morning. He couldn't even remember walking up to the counter at the gate and throwing himself onto his sword for the rest of the poor schmucks who were attempting to make it home for the holidays to their so-called loved ones.

People were entirely too horrible to one another in general, Deacon wasn't sure why he kept trying to connect with anyone at all. It inevitably brought him nothing but heartache.

"From boyfriend to bitterness in…" He glanced down at his watch. "Three hours and forty-two minutes. Impressive."

Deacon sighed, chuckling sarcastically over his disappointment, taking another quick sip. He became aware that someone else was snickering right along with him. There was no one sitting on his right, so that only left one other option, Mr. Smiley.

"Sorry, didn't mean to eavesdrop on your little rant there," Smiley said, though the expression on his face said otherwise.

"You look real torn up about it." Deacon smirked, shaking his head when Smiley began laughing harder.

The bartender had placed a Bud Light long neck on the bar in front of Smiley. Deacon was fairly certain he'd never actually ordered it, which meant his neighbor was somewhat of a regular.

Probably trolls for trade here a lot.

"From boyfriend to bitter, huh? Sounds like trouble. He dump you or the other way around?"

"He eviscerated me, if you must know." Deacon took a sip from his glass and scooped up his phone with his free hand. He tapped on the screen, bringing it to life once more before reading the same horrible paragraph aloud so Smiley could be brought up to speed.

"Jeez," Smiley said. "That was…wow." He held up his beer bottle to toast, clinking it against Deacon's glass. "I'm impressed you're in as good a shape as you appear to be. Did you love him?"

"It hurts, so I musta, right?" Deacon shrugged, not waiting for an answer before asking, "Say, what's your name anyway? Can't keep calling you Mr. Smiley in my head, it's distracting."

"Names Steve, Steven actually, but most people call me Steve."

"I'm Deacon Miller," he said, before adding flatly, "nice to meet you, Steven Actually."

"Funny," he said.

"Hey just 'cause I'm gay and newly eviscerated doesn't mean I'm tacky. If we end up doing it later, I wanna know your last name."

One of Smi—Steve…one of Steve's eyebrows arched as he took a swig off his beer bottle. "It's Steele. Steven Steele is my name."

Before he could manage further comment, Deacon interrupted, "Your name is Steve Steele?"

"Um…yeah?" Steve seemed confused. "Have we met before?"

"What are you, porn star or car salesman?"

Steve laughed, blushed slightly as well. "Car salesman, though I'm surprisingly flattered you thought I could pass for a porn star."

"I'll admit that porn seemed less likely in Detroit, but hey, who am I to judge, you know?"

"Um…okay," Steve grinned.

Deacon cringed. "That made sense in my head. Too much liquor, I guess."

"Considering the day you've had, I'd say you're entitled."

"Very kind of you, considering you're a car salesman."

"Ouch," Steve said. "I own the dealership if that helps raise my likability quotient."

"Might be worse, but I'm not really thinking clearly at this point. Sorry. I'm not usually this rude."

"It's okay, I am kind of a dick, too." Steve grinned as Deacon stared back at him in shock over the admission. "What is it you do? Cure nuns with cancer?"

Deacon laughed over the sarcastic delivery. "I'm a nobody, one of those cashier drones, I work at a Target."

Steve smiled, turning on his stool to face Deacon. "Bet you look awfully cute in those red shirts and khakis. Though I could offer a few suggestions for where they place that bull's eye."

Deacon laughed. "Knew I wasn't wrong about your proclivities."

He wiggled his eyebrows and took another swig off his beer. "How'd you manage to get time off working retail this close to

Christmas?"

"Had a family emergency kinda-thing."

"Everything okay, I hope? Aside from the ex dumping you, I mean. You know with your family?"

"Just peachy." Deacon faced Steve, propping up his elbow on the bar for support. "Say, you can't be too much of a dick, you at least asked how I'm doing, right?"

"Well, you did mention doing me before. I became infinitely more invested at that point."

Deacon started laughing.

"We'll blame your evil ex for your rude behavior." Steve said. "I take it he neglected to mention what a fucking asshole he was."

It wasn't a question, more of an assumption.

"No, I apparently suffer from low self-esteem and have an unfortunate attraction to loose-moraled men with little to no character."

"Sweet, so my chances of getting lucky just skyrocketed."

Deacon laughed but could feel the heat rushing to his cheeks. "Oh yeah, nothing short of you turning out to be a cannibalistic serial killer could spoil that, buddy."

Steve looked at him sideways. "At some point, I'll be inquiring about the fact your statement leaves the door open for non-cannibalistic serial killers, but at the moment. I'm too distracted by the possibility of sex to offer any further judgments."

"Makes sense." Deacon nodded. "Though as you heard before, I'm apparently not very passionate in the sack, so I wouldn't get overly excited if I were you."

"I don't buy that for one minute," he said.

"I'm not selling it, dude, so we're all good."

"Still don't believe it." Steve's voice lowered, getting slightly huskier in the process as he leaned closer and said, "Lips like yours were made for sucking cock, baby."

Steve's warm breath brushed across Deacon's face as he said the words, resulting in a positive reaction between his legs. He took a drink, using it as an excuse to break eye contact.

"That's the sweetest thing anyone's said to me all day."

"I'd be more impressed with myself were I not aware your ex shit all over you earlier today."

"So there's nowhere to go but up…up to my room…up to your room if you prefer…either way I can feel myself getting up as we speak so…whenever you're ready."

Steve smiled, showing off his pearly whites and the slash-like dimples in his cheeks. "I'm not actually staying here, so it will have to be your room if that's all right?"

"Christ, why would anyone come to this shit-hole if they weren't staying in the hotel?"

Clifford coughed, making sure Deacon was aware he'd overheard that. The guy was hacking into a lime with a paring knife, which made him seem slightly more menacing.

"My bad." Deacon shrugged an apology. "Put down the knife and step away from the fruit, buddy."

Clifford sighed, shaking his head and further signaling his disapproval.

"Let's just say that tonight is sort of an anniversary of mine and leave it at that," Steve said, picking at the label on his beer bottle. "I'm here…not celebrating so much as commiserating."

Deacon opened his mouth to demand more info but was interrupted by the drunkards in the booth.

"Hey, barkeep! It's almost Santa-fucking-Claus time already! How 'bout you be playin' some Christmas music? Let's cheer it up in here with a little Ho, Ho, Ho-ing!"

All the other idiots in his little group began clapping and cheering him on by heckling right along with him. Clifford rolled his eyes, reluctantly heading to the other end of the bar where he began fiddling with a remote. Magically the sound of sleigh bells filled the bar as Tony Bennett crooned 'Winter Wonderland'.

"Yeah, man, that's the stuff!" the guy screamed, before he began singing along…badly. "Come on, Scroogies, time to go caroling!"

Before anyone could manage to stop it, the table of women sitting in the next booth began singing, then it bled over into the next booth, and the next, like a virus that couldn't be neutralized. By the time Frosty the Snowman came on, the entire bar had joined in, even the sadistically judgey Clifford who kindly brought Steve and Deacon another round of drinks and some sort of Irish-creamy peppermint shots.

Deacon couldn't carry a tune to save his life, so he mainly mouthed along while trying not to laugh. Steven-Actually-Steele had quite the nice voice, however, deep and soothing in an odd way, which somehow made him seem completely un-dick-like, despite having claimed otherwise. Maybe it was the older guy thing, but he put off a disturbingly comforting protective-Dad-like vibe, and Deacon found himself wholly disarmed by it—though the booze likely helped.

They'd run through five or six songs and were both laughing hysterically when Deacon finally reached over, giving Steve's leg a squeeze. His laughing slowly subsided when Deacon didn't remove it.

Steve nodded, swigging the rest of his beer in one long gulp before hopping up off his bar stool, signaling he was ready to go. Deacon did the same, waving down the bartender so he could finally settle that tab. Steve tossed a couple of fifties on the bar and winked at Deacon before making sure Clifford had seen him leave the money.

'Santa Claus is Coming to Town' was being sung/screamed as they walked out. Deacon could hear Steve singing softly from behind him. They paused long enough for Steve to collect his coat, and Deacon realized he was already having trouble catching his breath, knowing what they were about to do. He was drunk enough to not overthink things, and his body was screaming for naked friction, yearning for the comfort that came from the heat of a hard body pressing into his.

Deacon wanted it so much he could feel the heat of his need burning his skin. Nothing else seemed quite as important to him in that moment. He was aware of the questions buzzing around in the back of his mind, most prominently dealing with Steve Steele's marital status. He pushed all that away. The man wasn't wearing a ring and as far as he could tell, didn't appear to have been wearing one recently.

Deacon was determined to let that be enough.

He needed this, if for no other reason than being wanted by someone, hell, anyone at this point. It was paramount to boosting his will to move forward into tomorrow.

There'd be time enough for sadness and heartache later, but tonight he wanted to be the object of someone else's desire, the object of Steven Steele's hard, wet affection.

They were staring at one another as the elevator doors closed. The younger couple with the whiney, cranky toddler was likely the only thing that kept them from attacking one another right then. The father was doing his best to soothe the spawn, but somehow, the young mother was aware of the animalistic lusty heat between Steve and himself. Perhaps it was some sort of pheromone thing that only gay men and women were genetically attuned to sniff out, but she was blushing with a slight grin and doing her best to avoid making eye contact.

Deacon, on the other hand, was barely able to tear his gaze away from Steve's—tension building with each and every ding as the elevator passed another floor. He could practically taste the anticipation—that sensation of the familiarly-unknown that came from a one-night stand with a total stranger.

Christmas was coming early, and Deacon was anxious to unwrap the package standing before him, ready to see what the universe had laid at his feet. He wanted to forget—was ready to have Steve fuck any lingering memories of the past twelve hours away, if only for a little while.

That's what Deacon needed most in that moment, and Steven-Actually-Steele was willing to help.

CHAPTER TWO

The metal scrape of the dead bolt clicked, and Deacon took a deep breath as he moved the safety bar into place, effectively locking out the rest of the world. He was already hard from anticipation.

Turning around slowly, Steve wasted no time pinning Deacon up against the hotel room door, sealing the deal with their first kiss. It was heated, lips burned and tongues tangled with the scrape of stubble. Surprisingly, Deacon found Steve's first move more sensual than expected. It wasn't the rushed groping he'd come to expect from the one-nighters he'd experienced in the past. It caught him off guard but pleasantly so, and Steve seemed to sense that, quickly taking the lead as he began removing Deacon's clothes, one piece at a time, only breaking the kiss when removing Deacon's shirt.

He was dizzy from the shortage of oxygen, as if Steve was sucking the very air from his lungs. The light-headed result was tingles as Steve slowly pushed Deacon's jeans and briefs down over his lean hips. Deacon groaned his approval as Steve ground his pelvis into him, the rough fabric from his jeans rubbing against the exposed skin of Deacon's erection.

The man's hands seemed to be everywhere at once, digging and kneading into Deacon's flesh as Steve sucked gently on his bottom lip—like he couldn't bear to completely let go of it. Each time Deacon attempted to get his hands on Steve, they were brushed aside and eventually forced above Deacon's head, pinned against the cool metal door.

"Leave them there, please," Steve said, though the tone in his voice didn't intimate it was something that was open for discussion.

Deacon complied, hissing in ecstasy when Steve palmed the head of his dick, applying some pressure as he twisted. The sweet friction sent fireworks off behind his now closed eyes. His lips quivered until Steve kissed him again. The scrape of stubble burned into the skin around his mouth, and he thought for a moment he might lose it and blow his wad prematurely.

His eyes popped back open when he heard the click of a light switch.

"Don't move," Steve whispered, taking a few steps back so he could inspect the merchandise more clearly.

It was exactly what he wanted to do, move or cover himself, fighting the urge to reach over and turn the lights back off. Instead, he looked away, unable to take the man's scrutiny, but he didn't move a muscle, just continued to breathe heavily, attempting to get his wind back.

Deacon caught his reflection in the long framed mirror on the wall, naked from the knees up, where his jeans and briefs had gotten tangled up. His hard-on was hanging there in midair, hard and pulsing, pleading for release. He shut his eyes, unable to take the very vulnerable sight of himself any longer.

He jumped slightly when Steve took him by the chin and forced his focus back to the man standing before him. The fact Steve was still dressed made Deacon feel strikingly exposed—defenseless.

"So fucking sexy," Steve said, kissing him again, lightly licking Deacon's full, swollen lips. "Love the way you taste, Deacon."

He started to respond, though the flash of heat that burned across his entire body likely said it all. He couldn't look away, Steve holding him there with a lusty longing gaze that made Deacon wonder if it had been a while since the man had gotten laid.

Before he had an opportunity to consider that further, Steve dropped to his knees and went about helping Deacon the rest of the way out his shoes and pants.

Deacon stopped breathing altogether after Steve's hot mouth engulfed his erection.

"Oh…*jeez*…yes, please," Deacon mumbled, desperate to take the man by the head and fuck his face. Steve had never told him it was okay to move so he hadn't, still standing there with his hands above his head. As Steve made love to him with his very proficient mouth, Deacon found himself unable to stand it, clawing at the door, then the wall, anything to keep from taking Steve by the hair and forcing himself down the man's throat.

Those thick, seductive fingers slowly wrapping around his ass, kneading the mounds of flesh and getting ever closer to Deacon's hot hole, it sent him over the edge.

"Gonna…come!" Deacon yelled in warning.

Steve relentlessly continued, swallowing each load as Deacon mumbled nonsensical bits of praise, grabbing hold of Steve's muscular shoulder for balance when he briefly lost all muscle control in his legs.

The tangy, salty kiss Steve returned upon standing back up only fueled Deacon's desire for more. They continued to make out as Steve led them toward the bed. He gently pushed Deacon backward, watching intently as he fell onto the bed.

Deacon was concentrating on the large bulge in Steve's jeans, right next to the wet spot in the denim. His mouth watered as if readying itself to return the favor, anxious to taste Steve, to breathe in that musky heat. He was so distracted he hadn't noticed the music at first. Steve had turned on the satellite using the television remote, and a saxophone began playing alongside Vanessa Williams singing 'I'll Be Home for Christmas'.

Steve dropped the remote onto the counter before he slowly began taking off his clothes while Deacon watched, completely enraptured. The man was thin at the waist but ripped. Deacon knew he would be. His type always was, had likely worked out every day of his adult life, and it showed. His chiseled chest was solid looking and dusted lightly with hair that hadn't been trimmed. Something about that made Steve seem even sexier, like he refused to alter his appearance in order to be a part of the status quo.

Steve smiled when he got down to his boxer briefs. Deacon's eyes had widened at the size of the bulge. Steve licked his lips, his thumbs lightly tugging on the elastic waistband, revealing another inch of skin.

"Glad to see you approve," Steve said.

Deacon was confused until he looked down to see he was hard again. He grinned, chewing on his lip as he scooted back across the bed, placing his hands behind his head and spreading his legs.

The invitation was unmistakable, and Steve groaned his approval as he slipped his briefs all the way off and stepped out of them. His cock wasn't that long, six, maybe seven inches, but it was thick and veiny, with a large head.

"Steele seems slightly more appropriate now," Deacon said, finding it difficult to swallow all of a sudden.

Steve laughed under his breath as he crossed the room, taking a small tube of lube and a couple of condoms out his coat pocket. It was a reminder that he'd come out looking for sex that night.

Deacon brushed that thought aside as Steve crossed the bed on his knees, stopping when he got between Deacon's legs, and sat on his ankles. He wasted no time ripping open the condom, and his eyelids fluttering as he rolled it over his sensitive dick.

"You'll go easy with that thing, right?" Deacon said, lifting his legs onto Steve's shoulders as Steve squirted lube over his beastly looking cock and grinned.

Deacon moaned, feeling Steve's wet fingers rubbing against his hole, no longer caring if he took it easy, feeling the digits slipping inside.

He was ready to be invaded—to be pushed over the edge.

He strained, fighting to relax his muscles as Steve forced his cock inside, stretching Deacon to the point he feared it might split him in two.

'Jingle Bell Rock' seemed an inappropriate soundtrack for that moment.

Sweat had broken out across his skin as he fought to steady his breath. He groaned in discomfort as Steve moaned in ecstasy—his full length finally all the way inside.

"Christ, Deacon," he whispered, eyelids half closed due to the pressure. "You feel incredible."

Deacon groaned a thank you.

"You all right?" Steve asked.

Deacon could tell the man was praying for a yes, and he nodded that all was good. His back started to arch when Steve began to slowly pull out, only to force himself back in. He could hear the joints in his toes popping as they curled.

It was slow going, and once again, Steve seemed more tuned into worshiping Deacon's body than he did power-fucking his way toward an orgasm. He was almost methodical, taking time to massage the tenseness from Deacon's muscles. He kept a vigilant watch over Deacon's erection, torturing his nipples until Deacon moaned for more.

He'd never been with anyone this patient, willing to take time working Deacon into a frenzied state before fucking him freely. The alcohol likely helped, but before long, Deacon was pleading for him to go faster, to be fucked harder.

Steve seemed to appreciate the prompts, Deacon could see it in his face that he was close, enjoying the effect he was having over him.

"So hot," Steve managed to get out just before screaming his orgasm.

Deacon grabbed his own erection and quickly jacked himself off, losing himself as Steve continued to lightly thrust.

When he reopened his eyes, Steve was still not moving, but the smile on his face said it all. He was clinging to Deacon's legs, which were still draped over the man's muscular shoulders. They were each wet with sweat, and the hair around Steve's face was damp as they fought to catch their breath.

"And here I thought you couldn't possibly look any sexier," Steve said upon opening his eyes.

Deacon smiled, unable to manage a full blown laugh as he glanced down at the cum streaked across his chest and stomach.

"Thank you, Steven Steele," Deacon said, using his fingers to comb the damp hair off his forehead. "And may I say that after having had sex with you, the name is *very* well deserved?"

Steve bit down on his lip, his voice quivering slightly while removing his softening cock. "May I say your ex is a god damned moron?"

Deacon smiled, but the mention of Seth did nothing to aid his mood. He watched Steve cross the room and head into the bathroom. He took a turn at washing up himself once Steve returned, falling onto the bed in heap.

The man looked incredible laid out naked across the bed. If he stared too long, Deacon knew he'd get hard once more, so he averted his eyes hoping to not embarrass himself by coming off like some kind of a nympho.

"You want me to go?" Steve asked as Deacon crawled back onto the bed.

Deacon felt his stomach drop. "Not particularly, though I get it if you're ready to jet."

Steve rolled onto his back, folding his hands across his abs while staring up at the ceiling. "I don't particularly wanna be alone tonight either, if it's all the same to you."

"That's cool." Deacon wasn't quite sure what else to say.

"Hey, I'll even kick in for the room," Steve finally said.

Deacon grinned, thinking his bedmate looked quite young all of a sudden, like a boy offering up some sort of trophy.

"You bought my drinks…and gave me two orgasms," Deacon pointed out. "I think you've done enough."

Steve laughed and went back to staring up at the ceiling.

The room quickly settled, nothing but the Christmas music still playing in the background and the hum of the window unit pumping out warm air. Deacon figured maybe Steve was ready for sleep, so he too began staring up at the white expanse, momentarily distracted by the tiny red light that periodically blinked. He was still a bit drunk, but the euphoric sensation was gone and he could feel the beginnings of a headache coming on. When Seth and his email popped back into his mind, it brought along that profound unhappiness he'd been trying to drown out with the gin.

He turned to look at Steve. "So what drove you out into the freezing cold looking for a warm piece of ass this evening, or is that too personal a question?"

Steve rolled onto his side. He stared into Deacon's eyes for a long moment before reaching over and running the back of his hand down the center of Deacon's chest. "Difficult to claim anything too personal, considering I was just inside you."

"I'm not sure most gay men see it that way," Deacon admitted. "Sharing your ass is probably considered way less personal than sharing your feelings…said the recently dumped twenty-seven year old slut lying naked next to a near perfect stranger."

"Don't be so hard on yourself," Steve said, scooting a little closer so he could stroke the hair off Deacon's forehead. "To be fair, you kinda wear your heart on your sleeve, buddy. I took one look at you at the bar earlier and could feel the sadness coming off you in waves."

"Yet you came and sat next to me anyway?" Deacon asked. "How old are you, by the way?"

"Forty-four." He felt a stab in the gut when Deacon's eyes bugged out of his head. "I know, it's a lot."

"Well, no, I mean yeah, but, hell…anyone that looks as good as you do is never too old." Deacon allowed his gaze to run along Steve's rock hard body. "Seriously, you look incredible, even more so considering you're so old."

He smirked. "Thanks…I think."

"Shit, that came out wrong." Deacon sat up a bit, propping himself up on his elbows.

Steve nodded, though he didn't look all that convinced as he rolled onto his back to watch the ceiling once again. "I am old, too old to be having sex with twenty-seven year olds at any rate."

"I beg to differ," Deacon muttered.

Steve grinned. "You did beg a little, there toward the end."

"Thanks to Steve's hard as Steele cock monster, I did indeed."

He sighed, reaching over to pat a thank you on Deacon's hip. "I'm a little new to the whole gay thing."

- 21 -

Deacon said a silent prayer before finally asking, "Please tell me you aren't married?"

"Not anymore," he said. "So no worries. I belong to no one."

Steve went quiet again and despite Deacon's initial instinct to try and fill the stillness that had taken over the hotel room, his mind went blank. The sound of their breathing was interrupted by a noisy group of people going down the hall to their room. That disruption followed by the slam of their door seemed to bring Steve back to the present.

He glanced over at Deacon who smiled tentatively.

"It was actually one year ago today that I went home after work and told my wife that I liked men."

"Oh," Deacon said, unsure what the right response for that situation might be. It wasn't something he considered to be a problem his generation had to deal with.

"So you see, I am kind of a dick, after all," he continued. "Not to mention a bit of a coward."

Steve nodded and looked away when Deacon didn't jump in to start arguing with him.

He ran his hands through his hair and went back to staring upward. "As clichéd as it sounds, things really are a lot different than they were when I was your age, but that's not an excuse, at least not one I care to use these days."

Deacon felt bad. He was able to see the man appeared to be genuinely tortured by it, but Deacon didn't know what the right thing to say might be.

"I knew who I was deep down, but I played it straight. I was a bachelor for a very long time before the rumors got to be too much. Married Clarissa in April of 2005, she was a widow with a three-year-old daughter, and I convinced myself that they needed me—that I could support them and be a decent father for Kylie."

Deacon scooted closer, tossing an arm over Steve's chest, partially because he was getting cool but also in an attempt to comfort Steve. "I'll confess that I don't really understand it, but I am sorry."

"I was faithful in the beginning—for several years, but my desire to be with men is stronger than I am. My guilt became more than I could bear, so I told her the truth. I broke her a little more that night. Her first husband died, leaving her all alone, then I come along and end up deserting her in a different way."

Steve glanced over at him. Deacon could tell his eyes were welling up a little.

"Never will forgive myself for that, so selfish. And all because I was terrified of what people would think of me? There were times when I literally became paralyzed by the thought of anyone finding out—all the guys who work for me knowing that I like to suck dick? I still get sick to my stomach. The auto industry, in general, is a pretty masculine driven business."

Steve looked at Deacon, who decided to nod that he understood, even though he wasn't sure he did.

Steve took a deep breath before running the palm of his hand over his face.

"Some of my friends and the guys I work with, I've known since high school. It all felt impossible—this insurmountable obstacle that I could never find my way around. Facing the disappointment of my mother?"

Deacon could feel the stress coming off of Steve in waves. He could sense this was an issue that Steve was still wrestling with. "If it makes you feel any better," he said, "my mother despises me because I'm gay. So not everything has changed in the world."

"Damn, I'm sorry, Deacon." Steve sighed, rolling onto his side to face Deacon once more. "My father passed away before I came out so I never had to face him. My parents divorced when I was in high school. My mom doesn't understand it, but she never cut me off. I mean, she's getting up there in years, so new things don't tend to go over too well. She was more furious with me for Clarissa than she was over the gay thing, but I guess those events are all tied up together."

"How are things with your ex-wife?" Deacon asked. "You still see her?"

"Not very much. I pay her child support, my choice, she never asked." He shrugged. "It's a small thing, but it helps me not feel as awful. I'd like to see Kylie more, still would like to be a father to her, but I don't feel like I have the right to ask, especially if my presence makes things tough for Clarissa."

Deacon was disappointed that he didn't seem to have any advice or knew what the right thing to say might be.

"Can't believe I'm laying all this on you, jeez." Steve shook his head. "Can't even be a decent trick who fucks you senseless while keeping his trap shut."

"You certainly accomplished the first part." Deacon grinned. "And I don't mind the rest, you know, the talking. It's nice to know I'm not the only miserable son of a bitch out there. Besides, I did ask."

"All I wanted to do from the moment you read that email to me was make you feel good, not dump all over you."

Deacon smiled. "Told you, you weren't a dick."

Steve scowled like he might not agree.

"Hey, at least you give a damn that you crushed your wife, which is more than I can say for Seth—who broke up with me and went on a cruise."

"That guy is a real piece of work." Steve looked genuinely angry. "If you were mine, I'd...well..."

Deacon smiled again when he trailed off, visibly too embarrassed to actually finish that statement. He thanked Steve with a soft, sweet kiss that quickly deepened into something more. Steve slid his fingers into Deacon's hair, holding his head steady so he could control the kiss.

It was mere minutes before they were each hard with Steve rolling on top of Deacon who wrapped his legs around the man's waist, holding on to him tightly.

"Guess it's true what they say about talking to strangers," Steve managed to get out between kisses.

Deacon reached down between them, taking Steve's hard cock in his hand. "No more talking."

Steve smothered Deacon with a kiss so deep Deacon began seeing stars behind his now closed eyes. They went from zero to sixty in a heartbeat as the heat between them quickly spiraled out of their control. He wasn't sure if it was an older guy thing, but Steve once again had his hands bound tightly above his head as he licked and sucked his way around Deacon's neck and ears—like he was hard at work and didn't want any interference from the peanut gallery.

Deacon was beginning not to mind as one thing became quite clear, Steve was very good at sex. He all but tortured Deacon's mouth, thrusting his tongue down his throat one minute, then seductively sucking on his lips the next.

He cried out when Steve started in on his nipples, which were still sensitive from before. His body was writhing underneath the assault, and Deacon found himself wanting to drown in the passion, willing to be swallowed up by Steve, intoxicated by the loss of control from the agonizingly sweet embrace where every inch of his body burned in needy heat.

He hadn't even realized he'd begun saying it aloud, pleading to be fucked, until Steve rolled him onto his stomach and began spreading him open. Strangely enough he wasn't embarrassed at having asked for it, only desperate to receive what Steve was only too happy to provide.

He grabbed onto the headboard as an anchor and allowed himself to fade into the haze, surrendering any and all control as Steve slowly drove him toward the edge. His sanity felt like an albatross he needed to rid himself of in order to stay right where he was for as long as possible.

The last thing he remembered was Steve whispering once again how sexy Deacon was.

As he concentrated on the sensations created by Steve entering him over and over again, his vision began to blur and he felt light for the very first time in a very long time—so light that he thought for a moment he might float away were it not for Steve keeping him pinned to the bed.

Despite knowing they were each racing toward an end,

Deacon shut his eyes and did his best to pretend otherwise…if only for a little while longer.

CHAPTER THREE

His eyes fluttered open, but it took Deacon a moment to remember where he was. Stirring under the blankets, the cotton sheet felt abrasive against his nipples. He would've smiled from the flood of erotic memories that followed, were it not for the pounding in his head. Rolling over onto his side, he was disappointed to see Steve wasn't there. He'd just begun to wonder if he'd dreamed it all when someone coughed behind him.

Deacon sat up too fast, instantly feeling woozy. He grabbed hold of the mattress to steady himself and focused in on the man perched on the edge of a chair watching the snow falling on the other side of the window.

So lost in his thoughts, Steve hadn't notice he'd risen. Even through the befuddled state of his hangover, Deacon was slightly mesmerized by the sight of his muscular naked frame.

Solid.

That was the best way he could think to describe his impression of the man who had mercifully fucked him within an inch of his sanity the night before. His ass throbbed in time with his head, but the result was an altogether different experience.

Steve finally turned, as if sensing he was being watched. He smiled with trepidation.

Deacon forced a grin.

"Hi."

He shifted in the chair so he no longer needed to strain to look at Deacon. "How you feeling?"

"Like I've been mauled," Deacon said.

Laughing under his breath, Steve nodded. "You most certainly were."

"Head is killing me." Deacon threw the blankets off, whimpering at the cool air in the room as he started to get out of bed. "Need pills."

"On the nightstand." Steve pointed at the medicine and small bottle of water. "I apologize for riffling through your luggage, but I thought you might need them."

Deacon nodded his appreciation as he quickly popped four pills into his mouth and swallowed them, not waiting to get the cap off the water bottle. He got up and stumbled into the bathroom to pee, stretching and listening to his back pop as he came back out into the room.

"I look like I have skin issues." Deacon frowned, taking in all the red patches of skin around his neck, mouth, chest and inner thighs as he stared at himself through the mirror. "Hope you're happy with yourself, mister."

"You look exceedingly sexy to me," Steve teased.

"Why do guys enjoy leaving marks behind so much?" He was getting slightly hard, despite his objections. "You got some serious stubble."

Steve ran his hand over his chin, and the scraping sound could be heard across the room. "Proof we were there to begin with, I guess."

Deacon grunted his agreement, taking a peek out the window. "That's a lot of freakin' snow."

"Airports been closed, looks like you're stranded."

Deacon nodded. "Figured that might happen."

"If you find yourself without any other commitments, I can certainly think of one or two ways to keep you distracted until they resume flights."

Rubbing his forehead in an attempt to soothe his headache, Deacon couldn't keep from grinning. "Don't you gotta work?"

Steve was up and out of the chair, crossing the room until they were face to face. "Being the boss comes with perks."

Deacon nodded, already lost in Steve's gaze. He smelled amazing, kinda musky with a hint of spice. He wanted to bury his head in Steve's chest and live there.

Steve's hand brushed lightly across Deacon's chest and stomach. "I can certainly try taking your mind off the hangover, if nothing else."

Deacon looked the man up and down, flattered that Steve was already half hard despite the otherwise sobering early morning hour. He kissed him, taking Steve in his arms. Their cocks were on the rise, dancing as both men allowed their hands to wander.

"You taste minty," Deacon said between kisses, having already seen that Steve had made use of the spare toothbrush Deacon had packed.

"Mmm," Steve grunted. "Found a spare toothbrush when I was rummaging for pain reliever. Appreciate you thinking of me." More lip smacking as they continued to make out. "Damn considerate of you."

The man hadn't lied. Deacon had nearly forgotten about his headache until his cell phone started to ring. Steve did his best to keep him distracted, but when whoever it was called for the third time in a row, Deacon pulled away.

"Sorry," he whispered, wiping the back of his hand over his mouth. "Man, you kiss good."

Eyebrows arching, visibly impressed by the ego stroking, Steve let go of him.

Deacon grumbled in frustration, looking the man up and down as he backed away. His stomach dropped the instant he saw his sister's name on the caller ID of his cell.

"Can't be good," he mumbled, scooping it up while making a silent promise that he wouldn't allow Ashley to talk him into going back to their mother's house.

I've suffered enough abuse already.

"Hello, Ash," Deacon said, hoping she'd understand and wouldn't be upset with him.

"Oh thank God," she said, a strained tone detectable in her voice. "You need to get on the next plane back, Deacon? I don't know what to do."

She was sniffling so he could tell she'd been crying.

"What's she done now?"

"I was so mad at her after you left, and we had a huge fight so I went to spend the night with Mel after Mom became belligerent.

She was a real mess, Deacon."

He was riffling through names trying to recall who Mel was. He sighed in relief, remembering it was short for Melanie. He took a seat on the edge of the mattress when Steve went back to staring out the window from his chair.

"She's in the hospital, Deacon," Ashley said, beginning to cry again.

He could feel his jaw tensing as he started to grind his teeth. "Which one?"

"St. John. She won't wake up, Deacon. I'm scared."

"I'm still in town, Ashley, got bumped from my flight. Might take me a bit to get there in this blizzard, but I'm coming, okay?"

Steve turned around hearing that.

"Please hurry."

"Was she driving, Ash?" he asked.

"Ya-huh," Ashley said, sniffling. "But she didn't hurt anyone. Just herself. Wrapped the Buick round a tree."

Deacon sighed, relieved no one else had lost a loved one at Patty's drunken hands. That had been his biggest fear growing up. He'd had nightmares of sitting in court and having the family of someone his mother had killed while driving drunk staring at her with hatred in their eyes—staring at him with hatred because he had come from her and was likely no good as well.

He was aware it was partially due to exhaustion, refusing to consider he might care about what happened to Patty, when his eyes began to well up. He knew he needed to pull it together, for Ashley's sake if not his own. Not to mention the fact he didn't want to lose it front of Steve who'd gotten up and come to sit next to him on the bed.

"I just woke up, Ash, but I'll be there as soon as I can. I won't leave you, you understand me?"

"'Kay," she said.

"I want you to stop crying now, everything's going to be fine."

"Yeah." More sniffling. "Okay…thanks."

"You don't need to thank me, Ash, you're my family. You'll always be my family, you hear? And as long as you have me, you'll never be alone."

"Stop talking like she's dead, Deacon!"

Steve's eyes bugged out, able to hear her squealing loudly through the phone.

"I—that's not what I meant." Deacon sighed.

"Okay. Just. She can't die, you know?" Ashley said, calming down.

"You'll be all right till I get there?"

"Yeah, I'm not a baby."

He rolled his eyes. *Deliver me from teenage hormone hell.*

"Well, call if you need to, but I'm on my way."

He was massaging his temple once again by the time he disconnected the call. "I'm really sorry, Steve, but my mother has apparently gone and driven her car into a tree."

"She going to be okay?" he asked.

Deacon nodded. *If she survived the car wreck, she'll be going to prison, so somehow I seriously doubt it*, he thought, deciding not to burden Steve with his family drama.

A wave of nausea swept over him.

This would be Patty's fourth DUI. The first two had each occurred years before, but she was out on bail, still awaiting a court date for the third offense—didn't even have a license anymore. Regardless of whether or not Patty survived the accident, his promise that Ashley would never be left alone was likely going to be put to the test.

"She's only sixteen," Deacon mumbled.

"You're sister?" Steve asked.

"Huh?" Deacon looked up, shaking the fuzz out of his head. "Sorry, lost in my thoughts."

Steve stood up, following Deacon's lead.

"I gotta figure out how the hell to get to the hospital in all this," Deacon motioned toward the snowstorm out the window.

"Go get in the shower, Deacon." Steve nudged his head toward the bathroom. "I've got a four-wheel drive parked outside the hotel. Might take me a bit to dig out, but I can take you wherever you need to go."

"I can't ask you to do that, Steve. You've already done too much."

"You didn't ask, I offered, and what the hell have I done thus far?"

Deacon opened his mouth, but nothing came out.

"Go on, Deacon. I'll get dressed and get my car cleared off."

"You did provide the incredible sex." Deacon pointed at him. "And bought my drinks!"

Those were the surface things the man had done, but Deacon knew there was something more. He couldn't seem to put it into words, though he recognized deep down that Steve had helped him in a way few people had in his life.

Steve chuckled, heading toward his clothes, which had been tossed across the dresser. "The incredible sex takes two, and the drinks weren't exactly of noble intent, considering I knew the more intoxicated you were, the more likely you'd be to say yes when it came time to propositioning you for said sex. Now will you please go get in the shower and let me help you?"

Deacon sighed, nodded that he would, before laying one last, short but smoldering kiss on Steve's lips. "For the record, I don't think you're the least bit dick-like."

Steve licked his lips and looked particularly tormented. "Kiss me like that again, and you'll discover just how wrong you are."

Reluctantly, Deacon stepped away, before turning to head for the bathroom despite wishing there was time for Steve to take some of those frustrations out on him.

By the time he'd stepped into the shower, Deacon heard the hotel room door closing. He'd now had a sufficient amount of distance from Steve to discover just how confusing the events of the last twenty-four hours had been.

A near perfect stranger had been kinder to him than both his own mother and the man who was supposed to have loved him.

How was that even possible?

Deacon knew himself well enough to understand that sort of generosity could easily go to his head—make him think intentions were there that actually weren't. Steve sure as hell deserved better than the mountainous heaps of shit that followed Deacon around like an albatross.

He shook the nonsense from his fuzzy, addled brain. "It was one night in a hotel room, asshole, he's not gonna propose."

And you wouldn't say yes even if he did. Deacon wilted slightly, Seth's cruel words still rattling around inside his head.

"Why would he want me?" Deacon shoved his head under the shower nozzle, attempting to drown the negativity. He apparently wasn't worthy of love in the first place, at least according to those who were supposed to love him most.

* * * *

Being at the hospital did little to lighten Deacon's mood, not that he really expected it to. The mechanical beeps and methodical rhythm of the respirator helping Patty breathe felt artificial and cold. She was so still, which was odd given her usual jittery restlessness—a nicer way of saying withdrawal shaking.

Her black hair was stringy—oily from sweat and stress no doubt, and he could see the evidence of premature gray hair along the roots. His mother looked old, a decade or more so than her actual years. The stark reality evidenced from her chain-smoking and alcoholism when not covered up with the pounds of makeup she typically caked on.

They'd moved her into intensive care, and he was thankful to be out of the ER. There wasn't another patient in the second bed so it was much quieter. Hopefully, they'd keep it that way, and he could avoid the awkward stares from complete strangers coming in to visit a loved one.

He hated hospitals. A few months before he'd met Seth,

Deacon had come down with pneumonia and spent four and a half days in the hospital. It had been an exhausting experience—one that left him reeling upon the realization that he was all alone in the world. No friends, lovers, or family who cared about him. No one had come to visit him. He literally could have died and no one would have missed him.

Up until that moment, Deacon had been unaware of exactly how isolated he'd truly become. It was his own doing; he knew that, though it hadn't been something he'd done intentionally. Trust wasn't something that came easily to him.

The entire experience had scared the hell out of him, being so sick with no one that cared aside from those who were being paid to. Deacon's entire life had flashed before him, an entire future where he continued to be withdrawn, hiding from everyone—all alone with no one to love and no one who loved him.

He sighed, feeling his eyes welling up as that same fear crept back over him now.

"Don't wanna be that guy, again."

He fought back the tears, forcing away the mental images of him lying in that bed instead of Patty. That all-too-familiar sense of helplessness swept over him, and Deacon had to fight to catch his breath.

He turned to look out the window in an attempt to distract himself.

The cloudy daylight from outside bathed the room in pale gray washed-out hues. He began concentrating on the snowflakes that were now falling peacefully as opposed to the spinning, whirling angered fury from earlier that morning. Each flake carelessly floating down, piling one on top of all the others that had fallen before as if attempting to bury everything offensive in a clean white, pristine blanket.

He turned toward the hall, distracted by the commotion when several nurses went rushing past as a code blue came over the intercom along with a room number. Deacon realized someone else's loved one was now fighting for their life. He was thankful Ashley had stepped out so she could call and report back to Mel and her parents on Patty's condition. She didn't need to see that after the morning she'd spent terrified and alone.

He could tell she was still spooked, despite her attempts to pretend otherwise. She and Patty never fought like Deacon and Patty had, and she wasn't equipped to deal with the fallout as a result. They had spats, but Ashley wasn't a freak like Deacon and for the most part had flown under the radar—never giving their mother any reason to attack her with negativity.

She was actually a pretty good kid. She'd been a little brat when she was younger but had somehow blossomed into a fairly well-balanced teenager.

No thanks to Patty, he guessed, turning to look at his mother once more.

She was eerily still and silent, her jaw slack, face completely relaxed and pale with no color in her cheeks. Tubes coming from her mouth and needles in her arms, this was how he'd always imagined Patty would die, hooked up to machines in a hospital. Deacon assumed it would be while waiting for a kidney, or maybe cancer from the chain-smoking, but never like this.

There was no life in her. Zero animation—the way he imagined dead people looked.

Deacon couldn't keep himself from thinking he and Ashley would both be better off if she never woke up.

It was a horrible thing, but Deacon blamed Patty for putting that thought in his head. Ashley was the type who'd forever be wasting her energy trying to take care of Patty, who was like a succubus that would slowly drain the life from her own daughter. Two lives ruined in a foolish attempt to salvage the one. His mother had snuffed out that instinct in him long ago, and the result was a sort of freedom from the responsibility.

Part of him wanted to cry over that fact because he knew it was more complicated than that. His mother had methodically murdered a tiny piece of his soul. It had been the price he'd paid for freedom, making him colder, more standoffish and less likely to believe himself worthy of too much of anything.

But he was free of her, and that was something. Still, there was a limit in place for Deacon where happiness was concerned, an invisible glass ceiling that would forever prevent him from rising to the top. He truly believed that.

If his own mother couldn't love him, why in the hell would anyone else?

He'd accepted all of that long ago.

No wonder Seth treated him like shit. It's all Deacon believed he deserved.

As he watched her now, knowing that she would indeed survive her injuries, which had been minimal outside of the concussion, Deacon wished he'd never come back in the first place.

He felt desperately isolated, more than he had in a very long time, and that cut through his chest, made him want to scream out.

Instead, Deacon did as he'd always done before and sat there, suffering silently.

One of the nurses came through, checking Patty's vitals. The hospital staff had all been exceedingly kind, but he was aware they all knew his mother had been drunk off her ass while operating a moving vehicle. He'd missed the police but had been informed they'd be returning.

He didn't understand much of the medical jargon, but basically, the doctor had placed Patty into a medically-induced coma because they were worried about the swelling in her brain from the concussion she received in the wreck. She'd cracked a rib but otherwise had been unharmed.

Deacon shoved his hands into his coat pockets. He'd never managed to warm up, frozen cold from the inside out. He felt some paper and glanced down, slipping Steve's business card out of his pocket. Running the tip of his finger over the glossy finish, Deacon stared at Steve's photo. It was the heavily airbrushed kind of photo, and Deacon couldn't help but think Steve looked so much sexier in person.

The font that spelled out Steele Automotive was in a chrome-like finish, very butch. It made him smile, recalling Steve's comment about car sales being a masculine business.

He flipped it over and examined the handwritten numbers scribbled onto the back.

"Call if you need anything, Deacon," Steve had said, placing the card into his hand as they sat in the unloading zone at the hospital. "In the meantime, I'll run home and clean up before I come back to the hospital."

Deacon was stunned, and it must have showed judging by Steve's reaction.

"I can't let you do that, Steve. That's too much. Things aren't going to be pretty, and I'm sure you've got like a million better things to do with your time."

"I don't mind."

"That's really nice of you, but honestly, I think you being there would make me uncomfortable."

"Well, you're going to need a ride later, right?"

"I imagine my sister will have driven herself here."

"Right." Steve glanced down at the steering wheel. "Well, what about food? I can bring you and your sister something to eat later?"

Deacon shook his head. "I don't wanna drag you into any of this, and to be honest, I'd rather have you remember me the way I was last night or this morning. Naked and grateful as opposed to sad, stressed out and utterly pathetic—which is the impression you'd be left with after witnessing the mess that is my family."

Steve hadn't seemed convinced, or very happy for that matter, but he didn't argue with Deacon, who had been surprised to discover that part of him wished Steve had put up more a fight. It was silly, he recognized that, yet he couldn't seem to stop himself.

"Who's the guy?" Ashley asked, hovering over Deacon's shoulder while staring at Steve's picture on the business card, which Deacon quickly put back into his pocket.

"A nice man who gave me a ride," he said.

She took a seat in the chair next to Patty's bed. "He's kinda hot for an old guy."

Deacon tried not to smile, knowing firsthand how much Steve would appreciate the backhanded compliment, but the grin on Ashley's face told him he'd failed miserably.

He could tell she was in better spirits; the break from their bedside vigil had done Ashley some good. She was so grown up. It made him feel old. She'd barely been a teenager when he'd left home at twenty-two—now she was practically an adult. Her shoulder-length blonde hair was bone straight and shiny, cut into a perky little bob. In contrast to their mother, Ashley was less flashy—every bit as pretty as Patty had once been but more natural and less painted up. She was dressed in girly pink sweat pants and multiple layers of tops like she'd come directly from her sleepover at Mel's.

He'd been livid Melanie's parents hadn't come with her to the hospital until he realized Ashley initially hadn't told them what was going on. Deacon recognized his sister most likely did everything possible to keep her friends and their families far away from Patty.

"I'm glad you missed your flight." Her voice became slightly softer as she stared across the room at Patty. "Was your boyfriend upset?"

"My boyfriend dumped me." His voice sounded flat, even to him. "Yesterday. Sent me an email."

"Sorry." Ashley said, not maintaining eye contact for long before she took to staring at the floor. "That why you been drinking?"

That question startled him.

Ashley shrugged. "I can smell it on you."

He'd showered and brushed his teeth, but he knew all too well the scent that comes from sweating the alcohol out of your system the next day. He'd grown up with it, as had she.

"Can't understand how you could ever touch the stuff."

He felt the heat rushing to his cheeks. "I don't normally, other than a glass of wine here and there when I go out to dinner with Seth or went out with Seth, I should say. Just...I had a real bad day yesterday, Ash, that's all."

"I won't touch it, not ever," she said, staring at Patty. "Don't ever wanna end up like her."

He'd felt that way too at one point. Part of him still did. He could count on one hand the amount of times he'd allowed himself to overindulge. There was always that fear deep down—that whatever demon was inside of Patty might also be in him—just waiting for Deacon to let his guard down long enough to take him over.

"You know Mom's going to jail, right?" she asked.

"I do. Wasn't sure you'd realized that."

"So what's going to happen to me?" she asked.

"You could probably go stay with Aunt Sara in Arizona, or you *could* come back to Chicago with me, if you wanted?"

Ashley sighed, rubbing her eyes. "Come on, Deacon, I only have a year and a half of high school left. Would you have wanted to start over senior year at a new school?"

"I was tormented in high school, so yeah, I would've jumped at the chance—did jump at the chance, not that it did much good."

"Couldn't you come back home? Just until I graduate? You could work at a Target here? It's not like you have a guy to get back to anymore?"

He watched her cringe and could tell Ashley wished she hadn't included that last bit.

"I don't want to go into a foster home, *please*. I'll be a model sister, I swear it." She looked at him all pleady with the big eyes.

The striking resemblance to their mother in that moment was unsettling. The way he'd remembered Patty looking when he was a young boy.

"It's free rent—you could get a job and save a little money. Maybe look into college. We could go to college together!"

Deacon was embarrassed that the free rent portion of her statement had ended up being the most appealing part to him. Homeless chic wasn't *en vogue* as far as he was aware, and thanks to Seth, he currently had nowhere to live.

"What about your dad?" Deacon asked.

"Good luck finding Mr. Deadbeat." Ashley frowned. "Honestly, I barely know the man so it wouldn't be any different than going into a foster home."

It was what he hoped she'd say, but it needed to be asked all the same. Ashley's father was the last person he'd want her staying with, as long as it wasn't something she wanted.

He couldn't think straight, partially due to all that had happened with his family and Seth, but also because his ass ached in a pained needy way that made concentration difficult. The sporadic sex flashbacks that occurred as a result were disorienting, and part of him wondered if that wasn't self-preservation at work, his body's way of clinging to the fact someone had wanted him— even if for only one night.

He didn't want her to see how close he was to unraveling.

Ashley sighed. "I know it's a lot to ask."

He could see it in her eyes that she'd hated having to do it. It was a quality they shared, an intense hatred of asking anyone for help. He shouldn't have let her ask, hadn't intended to, but she jumped the gun on him. He hadn't been expecting to have this conversation so soon.

In that moment, he realized Ashley had been the one who'd picked up the pieces and kept Patty pulled together in between boyfriends after he'd left home. It had changed her, and not for the better. He recognized that same sadness staring back at him from behind her eyes. She was more grown up than a sixteen year old should be.

"I'll come back, Ash," Deacon finally said.

She started to cry, but the huge smile on her face told him it was motivated by relief.

Deacon shook his head at her. "None of that, sis." He smiled, determined to make sure what remained of her high school years would be spent worrying about boys and dances and dresses. He couldn't take back everything Patty had put her through, but he could give Ashley that, and Deacon was surprised to discover it actually made him feel useful for the first time in a very long time.

* * * *

It was little more than twenty-four hours ago that he'd stormed out his mother's tiny little bungalow, vowing to never return again. As he passed over the threshold now, Deacon could feel the muscles in his stomach tightening. He hated this place.

It was a small, three-bedroom house with a tiny kitchen/dining combo and a decent-sized living area located in Vidale Heights, an older area of town filled with the sort of historic homes no one had any desire to fix up or restore. It was old-school low income housing, with little to no architectural style or embellishments that would inspire conservation or preservation. They hadn't been built to withstand the test of time either, and as such, many of the homes in the area had become run-down and most were like Patty's, tiny rooms and low ceilings.

Seth's loft in Chicago, while in reality wasn't large, seemed huge to Deacon when he'd first moved in. It was only one bedroom, but the high ceilings and huge windows took some getting used to. It had been like moving from a cave into a theatre. Seth didn't believe in curtains or blinds so the entire world was free to look in and watch the two of them cohabitate. He wondered if the voyeurs had been able to tell that their relationship had been doomed from the start.

He closed the front door, locking it while trying to ignore the echoes of two decades of arguments and anxiety over his own safety. The near crippling desperation he'd experienced growing up here, fearing that anyone might discover what his home life was like. Deacon avoided making friends at all because of it.

Even knowing Patty wouldn't be there, and would very likely not be returning for many years to come, didn't seem to set him at ease.

Too many ghosts.
Too many disappointments.
Too much unhappiness.

His sister, on the other hand, appeared more at ease now that they were home.

"Think I'm gonna go lay down, take a nap." She thumbed toward the hall that led back to the bedrooms. "We'll talk later, yeah?"

Deacon smiled, which seemed to relax her even more. She nodded before turning to head for the safety of her bedroom. All the drama wore on Ashley as much as it did him.

He dropped his bags on the floor and sighed, shaking his head slightly before flopping down onto the sofa.

The house reeked of cigarette smoke. Difficult to imagine why, looking at the three…no, make that four ashtrays currently sitting around the room, each with varying levels of snuffed out butts piled high. The pressed wood coffee table sat slightly askew, like someone had clumsily run into it, and one of the glass pane inserts had a long crack that snaked out from one corner. It was covered with mauled magazines and Patty's purse, the contents of which had been dumped out, alongside several empty liquor bottles.

"She'd left the night before because she'd run out booze."

He shook his head as he picked up her wallet, thinking she'd left her damn purse behind and wouldn't have been able to buy any had she managed to make it to the liquor store.

"Stupid drunk."

The layer of dust was thick enough that everything that had been dumped out of her purse had left tracks as the items scattered across the tabletop.

Patty had been meticulous when he was little. This house had always been clean if nothing else, but apparently, time and booze had made her lazy, or perhaps the disappointment of one soured relationship after another had simply taken its toll.

That had been what had sparked their argument the night before. Her latest drug and alcohol addicted boyfriend had broken up with her the day after Deacon had come back home. Somehow, in Patty's mind, that had made it Deacon's fault.

"You poison everything!" she screamed, stumbling around and clinging to the top of the sofa to keep from falling over. "You're like a cancer I can't manage to cut out of my life."

"Have another drink, Patty," Deacon snapped back. "You're not slurring your words yet so there's room for improvement."

"Will you two please stop it," Ashley pleaded, stomping her foot for emphasis as she hovered in the hallway.

"He left me 'cause of this...fag," Patty added, motioning toward Deacon while appearing truly stunned that Ashley didn't seem to understand. "No one wants a faggot around—he was afraid of getting attacked, no doubt."

"Right, since it couldn't possibly have anything to do with you?" Deacon asked. "Jesus Christ, have you taken a good hard look at yourself, or have you not been sober long enough to focus the past couple of years?"

"Please, guys," Ashley turned in a circle like she wasn't sure where to go before deciding to lean against the wall. "I just want one normal holiday with my family, just once."

"Then you shouldn'ta invited the cock sucker, nothing normal about that."

"'Cause I'm sure you've never done that," Deacon mumbled.

"I can't believe you'd talk to your mother like that," Patty spat out, her entire body now shaking she was so mad.

"You stopped being my mother somewhere around the time you told me you wished I was dead."

"More evidence that wishing for things is a waste of time," Patty muttered. "Not wasting my time with someone I won't see in the afterlife."

Deacon turned to his sister. "I'm sorry, Ash, but this was obviously a mistake. Maybe next year you can come to Chicago to see me for Christmas? We'll make a whole weekend out of it, but I'm not sticking around for another three days of this shit."

Ashley nodded that she understood, but the look on her face made him feel like a scum bag for leaving her. He wished he could take her with him, free her from the crypt keeper and all the madness that came from a life lived with Patty. But that wasn't an option, and he was determined to once again save himself, if no one else.

Deacon sighed, doing his best to push that entire episode far away into the very back of his brain, where he attempted to store all the memories he didn't need or want, yet couldn't seem to rid himself of completely.

He glanced around the rest of the room, and everything felt dingy, even the depressing looking Christmas tree that was slightly lopsided. It had seen better days, and those days had long passed. He could tell Ashley had tried covering it up using extra tinsel, but that hadn't improved things. It looked so sad with its scratched, mismatched ornaments…like a glittery blob with a bad skin condition…and scoliosis.

As if on cue, the lights in the tree flickered, then sparked at the outlet before going dark.

He was up off the sofa in a flash, hissing in pain when he snatched the cord and ripped it from the wall. He shook his hand after dropping the cord that had been hot to the touch.

"Fucking hell." He was fairly certain he'd just been electrocuted in the process of attempting to save this shit-shack from the flames of hell.

It was difficult to imagine any place being more depressing than the hospital. This house managed it. He felt dirty, all the way down to his soul.

Deacon stood there for a moment, watching the wall and outlet, half expecting the house to go up in flames.

"Like the gates of Hell opening up to reclaim what rightfully belongs there."

Taking a few deep breaths to calm himself, he wiped the sweat now forming on his brow, and he laughed under his breath.

After several minutes, he realized the house would not be catching fire after all and shoved his hands into his coat pockets, still a little too spooked to completely walk away. He could feel the corner of Steve's business card poking into the back of his hand. He pulled it out and stared at the photograph once more while chewing on his lip. Part of him wanted to go back to that morning when it was just the two of them naked and kissing.

Deacon had felt safer within the confines of that hotel room than he had anywhere else in a very long time.

He sighed, crossed the room and grabbed his bags, shoving the card into the side pocket of his rollaway. He'd unpack first, then start cleaning. Tomorrow, he'd call his boss and quit his job—maybe see about getting transferred to a store up here, though he wasn't holding his breath. They'd be trying to cut back after the holidays as it was.

All stuff he'd have to deal with in the upcoming weeks, not to mention going back to Chicago to stuff all his crap into his car and drive it back to Detroit. Ashley was out of school for the next week, maybe she'd wanna come with him. For now, he decided to try getting through the rest of the day and see how that went before committing fully to his next move.

He sighed, thinking how much he hated change while attempting to figure why the hell he seemed to be forever suffering from it.

CHAPTER FOUR ~ MARCH

Steve glanced down at the clock before changing lanes, making a last minute decision to stop at Garibaldi's Gourmet Market. It was nearly a quarter after nine p.m. as he pulled into the parking lot, and if he remembered correctly, they stayed open until at least ten on weekdays. He'd be in and out without holding anyone up. It was one of his pet peeves, having people stroll in right before closing, forcing everyone to stay late. That happened a lot at the dealership. Often times when people were looking at cars, it ended up being all they were doing, and they didn't tend to care whose time they were wasting in the process.

Hell, even hookers have sense enough to get paid first.

It's part of the game, though, he thought, getting out of his car. *Guys who work on commission often end up working for free.*

Heading across the small parking lot toward the store Steve eyed the tiny Smart ForTwo coupe parked under the streetlamp—bathed in light as if whoever owned the damn thing was actually proud of the fact.

He shook his head, a little embarrassed for whoever had the balls to drive that trinket in Motor City. It was nothing but a glorified shiny chunk of plastic that had him longing to race back to his fully restored, American made, '67 Raven Black Mustang Fastback to issue an apology for being parked anywhere near such an eyesore.

Silly thing looks like a damn toy.

"Plugs into the wall like a damn toaster," he muttered, listening to the bell chime as he pulled open the door and entered the building. "What's the world coming to?"

The small grocery store was owned by the Garibaldi family. Originally a butcher shop, it had grown and changed with the times and now carried an impressive array of gourmet foods and wine from all over the globe.

The wide barn-plank style flooring and wood shelving gave

the place an old-time general store feel. It wasn't a huge space, but every shelf was crammed full. The first time he'd been inside the place, Steve had actually been impressed by the amount of stuff they'd managed to squeeze into such a small space.

It was the kind of store where everyone smiled all the time, patrons and employees alike. The owners were that type of people—everyone was family. It's how they were able to survive the larger chain stores. They couldn't compete with the prices, but the primo service and personal touch was worth the extra coin, plus they carried things the typical grocery store didn't.

The Garibaldi's had purchased several family cars and delivery vans from the dealership over the past twelve years, and Steve liked to pay it forward by stopping in a couple times a month. He was there more over the summer months when he grilled outdoors—Garibaldi's was still the only place he'd shop for fresh meat.

Tonight, he was craving that imported smoked Gouda from Holland he'd picked up here last month. It was delicious, thinly sliced and baked on bruschetta topped with chopped fresh Roma tomatoes with garlic, basil, and olive oil.

His mouth was watering already, and he'd just eaten dinner.

"Too bad the meal had been better than the company," he muttered as he snagged a basket and headed down the first aisle toward the deli counter located in the back of store, right next to the butcher. He'd just survived what was officially his third shitty date in a row, all of them different guys, yet none he'd felt any sort of connection with.

Steve smiled as he passed by the young woman who was singing a song under her breath to the antsy toddler sitting unhappily in the shopping cart, legs dangling lifelessly over the side.

Itsy bitsy spider. Horrible song, he'd hated it when he was a kid. Never liked spiders much, something his father enjoyed teasing him about when he was little.

He reached the back of the store only to discover there was a line. He grumbled under his breath, ready to get home and relax for the rest of the night. He'd put off his laundry for far too long and was doing his best to ignore the fact it would suck up an entire day in order to get caught up.

It seemed like a complete injustice having to wash clothes, then fold *and* put them away on top of everything else. His suits went to the dry cleaners, but he was too embarrassed to ask what they'd charge to do his regular laundry.

My mother would kill me.

"You're a grown man and you can't manage to clean up after yourself?" she'd no doubt ask. "That's not who I raised you to be."

Thinking about all he could with a full day off minus the laundry and he was tempted to weather his mother's wrath after all.

Steve sighed, watching as the same woman continued to grill the poor guy behind the deli counter about each and every item in the case, not seeming to give a damn about the people waiting behind her.

Selfish.

That had been the same vibe Steve had gotten from the guy he'd been out to dinner with earlier that evening. Dude was severely into himself, and to an extent, deservedly so considering how hot the guy was. Unfortunately, he'd left Steve feeling more like a meal ticket than a man. He'd been tempted to take the bastard home and screw the selfish out of him, but it wasn't worth all the drama he was sure to bring to Steve's doorstep.

Not to mention he seemed like the type who'd enjoy the lesson a little *too* much.

That thought had him grinning and made him wonder if he'd done the right thing in letting the guy get away.

Considering how many years he spent lying to women because he was too chicken shit to be out of the closet, Steve had decided not to mix fucking and dating. No more lying. If he wanted sex, he went out and found it. When he went out to a bar, it became purely about physicality; was the guy hot and did he like to take it up the ass? That was it, end of criteria. But screwing a guy he went out on a date with when he knew there wasn't going to be a second date seemed like bad karma. The whole intent behind a date was different. Agreeing to sit across the table from a guy for an hour or two—that was a commitment, sending the message that he had an interest in getting to know the man beyond the physical.

Maybe that was his real issue. He wasn't spending enough time vetting the people he went out with. Still allowing his cock to make all his decisions.

He rolled his eyes and grumbled under his breath, and the old battle axe holding up the line turned around to see there were several others waiting behind her. She then went back to grilling the deli counter guy.

He glanced up at the round security mirror hanging in the corner of the store, and his breath caught in his chest, swearing for a moment that he'd seen Deacon passing by behind him. He froze, as this hadn't been the first time Steve *thought* he'd spotted his hotel trick from two months before.

The fact of the matter was Steve had been unable to get the sad and sexy Deacon Miller out his head. Practically every time he closed his eyes at night, it was Deacon's face that he saw there. It was beginning to feel like he was being haunted.

He grinned after turning around to find that no one was actually there, and he shook his head. Usually, he found someone that looked like Deacon, but this time he'd imagined it completely.

"Going nuts in your old age, buddy," he muttered.

Steve was still kicking himself for not getting the man's phone number before driving away from the hospital that day. Steve recognized he'd done so intentionally. At the time, he'd been mildly freaked over the connection they'd had. It was unnerving. Within a week, the regret started to sink in. He'd even resorted to searching online, thinking Deacon Miller was probably not that common of a name, but Steve had been unable to find him on Facebook or Twitter, and he'd found no listing for him in Chicago.

That last bit had him thinking perhaps Deacon had gone

back home and gotten back together with his ex. That pissed him off, considering the way the ex had treated Deacon, but people did dumb-ass shit all the time, including staying in a relationship with people who were no good for them.

Steve quickly shoved all of that out of his mind once he finally made it up to the counter. He ordered his Gouda, along with some Swiss, and a couple of varieties of cheddar. He topped off his order with some thin shaved salami, roast beef and apple smoked ham before heading off to nab crackers and a couple of day-old baguettes from the bakery.

Checking his watch as he rounded the cracker aisle, it was twenty till, so he reminded himself not to dawdle. He froze in place upon looking up to find Deacon midway down the aisle, restocking tortilla chips as he fended off questions from the same nosy bitch who'd held up the line at the deli.

Steve shook his head and rubbed at his eye sockets before focusing in once again.

There was still a guy standing there looking clueless about the different varieties of corn used in the production of tortilla chips, and that guy was Deacon Miller.

He feared his heart might pop right out of his chest when Deacon finally noticed Steve. The smile that formed across Deacon's face was instantaneous and appeared quite genuine. It also made Steve a little weak in the knees.

The fact Deacon tripped coming off the step stool, nearly falling into the shelving on the opposite side of the aisle made him think for a moment that Deacon might be unnerved by seeing him as well.

Then the realization sunk in that Deacon had apparently moved back to Detroit yet had never called him. His disappointment was instantaneous and quite severe, leaving Steve with what felt like a cavernous vacant hole inside his gut. He wasn't a fan of that particular sensation and was already regretting the experience as a whole.

"Hi!" Deacon said, now completely ignoring the old hag and her nagging questions.

Steve quickly snagged a box of crackers off the shelf, not paying attention to what he'd taken. "Good to see you, Deacon. Family all right?"

"Uh, sure, yeah…fine." Deacon was fidgeting with the string that tied the black and white striped apron all the employees wore around his waist. "How are you? How've you been?"

"Good." Steve nodded, ignoring the woman who was now impatiently waiting for them to dispense with the pleasantries so Deacon could get back to helping her. "You guys are getting ready to close."

Deacon nodded, looking adorably awkward.

Steve wanted to kiss him.

"Guess I better head for the register—get out of your hair."

"Right, sure." Deacon smiled, but his forehead was all crinkled up like he might be frustrated despite trying to project otherwise.

"I meant to call, but—"

"It's okay," Steve interrupted. He reached over, giving Deacon's shoulder a squeeze of reassurance before continuing on, leaving Deacon to his own devices with the Question Queen.

His urge to turn around and go back was nearly crippling.

Ridiculously elaborate fantasies about abduction popped into his head, yet it was exactly what Steve wanted to do in that moment.

He kept moving forward nonetheless—one foot in front of the other, reminding himself to not look back. For some reason, Steve knew that doing so would mean he might not have the strength to turn away a second time, and he was scared shitless Deacon likely wouldn't feel the same.

* * * *

He admitted to himself that his behavior was quite likely bordering on the bizarre, but Steve hadn't been able to make himself leave the parking lot of the grocery store. He'd definitely worked himself up into some sort of a frenzy during the past forty-five minutes and was now searching the Internet on his phone attempting to determine how long cheese would last without refrigeration. In the end, he decided it was plenty cold outside and thus had nothing to worry about.

It made for a nice momentary diversion, but he was anxious and frustrated as a result.

Would it have really killed the little bastard to take five minutes and make a phone call?

"Hey, thanks for the ride to the hospital *during* the blizzard," he muttered. "My verbally abusive mom's going to live by the way, so no need to worry."

Steve tossed his phone onto the dash, watching a few more employees come out of the store and walk to their cars. Deacon wasn't among them.

"People have no manners anymore." He looked at his reflection in the rearview mirror, trying not to think about the fact that perhaps Deacon hadn't enjoyed the sex as much as he'd seemed to after all. "You brought your A-game to that hotel room, Steele so if that didn't cut it, you're fucking toast, buddy. Not a chance in hell this guy's going out with you again—let alone jumping back into the sack."

That's what was truly bugging him and deep down he knew it. Steve wanted more, a lot more, but it went beyond the physical. Something else had happened that night—a deeper connection. At least he'd thought there had been, but perhaps it had all been one-sided? He'd told Deacon things, stuff he'd never talked about with anyone else, and Steve had done so freely. Deacon hadn't coerced the information from him, and it hadn't felt weird or awkward afterward, which seemed like a big deal.

Steve was well aware he could continue to sit there in his car, waiting around like some sort of stalker freak or leave now and perhaps maintain what little dignity he had left. He was equally afraid of the repercussions either way, aware the unknown would eat away at him slowly but being rebuffed might kill him outright.

The danger alarms were going off inside his head, sirens blazing, along with his libido. Steve tried convincing himself he'd be okay with one more taste but knew one would lead to two, then a third and on and on until he was drowning in Deacon Miller.

He glanced back out the windshield, watching as Deacon came out the door, digging around inside a beat-up brown leather messenger bag, presumably for his keys. Steve got out of his car, watching as Deacon tripped and stumbled because he wasn't paying attention to the terrain.

He looked up, startled by the sound of Steve shutting his car door, and Deacon slowed to a stop. He was visibly confused, staring intently at Steve for a moment before he started walking again, changing course slightly to head in Steve's direction.

"Hey," Deacon finally said once they were face to face.

"You never called me?" Steve blurted out, not intending to sound quite so pissy.

Christ, I sound like a fucking chick.

"Well, I...um."

"What's up with that?" he asked, once again, wishing he hadn't sounded so irritatingly grating.

"Well...you sound... mad?" Deacon asked, visibly confused.

"I'm not mad," Steve scoffed. "Come on, jeez...I'm pissed."

Deacon's mouth opened, but nothing came out.

Steve shifted his weight, feeling silly all of a sudden. "Not to sound all girly or anything but that night...you and me...it felt..."

"Like we'd shared something?" Deacon sighed, nodding his head.

"Kind of, yeah," Steve said, shoving his hands in pockets. "You apparently moved back at some point over the last two months, yet you never called? I wanna know why."

"Honestly, Steve, I just assumed it was me, you know? I was drunk, a teensy bit unhinged and most definitely vulnerable, even without the booze. Thought I like, imagined it all or something."

"Well, you didn't," Steve snapped.

Deacon's eyes bugged out slightly. "All right, Steve, I'm sorry. I didn't think. Guess I figured either way I was doing you a favor by leaving you alone. It's not like I didn't *want* to call."

"You did, huh?" he asked, looking around and feeling more than a little stupid. "Guess that's something."

"Thought about calling a lot, actually."

"Just a lot?"

"Like every day, sheesh." Deacon started to fidget again, like he might be getting uncomfortable until he saw the corners of Steve's mouth curling up. "Asshole, you're giving me grief?"

"Knowing you thought about me daily helps. That's good for my fragile ego."

Deacon laughed. "Nearly gave me a heart attack just then, you jerk."

Steve chuckled. "Serves you right for making decisions for me."

"Think you're awfully cute, I suppose."

"So do you, the everyday kinda cute, apparently. You youngins are so *clingy*."

"Such an asshole."

"Difficult to argue that at this point, but nevertheless, can this ass buy your ass a drink?"

"Pfft, this ass can't be had for anything less than a burger… and some fries come to think of it." Deacon nodded abruptly, like he'd decided that would indeed be reward enough after all, so long as fries were included.

"Hungry, huh?" Steve asked.

"I am, starving in fact."

"All right, I guess I can feed ya."

Deacon's eyes got all squinty, and he looked put out. "Well, don't strain yourself, pal."

Steve laughed under his breath, and they each stood there for a moment staring at one another before Steve finally broke the spell by saying, "I'm gonna kiss you later on, so prepare yourself."

Deacon grinned, and once again Steve was surprised to feel his stomach flutter in response.

"Now get in the car," Steve ordered, walking around to the passenger side of the Mustang so he could open the door for Deacon.

"Yes, sir, Mr. Bossy-butt." Deacon saluted, then glanced down at his cell phone and frowned. "Better call and check in on my sister, make sure she's okay and stuff, let her know I'll be late tonight."

Steve grabbed Deacon's arm as he was about to get into the car and planted a kiss on those thick, pouty lips. He could tell Deacon hadn't expected later on to come quite so soon, but his quick recovery and favorable response told Steve the man wasn't disappointed either way.

Steve backed him up against the car, enjoying the feel of Deacon's tongue in his mouth—the heat from their bodies pressing into one another in contrast to the cold air surrounding them. He moaned softly, a sound that made Steve hard, fast. He realized how badly he wanted to make Deacon feel something, anything at this point.

When he finally pulled away, it was Steve who groaned, witnessing the lust playing out across Deacon's face from that kiss.

"Guys like you should come with a warning label," Deacon said, still sounding out of breath. "You're a little too good at that."

"Just thinking the same thing about you." Steve nudged his head toward the open car door, and Deacon licked his lips before finally crawling inside.

Steve cleared his throat and adjusted his now near-painful erection after shutting the car door. Rounding the trunk of the car as he headed for the driver's side, it dawned on him that the only other car left in the parking lot was that oversized plastic toy sitting under the street lamp, and Steve shook his head.

"Of course it had to be his," he mumbled as he climbed behind the wheel of his 'Stang.

Deacon was messing with his phone, not looking up when he said, "I'll just text her for now, and I'll call later."

The V-8 engine roared to life, and Steve smiled, comforted, thinking it the sweetest sound he'd ever heard while backing out of the parking spot.

He stopped the car and rubbed at his chest, resisting his urge to kiss the little bastard again. "I can't believe you drive that thing."

Deacon looked out the passenger side window at the metallic gray Smart ForTwo coupe. "What's wrong with my car?"

Steve was flabbergasted. "You call that a car?"

"It's electric. Gets real good gas mileage." Deacon shrugged. "I think it's cute. Don't you?"

"Jesus." Steve hunched over the steering wheel, resting his forehead against the leather. "Cute?" He glanced over at Deacon. "What's it got under the hood, a couple of triple As? Did it come with a remote control?"

"Oh, shut up." Deacon rolled his eyes. "Take me to dinner already, before I decide to take my toy and go home to play with myself."

Steve laughed, deciding to ignore the playing with himself part of that comment as he fully intended to be the one playing with Deacon. "This conversation is nowhere near over."

Deacon mumbled something under his breath, which made Steve chuckle despite not having heard what he said.

He couldn't keep himself from grinning as he pulled out into traffic, thinking life was about to get interesting once again. He prayed that for once, he wasn't wrong.

CHAPTER FIVE

Steve nursed his beer, watching Deacon finish up the last of the fries on his plate. Things had been pretty quiet since Deacon finished explaining why he hadn't tried contacting Steve after moving back. He was feeling like a bit of a heel for giving the poor guy such a hard time over the fact. It hadn't occurred to him someone Deacon's age would be dealing with so much.

He might have guessed, considering the last time they'd seen one another Steve had dropped the guy off at the hospital. The details had been a bit fuzzy, though, and he'd been aware Deacon had been intentionally holding back at the time, not mentioning more than the fact his mother had wrapped her car around a tree.

Watching him even now, Steve got the impression things were quite a bit worse than Deacon was letting on—the way he avoided eye contact shy of quick glances up from his plate, like a child waiting to be scolded at a moment's notice. He wasn't just bashful, there was something else going on underneath.

Sifting through the little information he'd been given, the fact Deacon's mother was in prison for driving under the influence told Steve it wasn't her first offense, which hinted toward a pattern of behavior on the part of the woman Deacon referred to as Patty, as opposed to Mom or Mother. Steve assumed some sort of long-term abuse was the reason behind Deacon distancing himself from the woman who'd given birth to him.

Deacon belched after taking a sip from his soda. Both men started to laugh, and Deacon apologized for his rudeness. He wiped his mouth again. "I feel bad I forced you to dinner, you've already eaten."

Steve winked. "I had fun watching you."

"That's kinda odd, dude, possibly a bit pervy, too." Deacon said.

Steve could tell Deacon enjoyed the reaction his comment received.

They each fell silent and just sat there staring at one another. Whatever it was that had drawn them to one another all those months ago was still there, tugging at Steve's chest. Even through the low lighting of the TGIF, he found himself lost in it until Deacon broke their gaze to check his cell phone again, frowning slightly at the lack of response he'd received from the text to his sister.

"Being a guardian agrees with you," Steve said sarcastically.

Deacon grinned, tossing the phone back onto the table. "Sorry. I have no reason to worry, Ashley's incredibly responsible for someone her age, but—"

"You worry about her all the same," Steve interrupted. "I get it."

"It's just, we're sort of in a probationary period. Patty was reluctant to sign over guardianship to me to begin with, and I don't think the judge would've agreed to it had the Hendersons not stepped in and testified on my behalf."

"And the Hendersons are—"

"Mel's parents, that's Ashley's best friend," Deacon told him. "Still a little shocked they did that for us. They really don't know me all that well. It's temporary custody, but now that I have a job and a steady paycheck, I'm hoping everything will iron out in my favor next time we meet with the judge. The Garibaldi's have written a glowing letter of recommendation on my behalf, that should help."

"They're good people." Steve took another sip of beer before pushing the mug away. The alcohol seemed inappropriate in retrospect. He wouldn't have ordered it had he known then what he knew now, even though Deacon had been drinking the first night they met.

Deacon seemed aware of the fact Steve wasn't going to finish drinking it, but he didn't say anything one way or the other. Deacon smiled suddenly, which caused a chain reaction as Steve did the same, pointing at Deacon's mouth.

"What's that for?"

Deacon shrugged. "It's really good to see you, Steven Actually Steele."

That particular memory had Steve's gut doing a couple of backflips.

"I really did think about calling you, you know?"

Steve sighed, a bit flustered over the implied compliment. "Bet you say that to all the guys you pick up in cheesy hotel bars."

"I've never been one for lying, Steve. It's like one of my few good qualities."

"That I do not believe." Steve sat up in the booth and leaned over the table slightly. "The part about you only having a few good qualities, that is. I can think of at least half a dozen off the top of my head from just having seen you naked."

Deacon inhaled a short breath of air, and Steve could tell the man was blushing, despite not being able to witness it firsthand due to the dark lighting in the restaurant.

"But now that I know you never lie, I thank you for admitting that you've been thinking about me. My fragile ego is once again firmly in place." Steve chuckled when Deacon shook his head. "For the record, I wish you had called me."

The look on Deacon's face seemed to indicate he was wishing the same. "I'm apparently not very bright, you see? That would be one of those negative qualities I was talking about."

"You forget I was out on a date earlier this evening. By comparison, you, sir, have more inherently good qualities in the tip of your pinky than that guy could claim."

It made Steve feel incredible, making Deacon smile.

"I actually missed you, as odd as that sounds." Steve stared down at the top of the table, avoiding eye contact. He was no longer sure he might be saying too much. "I'm sorry about your mother, and you've had a lot on your plate, so I get it."

Deacon began squirming around in the booth like the return to the topic of his family was an unwelcome one. "For some odd reason, I felt like I owed you the truth."

"Thank you for trusting me with it." Steve started to reach

across the table, then stopped himself, smiling at the waitress who was asking if they needed anything else. He told her it was fine to bring the check. The instant she departed, he began to panic at the thought their time together was coming to a close. He wasn't ready to let go of Deacon for the evening and began struggling to come up with an excuse to keep him from going home.

"I wish you'd have let me in sooner, though, I could've helped."

"Really?" Deacon asked. "Is that what you would've done had the roles been reversed?" Deacon shook his head, and Steve became aware of the fact he'd made a piss poor attempt at hiding his true feelings. "Not exactly the type of stuff you wanna open up to about with the great new guy you just met."

Steve sighed but nodded his head. "I get it, I do, but I'm good in a crisis, that's all I'm saying. I'm sorry you've had to deal with it all by yourself."

"Makes you appreciate your parents more, no doubt."

"Makes me appreciate the kind of man you are, Deacon," Steve said, those big brown eyes once again piercing his chest like a laser beam to the heart.

"God, you're pretty," Deacon blurted out.

Steve blushed and started to laugh quietly. That wasn't the typical compliment he got from other men.

"Seriously, those baby-blues practically destroy me." Deacon cleared his throat.

Steve got the impression Deacon might be wishing he could learn to think before speaking.

"Thank you, Deacon, that's not one I get very often."

"Find that hard to believe." Deacon shifted in his seat.

"I think you're very pretty, too." Steve was grinning in that slightly teasing way, back to flirting once again.

"Shut up, and stop leering at me for crying out loud, makes me feel all naked and shit."

"I'm most certainly picturing you all naked and shit." Steve tapped his index finger against his temple a couple of times, taking an immense amount of pleasure watching Deacon squirm under his gaze.

Deacon sighed, visibly relieved for the distraction when his cell phone blurted out a little chirping tune, signaling he'd received a text. He grabbed for it a little too quickly, which had Steve chuckling.

He tapped the screen, his lips moving as he read the text. "Ashley's studying late at Mel's, decided to spend the night and go to school with her in the morning."

"Glad to hear she's okay." Steve said.

Deacon went back to tapping on the screen, texting her back to let her know he'd received the message. "Nothing new there, she ends up spending the night over there two or three nights a week. Mel's parents never liked them staying over at our house because of Patty. I work late most of the time plus it gives me a break, you know?"

Steve nodded that he understood.

"The fact the Hendersons are so overprotective means I don't have to worry as much about Ashley when she's over there."

"Sounds to me like you also don't have any reason to rush home tonight, as a result."

Steve was once again leering across the table at him.

"Pfft, you don't know," Deacon said. "I might have to work early in the morning."

Steve shrugged. "You told me you work nights at the store?"

Deacon curled up his lip. "I could have another date lined up, you know…a midnight rendezvous waiting for me."

"You better not,' Steve said, looking indignant.

"That's rich coming from the guy who was on a date earlier this evening. Double standard much?"

"Whose fault is that?" Steve asked, looking incredulous. "Were I aware of your presence sooner, let me assure you, I would have been all up in your business long before tonight."

Deacon smiled, apparently enjoying the sound of that.

"Sex would certainly go a long way toward easing the blow that you never called." Steve added.

"Oh brother," Deacon said, a little louder than he'd intended. "Tell me now, exactly how long are you planning to milk that one?"

Steve shrugged. "For as long as I can, I'd imagine."

"At least you're honest about your emotional treachery."

"Ain't too proud to beg." Steve sang along with the doo-wop dudes playing over the restaurants sound system before adding under his breath, "Or make you beg as the case might be."

Deacon folded his arms across his chest as Steve continued singing along.

"I can't believe you know the words, sheesh, how old is this song anyway?" Deacon asked, doing his best to feign disinterest.

"It's the Temptations for crying out loud." Steve shook his head, disapproving of Deacon's apparent lack of musical prowess. "The electric car, the lack of musical taste…it's a wonder anyone is willing to take you on."

Steve made sure his behavior was over the top so Deacon wouldn't take him seriously for even a moment.

"Too bad you're so upset, I *was* gonna go home with you, but—"

"I'll get over it," Steve interrupted.

They both started to laugh as the waitress swung by to clear the dirty plates and drop off the check. She'd get an extra bump in gratuity for her fortuitous timing, Steve thought, reaching for his wallet.

"You don't actually have to pay for my dinner," Deacon said, reaching for the receipt.

Steve snatched it up off the table. "I insist, but feel free to thank me later if you're so inclined."

Deacon scoffed. "Like I can be had for the price of a meal?"

Steve laughed evilly. "What else am I supposed to think? I had you for the price of a couple of cocktails the first time around."

Deacon laughed, rubbing at his nose like he might be ready to sneeze. "That was a fluke! You caught me in a moment of weakness, not likely to happen again, buddy."

Steve tossed some bills onto the table, unable to keep himself from grinning from ear to ear as he scooted across the seat, getting out of the booth. "Let's get outta here so I can get you someplace we can put your objections to the test."

Deacon was shaking his head as he followed suit. "Guess it's true what they say, you really can't teach an old dog new tricks."

Steve's mouth fell open, watching as Deacon walked away toward the exit. He began to follow the little shit, muttering, "You haven't seen half my tricks."

* * * *

"What you do to me, Deacon Miller." Steve thrust his cock deep inside, watching the expression on Deacon's face as he moaned while biting down on his bottom lip. "Like someone set a fire inside, one that threatens to burn me alive."

"Steve," was all Deacon managed to get out in return before Steve took him by the ankles, forcing his legs back and his ass farther up into the air.

Steve knew he wasn't going to last much longer so he picked up the pace.

"Fuck yes," Deacon muttered, already jacking himself off and groaning louder with each forceful thrust.

"Want you to come for me, Deacon," Steve said, his voice trembling as he teetered right on the edge, got closer and closer each time he forced his hard cock deep inside Deacon's warm tight ass.

Deacon called out that he was going to come, and Steve drove his cock in at just the right angle, causing Deacon to lose it. Several shots of cum sprayed across Deacon's abs, and Steve soon followed, screaming his own orgasm.

Steve was still muttering Deacon's name over and over in a soft whisper when he collapsed on top of him. His body was still twitching, and his pelvis lightly thrusting, unable to pull out just yet—not sure he ever wanted to.

"Fucking Christ," Deacon whispered, making Steve laugh for a moment. "You do that really, *really* well for a guy that's been hiding out in a closet for a couple of decades."

"Think so?" Steve asked, attempting to get his wind back.

"Still seeing stars." Deacon was smiling, lying back with his eyes shut tight.

"Damn beautiful," Steve whispered, closing off any attempt at further discussion by kissing Deacon.

It was slow and passionate, tongues dancing, no longer warring for control, merely tasting one another as they continued to lick and suck. After several minutes passed, Steve pulled out of Deacon, his own dick beginning to soften despite the fact Deacon was getting hard again.

Steve moaned, breaking their kiss as he reached down, slipping off the condom. "Cannot believe you're getting another erection."

Deacon chuckled. "I get hard easily."

"You don't say?" Steve said sarcastically.

"To be fair, I'm not as big as you are. Doesn't require as much wind to raise my sail. It'll take a bit before I can come again, though, if that makes you feel any better."

"I love that you're attempting to soothe my ego right now. You've got to be the sweetest man I've ever had the pleasure of… knowing."

Deacon frowned, and Steve laughed, realizing his attempt to change the direction of that last comment came too little too late.

"Sorry, baby," Steve said, before getting up off the bed and heading into the attached bathroom.

Deacon came padding in behind him, heading straight for the shower as he tried not to leave a trail of cum, which had begun to run down his stomach and thigh.

"I was gonna bring in a washcloth to clean you up." Steve held the item up into the air as an offering of proof.

"Oh, um." Deacon fumbled with the knobs, turning on the water. "Well, come in here and bring it with you."

The water shot to life from the showerhead, and Deacon squealed when the blast of cold water hit his skin. Steve tried not to laugh as Deacon clung to the side of the stall, trying to avoid further contact until the water warmed.

"So not funny," Deacon said in a whisper.

"It's a little bit funny." Steve stepped into the stall, the washcloth dangling from his right hand as the now lukewarm water hit his legs.

"You're not looking all that helpful either," Deacon said as Steve pulled the glass door closed behind him and dropped to his knees.

"Here, hold this." Steve held the washcloth up until Deacon took it from him.

"What'cha doin' down there?" Deacon was trying to hold back a grin as Steve shook his head, watching Deacon's cock begin to swell.

"Horny little bastard," Steve said, licking his lips.

"Real nice, and a little judge-y coming from the man currently on his knees."

Steve smiled, wrapping his thumb and index finger just above Deacon's balls, giving them a gentle tug. "What makes you think I wasn't referring to myself?"

"Were you?" Deacon's breathing had become shallow.

Steve hovered there, his lips partially opened and only centimeters away from the head of Deacon's cock. "Certainly could've been."

"I take it all back," Deacon said as Steve licked the head, using only the tip of his tongue. "You're not a very nice man after all."

"Want me to show exactly how not-nice I can be?" Steve

asked.

Deacon nodded while chewing nervously on his bottom lip. "Yes, please."

* * * *

There was nothing but the sound of rustling sheets and blankets as they each crawled back into bed. Steve had decided to personally accept full responsibility for the smile currently on Deacon's face.

"The way you say my name when you're coming…" Deacon shut his eyes briefly as if attempting to recall the way it sounded.

"I tend to get a little worked up."

"Like some sort of heated prayer or something." Deacon reopened his eyes. "You almost make me not hate my name."

"I like your name, think it's sexy," Steve said.

"It's kind of a religious name, which is weird to me."

Steve ran his fingertips along Deacon's thigh. "Then allow me to be the first to worship at the altar of all that is you, baby."

"That's both disturbing and mildly erotic at the same time."

"Only mildly erotic?" Steve kissed his way up along Deacon's rib cage before briefly sucking on a nipple. "I need to work on my delivery."

Deacon hissed, his toes curling. "God, still sore there, buddy."

"Sorry about that, but nipple play is just too damn fun when it makes a boy squirm and pant as much as it does you." Steve wiggled his eyebrows, tweaking the hard, red nub once more with the tip of his tongue, causing Deacon's entire body to tense briefly. "Why don't you like it, family name or something?"

"You could say that." Deacon ran his hand through Steve's short blond wavy curls, fingers lacing through the baby soft hair. "Sorta named after my father, but that's a whole other crummy story. I promise you don't wanna hear that one."

Steve settled back into the bed. "I want to know everything

about you."

"That's just sick, dude." Deacon rolled his eyes when Steve didn't crack a smile, letting him off the hook gracefully. "Fine, but don't say you weren't warned."

Steve offered a quick thank-you peck. "You've done your due diligence."

"I only know this because at one point, my Aunt Sara overheard my mother telling me it was my fault that my father had left her. Think I was like eleven or twelve at the time. It was just before Ashley was born, or right after, can't recall exactly at this point."

Steve frowned.

"See, I told you, my past is a real downer. We should talk about something else?"

"Is it wrong of me to say I'm *happy* your mom is in jail?"

"Not the typical sentiment one expects, but I get it. This is why I don't like to talk about my family. It makes normal people feel uncomfortable."

"It makes me sad for you, not uncomfortable. You can tell me anything, but I don't want to pressure you to. I'd prefer you want to tell me as opposed to me prying it out of you."

"It wasn't a new thing for me. Patty saying it was my fault my father left her, she'd said it many times before. It was the sort of accusations that came after a certain number of cocktails."

"I'd have had a few words for your mother," Steve said, visibly pissed.

"Aunt Sara tried several times over the years to convince me to move to Arizona and live with her."

"Why didn't you?" Steve asked.

Deacon shrugged. "Guess I felt like I couldn't leave Patty all alone. I was constantly afraid she'd hurt herself or worse, that whatever guy she was dating at the time might hurt her. She dated a couple of abusers over the years."

"Your aunt should've fought harder for you, reported your

mother, something." Steve was livid.

"Things aren't always so simple, Steve. Patty comes by her homophobia honestly. My grandparents were very strict, devoutly religious and very homophobic. And Aunt Sara has had a female *roommate* for thirty-some-odd years now."

Steve sighed, nodding he understood. "Your aunt's a lesbian."

"She's still in the closet even though my grandparents are both dead. She's aware that I know, and even though I've been out since my early teens, she's never actually said the words aloud to me."

Steve reached underneath the blanket and scratched his thigh. "They can be very difficult words to say."

"Patty threatened to expose her whenever Sara pushed too hard. Stupid considering my grandparents cut Patty out of their lives after I was born. I hardly saw them, growing up."

"Which is probably a good thing from the sound of it."

Deacon nodded, making a soft humming sound. "Once Ashley came along I was afraid to leave for her sake—at least until things got so bad with all the gay stuff that I simply couldn't bear it any longer."

"You're a damn fine brother and a much better son than your mother deserved. I always hated being an only child."

"I wouldn't trade Ash for anything, and as bad as it sounds, it does help knowing that there's someone else in the world who understands me, who has gone through the same things I have, shared the experience, regardless of how awful it was."

"That's not bad, Deacon. You are human."

"It's a bit selfish. If I were a better person, I'd wish she'd never gone through any of it."

"May I remind you that your name is Deacon not Saint?"

"Ah yes, back around to the question of my name. Sorry, I got kinda sidetracked there."

Steve winked. "I'm along for the ride regardless."

"You're back to being sweet again." Deacon pointed out, an

observation that had Steve blushing. "Anyway, according to Sara, at the ripe old age of nineteen, my mother had an affair with a married man from the church they'd grown up attending. He was a very powerful member of the congregation, more than twice her age and her best friend's father."

"Christ, she was self-destructive from the get-go," Steve said, wide-eyed.

"Apparently. His name was Dan Mason, he was a deacon at the church, who brought in a lot of money. Needless to say, he was quite a popular guy."

"Oh shit," Steve mumbled.

"Sara did say Deacon Dan was pretty scummy, stringing Patty along for quite some time after discovering she was knocked up. Patty swore that Dan had promised to leave his family for her, that they'd run away together."

Steve cut in. "And of course, he dropped Patty instead."

"Cut off all contact."

"I imagine being pregnant at her age back then didn't go over real well."

"Sara said that my grandparents wore themselves out trying to get Patty to tell them who the father was, but she never would say. Why Sara never told anyone else aside from me, I don't know, but my mother seemed to believe that Dan would come back to her once I was born. I went nameless for nearly two weeks, known only as Baby Boy Miller while Patty waited for my father to come forward."

"And when he didn't, she named you Deacon so everyone would know…subtle."

"People realized what had happened, but everyone blamed her, assuming Patty had seduced him. She never went after him for money, but she did exact her revenge by simply refusing to disappear. Patty never stopped going to church—always sat just a few pews behind my father and his family. Sara said she would sometimes pinch me, making me cry in the middle of service, creating a scene and intentionally drawing attention to us. It eventually drove my father, and the family he did want, to move away."

"Fuck, Deacon, that's messed up."

"I don't actually remember any of it, but I am glad Sara told me. Eventually, I understood the kind of person Patty was. That her behavior and the things she said to me were not normal."

"Your father's a real dick too." Steve was visibly irritated. "Not that I'm a real beacon of morality with some of the shit I've pulled in my life, but to treat your own child like that? Kylie isn't even mine by blood, but it kills me that I hardly get to see her."

"I called him once, my dad. I was thirteen, maybe fourteen, can't quite remember now. The silence on the other end of the line was deafening. I could hear him breathing, though, so I knew he was still there. I told him I didn't want anything from him, just wanted to meet him face to face, to see him. Just once, you know—to know the man I came from."

Deacon was looking in his direction, but Steve could tell he was staring off into space.

"What happened?" Steve asked, bringing him back to the present.

"Deacon Dan told me there was nothing he could do for me. Asked me to never contact him again, before hanging up."

Steve sat up in bed, propping up his elbows on his knees. "What a goddamn, good for nothing prick."

Deacon shrugged it off. "It is what it is."

"You're better off, Deacon, and I truly mean that. There is nothing someone like that can do for you, he wasn't lying about that."

"It would have been nice, though, you know? To have been able to get to know him?"

Steve crawled on top of him, pinning Deacon to the bed with his body. "It was most definitely his loss."

Steve kissed him softly…slowly, pulling Deacon back from the shadows of the past and into the warm and fuzzy present.

"I barely know you, and I think you're pretty incredible," Steve said, breaking the kiss and doing that whole stare-into-Deacon's-soul bit.

"Keep looking at me like that, and I'm going to require another dinner, buddy."

Steve grinned and leaned in for another kiss. Mere minutes passed before they were both hard and grinding into one another. The urgency had been replaced with something else—something Steve was unfamiliar with but didn't dislike. He was certain of one thing for sure—he longed to get lost in Deacon. Ached to be inside him again—tied to the human race by the comfort of heat and need. He wanted to be able to give Deacon something, a safe harbor where he might find shelter from the rest of the world?

In that precise moment, it didn't feel like too much for him to give.

As he sucked on Deacon's neck and possessively cupped his ass with the palm of his hand, fingers inching toward his hole, Steve allowed any doubts he had to drift away. For now, he'd take whatever the man in his arms wanted to offer, and that would have to be enough.

CHAPTER SIX

Quietly, Deacon stood at the counter next to the sink in the break room, packing up a basket with the food he'd purchased from the bakery and deli. He'd noticed the Garibaldi stamped plastic baggies filled with cheese and deli meat in Steve's fridge the last time he'd spent the night and had gleaned some sense of what the man liked to eat.

It had been his fourth time spending the night at Steve's, yet the first time he'd felt comfortable enough to open the fridge door and get himself a bottle of water. Steve had told him to make himself at home, which Deacon thought was funny at the time as he'd never truly felt like he'd had a home—at least not in the traditional sense of the word. Patty had done a great job of ensuring he never received a moment of peace while under her roof, and as a result the h-word had been somewhat tainted.

He'd only lived by himself once, when he'd first moved to Chicago, but even then, it was a room that he rented in someone else's house, so not really his place. From there, he'd moved in with Seth, who never really let him forget that fact. Even now, despite all the painting and redecorating he and Ashley had done to Patty's, it was still her place, not his. They'd scrubbed it clean and given it a facelift, but the place still seemed…haunted. Too much had happened underneath that roof, too many bad memories.

He turned around briefly, ripped out of his own thoughts hearing Isabelle clearing her throat. She was thirteen and the youngest child of her employers. She acted like it as well and was the nosiest little girl Deacon had ever met. Her sweet, round and innocent looking face masked the fact she'd waterboard your ass if it meant getting the information she wanted out of you.

Her long, straight black hair hung loosely, the bangs tied back off her face with a simple barrette. She was currently absentmindedly gnawing on the eraser of her pencil while doing her homework. School was out for a teacher's conference, though

Deacon thought it was odd for her to be here, nevertheless.

Ashley had gone with Mel and her parents for a weekend trip to Toledo to visit relatives. That combined with the fact this was Deacon's one weekend off for the month was responsible for his current predicament. He'd decided to surprise Steve by taking him lunch.

It had been total impulse. He'd been awake since seeing Ashley off at eight that morning. He'd cleaned the house and done a couple loads of laundry before settling onto the couch with a new book that he found himself too antsy to read. He'd driven all the way to the store before giving the idea much thought, and now, as he packed one of the stupid-ass baskets that they sold in the store, he was second-guessing himself.

They were set to see each other that night, and Deacon was now wondering if showing up unannounced was going to come off looking needy. In truth, he was just bored. At least that was the current party line he was touting inside his head. Even as he stood there, chewing on his lip, he somehow believed Steve would be happy to see him regardless of the reason.

Now or later or both.

That felt right in his gut, but it seemed all wrong based upon experience. They liked each other too much—more than they should, considering they'd only known each other for a few weeks, aside from that one-nighter months before.

"What are you doing?" Isabelle asked, sounding annoyed, as if his silent fretting had disturbed her studying.

"Taking lunch to a friend," Deacon said, getting on with it.

He hadn't hidden the fact he was gay from his coworkers, everyone knew, but he wasn't a fan of questions. Unfortunately, the Garibaldi family wasn't one to shy away from interrogations… and relentless teasing. They were great, but he'd been raised in a non-communicative environment where you didn't say much of anything unless it was hateful and directed at a so-called, would-be loved one. That left Deacon ill-equipped to deal with intrigue because, growing up, no one particularly gave a shit what he did so long as he did it quietly and kept out of Patty's hair.

Mrs. Garibaldi strolled in, glancing at her daughter and not looking all that happy before smiling warmly at Deacon. "Aren't you supposed to be off today?"

He smiled back, never could seem to help himself when it came to Gilda Garibaldi. She'd asked him to call her by her first name on several occasions, but it just didn't feel appropriate. The woman was all-Mom. She fit the title so well that he'd be more inclined to call Gilda "mom", than he would Patty. She'd been so nice to him and Ashley from the word go, and he felt like she deserved to be treated with respect as a result.

She still made them friggin' casseroles or lasagna every now and again. It was a gesture that had touched him so profoundly—that she would actually spend her free time doing that for him. She said it wasn't such a big thing. She was used to cooking for a houseful, and now that most her kids had moved out, she suffered from excessive leftovers disease, and Deacon was doing her the favor by taking some of it off her hands.

"He's taking lunch to his boyfriend," Isabelle said, using a snotty tone.

He felt his face burn red, and Mrs. Garibaldi grinned momentarily before berating her daughter. "You mind your business, young lady, and get back to writing that report before I ground you for another week."

Deacon had no clue what Isabelle had done, and he didn't intend on asking as it would inevitably lead to an hour-long discussion. Nearly every conversation with a Garibaldi would if allowed to.

Deacon stepped back when Gilda came peeking over his shoulder to see what he'd chosen. She had a very pretty face, round with a clean complexion. Even with the little bits of gray through her dark hair, she was one of those people who looked eternally young. She wore a lot of dresses, which made her seem like a bit of a throwback, though she rarely wore heels, preferring flats or sandals, sometimes even snow boots in the winter, which Deacon found to be kind of adorable.

He knew without asking that Mrs. Garibaldi was merely

attempting to be helpful. He was also happy for any advice she might have, as the woman knew food like no one else he'd ever known. She was like a foodie scientist, able to pair combinations together that complemented one another, making the simplest of cuisines taste unique and more flavorful.

"Not bad," she said, appearing to be impressed. "Though you're missing something sweet."

"So you're saying I'm not enough?" he asked dryly.

She giggled, shaking her head at him.

"The gays don't eat sugar, Mom," Isabelle said, her tone tinged with condescension.

"Idiot child." Gilda sighed like she might be reaching the end her rope with her youngest, then grinned at Deacon. "I'll be right back, I know just the thing."

He was once again touched that she seemed invested in Deacon's happiness. Isabelle was watching him, visibly not caring for the fact her mother currently liked him more than her. He almost asked why she was in trouble, then quietly turned away.

Elena came rushing through the door, coffee cup in hand as she made a beeline for the fresh pot. She was the oldest of the Garibaldi children and currently in the process of taking over the handling of the business from her father. She'd said hello to him, even though she hadn't actually made eye contact. Her brothers had started referring to her as The Blur. There had been a lot of push and pull amongst the children, and a few of the older sons weren't happy Elena had become their father's 'chosen one'.

From what Deacon could tell, Elena seemed like a good choice, more even tempered and diplomatic. He had no clue if she had the business chops, but as far as a public face for the company, she was a total rock star. She'd interviewed him and been the one that had hired him, so it was entirely possible he was biased.

"Romantic picnic for Mr. Steele?" Elena asked, having stopped long enough to a breath as she dumped sugar and creamer into her cup.

Gilda came rushing back in with two plastic containers. "Fresh assortment of berries and some *crème fraîche* on the side." She nodded curtly at Isabelle in a take-that sort of way. "So it's a somewhat healthier dessert."

"That's perfect, thank you, Mrs. Garibaldi." Deacon packed it, slipping the two bottles of water into the corners before closing the lid. "I'll pay for them on my way out."

"You most certainly will not," she insisted, getting that 'don't fuck with mama' look. "Dessert is on me."

"Isn't Mr. Steele kinda old for you?" Isabelle asked, grinning evilly.

Elena rolled her eyes, then smacked her sister upside the head. "Mind your business."

"Ouch," Isabelle whined.

"Not when the man—" Gilda reached over and straightening out Deacon's faded T-shirt like she did with her own sons. "—is as attractive and successful as Mr. Steele."

Deacon smiled at her, thinking if he could choose any mom in the world for his mother he would pick her.

"I'm a little jealous," Elena mumbled, brushing aside the long curls that had gone rogue, falling across her face.

"I think he's old," Isabelle said defiantly.

"I think I'm mortified," Deacon said, wishing to God or Beelzebub or the friggin' Tooth Fairy that he'd not been spotted kissing Steve in the parking lot last weekend.

All three of them giggled, like he was silly for believing he was around for anything other than their own amusement.

"He's very kind," Deacon finally admitted, realizing they weren't going to allow him to leave until he gave them something. "The fact he's smoking hot is just a bonus."

Elena shot him a slightly hateful look like she might be jealous before sighing away her frustration and whizzing back out the door.

"He's a nice man, I agree," Gilda said. "Will be nice to see you taking care of one another, perhaps?"

Deacon glanced down at his T-shirt. "I shoulda dressed nicer, huh?"

"I don't think it'll matter all that much if he likes you for the right reasons, no?" Gilda asked.

"You're a very nice lady," Deacon said, making Gilda smile like someone had just given her a car.

"Oh brother," Isabelle moaned.

"Go on…you get outta here before you end up sucked into any more of our nonsense," Gilda said, giving her daughter the evil eye. "Have a good weekend, Deacon."

"You too." He grunted slightly, lifting the basket off the counter and thinking he'd obviously packed too much shit in it, then grabbed his coat off the chair on his way out.

As he walked along the back hall and out the employee and service entrance, Deacon could feel the butterflies flapping around inside his gut. He wasn't used to such blatant giddiness, and the fact any sort of happiness made him uncomfortable wasn't lost on him. He knew it was going to be a very long war before he allowed himself to relax long enough to fully accept the fact Steve made him happy. Considering how new they were, it felt a tad ridiculous to be having such thoughts in the first place. He couldn't seem to keep himself from smiling all the same.

CHAPTER SEVEN

It was one of those days when the sun was almost too bright, Steve thought as he yawned and stared out the window walls of his office that overlooked the showroom. The entire front façade of the dealership was glass, which let in a butt-load of natural light. The unfortunate side effect was, when it was nice out, Steve had to force himself to stay inside and work. Of course on deceptive days like this one, when it only seemed nice until venturing out into the cock-shrinking, cold-ass air, it only served to make him long for the nearly-naked days of summer.

The fact it was rapidly nearing the end of the month and they hadn't sold their quota did little to lift his spirits. He'd dropped out of college and taken Steele Automotive over after his father had passed away back in the early nineties. It hadn't been his dream, per se; it was the restoration side business Steve co-owned with three of his friends that he loved. The cars were certainly a passion—even as a child, he'd been mesmerized by the shapes and lines, the way each style or body type managed to evoke an entirely different mood or feeling.

The dealership helped fund the restoration side business, but Steve had never been a fan of the stress that came from a sales-driven occupation. It was a bottom line business. He enjoyed being the boss, enjoyed the sense of pride that came from providing others with a paycheck, allowing them to put a roof over their heads and provide for their families. However, he could live without the stress of monthly quotas, keeping a laser-focused eye on the profit margins built into the sticker prices in conjunction with the rebates they received from the manufacturer—figuring in the commissions received from the financing deals and warranties sold.

Steve massaged his temple, his head throbbing as he tried not to think about the inventory that needed to be moved.

The bright side was they were coming up on the weekend and despite the cold weather, the sun had been forecasted to stick around until the beginning of next week. All the ingredients were on hand to push them over their minimum and move some units out the door.

They'd moved into the new location a year and a half ago, having expanded considerably despite the recession, which had hit many of his competitors hard. Many had either gone under or consolidated. Steve had always been fairly conservative when it came to spending money; the reserves he'd built up allowed Steele Automotive to do more than merely weather the storm.

While the building itself was fairly new, the exterior was fairly ordinary architecturally speaking. The inside had been a whole other matter. Steve had brought in an interior designer to ensure the finishes felt as classy and detailed as those of the classic cars he loved. Everything sparkled, from the thick black slate tiled floor to the black leather and chrome seating scattered throughout that had been inspired by vintage Deco designs of the thirties.

There were three conference rooms, one in the center and the other two on opposite sides of the building, Steve's office was tucked in between two of them. The one glass wall looked out across the showroom, but the entrance was just off a hallway that led back to the service department, the employee break room, and bathrooms.

Marjorie was technically his secretary, whom he shared with his GM, but in reality, she was the glue that held Steele Automotive together. She sat on the opposite side of his window in an enclosed front desk with the receptionist. She was both gatekeeper and micromanager. No one did anything without running it past her, even Steve. She'd been a part of the automotive industry for the past fifty-three years in one form or another, and she knew her shit. Nobody got anything past Marjorie, and as such, she'd been awarded the respect and pay she was entitled to.

Steve liked to keep the atmosphere comfortable for his employees but demanded they maintain a level of professionalism, especially when out front on the showroom floor. Aside from the consumer walking through the front door, who was king, nobody that worked for him was more important than anyone else, from janitor to gear jockey and everyone in between, Steve treated each person that worked for him the same. Without them, he had no business and he knew it.

Other than a few bumps in the road over the years due to one or two personality conflicts, most of his staff had been with him from the time he took over. Steve took that fact in particular to be a personal triumph, considering the turnover in the front end of a dealership was typically pretty high—the sales guys had a tendency to jump around a lot.

The buzz in the air that day was a positive one due to the decent amount of foot traffic they'd seen already. He was optimistic they'd be able to pull themselves out of the sales slump. Business woes aside, Steve was finding it difficult to concentrate on work. He wanted to be someplace else—anywhere with a naked and sweaty Deacon Miller to be exact.

Bent over the kitchen island at home would work. Or Deacon on his back in front of a roaring fire, legs in the air and pleading for me to fuck him harder. On his side so I can fuck him from behind while we make out to the point we're both dizzy.

He smiled, adjusting himself in his chair due to the erection that was painfully pushing against the fabric of his briefs. He'd experienced more midday boners in the past few weeks than he had in many years.

"Like you're sixteen again with no goddamn self-control."

He'd said it as a condemnation of his out-of-control behavior, but he was still grinning. Continued thoughts of a naked and pleading Deacon weren't helping matters.

"That's the one, right there," Jimmy said, pointing at Steve's face as he pushed away from the doorjamb and entered the office.

Jimmy Newland had been his best friend since high school and was now the General Sales Manager for the dealership. He strolled in, eyes all squinty, like Clint Eastwood in pretty much every movie the man had ever starred in. Steve watched him flop down into one of the black leather and chrome chairs on the opposite side of his desk.

He cleared his throat while scooting his chair under the desk and went back to staring at his computer monitor. "What do you need, Jimmy?"

Like Steve, Jimmy had aged well. They'd been nearly inseparable since seventh grade. Roomed together through college and they shared a passion for cars. Even now they spent all day at the dealership together, typically ate lunch with one another, they worked out together and up until the time Steve had come out—with the exception of when either of them had been married—they'd gone out drinking and picking up women with one another.

Jimmy had left his suit jacket somewhere else, and as usual, his too-colorful tie was slightly askew, like he'd been tugging on it in silent, agonizing protest. He was lanky, taller than Steve and prettier by Steve's calculations. He'd never had any trouble getting laid, but he'd been married and divorced twice.

"Everyone's been talking about that grin of yours all week. You're freaking people out, Hoss."

Jimmy was now smiling, chewing on some gum and looking like he knew something no one else did. Steve sneered, thinking this right here was reason enough to never keep friends for more than a few years before cycling in a brand new batch.

"You don't know me." Steve sniffed, finally flipping Jimmy off when he didn't take the hint.

"You find yourself a little piece of ass?" Jimmy shuttered slightly. "Jeez, that means something totally different now. You sure you're a homo?"

Steve didn't react to the intended shudder of repulsion from his oldest friend because he was shocked Jimmy had brought up the topic to begin with. In the months since he'd come out to everyone at work, Jimmy had avoided this topic in general. It was the first sign that there might be a light at the end of the tunnel for the two of them. Steve had pretty much decided Jimmy would never come around, and that thought ate him up inside. It had been exactly what he'd feared most, the thing that had kept him in the closet all those years.

"Don't get high and mighty with me, shithead." Steve pointed across the desk at him. "Don't forget I know all your secrets, and you, my friend, have most certainly stuck your pecker up more than one asshole over the years."

"Not with a dude!" Jimmy tossed one of his long, lanky legs over the arm of the chair.

It was a habit of Jimmy's, which at one point, long ago in the very distant past, had been more than a little distracting to a closeted Steve Steele.

"Honestly, one asshole doesn't really look all that different from another," Steve said. "Though men tend to be hairier."

Jimmy made a slight gagging sound that had Steve laughing. He didn't actually want to be having this discussion with his best friend. It was something he couldn't imagine ever being completely comfortable discussing with any of the guys he worked with—though several had made somewhat strained and uncomfortable attempts to do so over the past few months.

For now, he was willing to swallow the discomfort. Lord knows he'd swallowed a lot more than that in the past. Steve decided to take it as a sign of support.

It didn't help that all the guys at work seemed interested in talking about was either sex or sports, but Steve had zero interest in becoming the in-house gay sex information kiosk. It was pretty easy to discourage Jimmy from pushing too hard for details, since the details tended to gross him out.

"I don't know I'll ever get used to it, Stevie," Jimmy added. "But you know I want you happy, right?"

"I do, and thanks for that." Steve sighed. "It actually means a lot to me. I was afraid I might end up with no friends after… you know?"

"No way, I don't get it, how you can go from banging chicks to screwing dudes, but hey…too much water under the bridge to lose my best friend at this point. Had you done it back in high school or college, no problem… I'd've tossed your ass over in a heartbeat."

"That's real nice." Steve shook his head as he leaned back in his seat. "I do actually have work to do, you know that, right?"

"Please, you're just trying to look busy so Margie doesn't get after you."

Steve laughed, despite not being true in that particular moment, he'd certainly been guilty of that in the past.

"You're trying to avoid the fact that I know you're gettin' some." Jimmy started squinting again. "Walking around the joint like you're the cock-of-the-walk. You don't wanna talk about it… makes me think you might be ashamed of him or something. But I know your stud-strut when I see it."

"Christ, fine, sheesh, you're like a girl all of sudden, wanting all the details." Steve tossed his arms through the air. "I'm seeing someone, we met over Christmas, he's moved back to town since then, and we've been dating for a couple of weeks." Jimmy opened his mouth to ask another question, but Steve cut him off. "He's very dreamy, and yes, I'm planning to ask him to the prom so we can totally double."

"Shit." Jimmy sat there, staring blankly across the desk at him. "You really like him?"

It sounded more like an accusation than a question, and Steve placed his head in hands and faux-wept.

"So when do we meet him?" Jimmy asked.

Steve looked up, his arms falling to a thud across the top of his desk. "If I thought I could get away with it? Never."

Jimmy smiled evilly. "I gotta make sure he's good enough to date my little sister."

"Fuck you."

"Sick!" Jimmy shuddered. "You're practically family, that would be incestuous."

"Will you get out? Surely, you can find some work to do."

"You leave your sense of humor up some guy's ass?" Jimmy forced back a grin as he tried to sell his own indignation. "Gay means happy, Stevie. Get with the program, or I'll have to sic the fairies on you."

"How anyone could think *you* homophobic, I don't know."

"I know, right? I'm practically parade-ready."

The intercom from the phone on his desk buzzed, and they both looked out the window at his secretary, Margie.

Steve's stomach dropped as Margie announced he had a visitor. There was Deacon standing on the opposite side of her desk, holding a large basket. He was up and out of his seat in a flash, despite his best efforts to remain cool and collected; he couldn't manage to prevent the big cheesy grin now plastered across his face.

He signaled for Deacon to come on in.

"Holy shit, is that the guy?" Jimmy asked, making no signs to vacate nor offering any evidence he intended to act cool.

Deacon was smiling like an idiot as well as he watched Margie point toward the hall around the corner, giving him directions to Steve's office.

"Christ, Stevie, you been trolling Toys R Us…how old is he, twelve?"

Steve backhanded Jimmy in the arm as he passed by. "He's twenty-seven, thank you."

"Hope you checked his ID, that's all I'm saying."

"He's older than that bimbo you're screwing at the moment."

Jimmy scowled, apparently not enjoying the reminder. "I don't think it's the same thing."

"Can you not be an asshole," Steve muttered, opening the door to his office for Deacon who had his hands full. "Hi."

"Hey," Deacon said, planting a quick peck on Steve's lips before hobbling over to the desk and using both hands to place the basket on top of his desk with a thud.

Steve licked his lips and noticed Margie was now staring wide-eyed, having witnessed 'the kiss'. Jimmy's mouth currently hung open in shock as well.

It was little more than a peck, but he and Deacon had not really had the discussion about PDA, which Steve was not too comfy with, especially at his place of business, though when he thought about, he wasn't big on it anywhere.

When he turned, Jimmy was once again smiling like the cat about to eat the canary.

"Jimmy was just leaving," Steve announced.

"Not before an introduction, Hoss," Jimmy said, holding out his hand for Deacon. "I'm Steve's oldest and best friend, so I'll be the best man when the time comes, just so you know."

Deacon was stunned into silence momentarily before he seemed to understand Jimmy was being a smart ass. They shook hands briefly. "Good to meet you."

"He's getting a little ahead of us." Steve tried not to enjoy the fact Deacon was blushing as he grabbed Jimmy by the arm and dragged him toward the door. "And he's leaving."

"It was very nice meeting you," Jimmy said as he was shoved through the door. "Give Stevie and me a heads up for the next frat party," he added before Steve slammed the door in his face.

He took a deep breath, doing his best not to think about the hazing he'd have to endure over the next couple of days. He glanced up, saying a quick prayer pleading for mercy before he turned to see Deacon was now chewing nervously on his lip.

"This wasn't such a good idea, huh?" Deacon asked.

"I'm not sure what this is, just yet, though from the smell coming from that basket, I'm assuming you brought me lunch?"

"Yeah." Deacon was nodding, staring down at the basket. "I shoulda called first, huh? Damn. I'm sorry, I didn't think."

Now Steve felt bad. "Are you kidding? This is...very nice of you, Deacon. Really."

Steve crossed the office and gave Deacon's arm a squeeze of reassurance before he looked down at the basket. His stomach started to growl.

Deacon snickered hearing the tummy-grumble. "I have good timing, despite having no tact. Please tell me I didn't just out you at work or anything."

"No, they all know, but I've never really had anyone show up here before." He glanced out the window and saw several employees passing by as they walked through the showroom, doing a terrible job of pretending not to be watching as they glanced up from their cell phones.

Further evidence that texting should be outlawed.

Seeing the nervous fidgeting return as Deacon hovered next to the desk, Steve swallowed his own discomfort long enough to give Deacon a quick peck on the lips, falling on his own sword in an attempt to put the man at ease.

"What did you bring me?"

The distraction of lunch seemed to do the trick as Deacon stopped looking out the window at the onlookers and went about unpacking the basket. It was a mouthwatering spread including gourmet meats and cheeses direct from the deli counter at Garibaldi's. There was an array of olives, crusty French loaf, German potato salad and some of the garlicy-hummus Steve had become addicted to ever since Deacon had recommended it the weekend before when Steve went in to see him under the pretense of needing groceries.

They'd met for dinner three times, lunch twice and Deacon had spent the night a couple more times since Steve had run into him in the chip and cracker aisle of Garibaldi's three weeks before. They hadn't been able to see much of one another the weekend before. Deacon had taken his sister Ashley to the penitentiary to see their mother. The experience apparently hadn't been a very positive one for Deacon who'd been a bit closed off ever since.

"I wasn't sure if I should come or not," Deacon said, snapping Steve out of his own thoughts as he folded a couple of napkins. "I know we're supposed to see each other tonight. Wouldn't want you to get sick of me."

"Don't think that's possible," Steve said. "If anything, I'd like to see more of you than I already do."

"I was kind of out of it last weekend." Deacon stopped unpacking the basket and glanced down at the floor. "Sorry about that."

"You okay?" Steve asked, smiling when Deacon nodded that he was. "I was disappointed I didn't get to see much of you, but I didn't mean to make you feel bad about that fact. You have responsibilities, other commitments, I understand that. Besides, we're still new. I don't expect to be a priority for you at this point."

"But you expect to be one at some point?" Deacon was grinning as he popped a marinated Kalamata olive into his mouth.

Steve felt his cheeks flush with heat so he pointed for Deacon to take a seat. He took the paper plate and napkin from his side of the desk and went about making himself a sandwich. "Damn right I do."

"I am sorry for showing up here without calling first. That was dumb."

Steve shrugged it off, not really caring at this particular point, considering Deacon was here, with him, and then he cringed. "Please tell me you parked down the block and walked up?"

The comment Jimmy had made about how young Deacon looked made the fact he drove that tiny-ass plug-in toy car seem even more likely to be a source of endless Daddy-jibes. It had taken him back a bit when Jimmy mentioned it because most of the time Steve had a tendency to forget about the age difference, due to the fact Deacon seemed more mature than your typical twenty-something.

"No...why would I—" Deacon groaned, falling back into his chair as he nibbled on a slice of pita. "Not my car again."

"You're using the word car loosely," Steve said, grinning when Deacon whimpered like he was near surrendering any argument over that point.

"You're such a snob," Deacon said. "I've met label queens before, but this is the first time I've seen it applied to automobiles."

Steve snarled up his lip, which appeared to please Deacon, who'd apparently picked up on the fact Steve didn't care for the word queen. "I'll be ribbed over your car more than anything else."

"Like the fact I kissed you when I came in." Deacon's face got all scrunched up. "That was pure reflex, my bad."

"That was a fair trade off for any shit I receive. I can't say the same for that piece of plastic you drive around in. And I kissed you as well, if you remember."

"Aren't you like, their boss?" Deacon asked.

Steve nodded, rolling his eyes as he tried to finish chewing so he could swallow. "I foolishly decided to be one of those employers who encouraged a friendly, we're-all-pals work atmosphere as opposed to striking fear into the hearts of my employees by being a dick."

Steve glanced out across the sales floor and sighed as two of his salesmen and a mechanic quickly glanced down at the yellow legal pad and pretended to be discussing something important.

"Really regretting that decision right about now."

Deacon laughed, cracking open one of the bottles of water and taking a drink. "I'm assuming they don't realize we can tell they're pointing at a blank piece of paper?"

"Idiots, the lot of them." Steve shook his head.

"Allow me to change the subject by reminding you that I managed the entire weekend off, and with Ash out of town with Mel, I'm available to lick your wounds later, assuming you don't have other plans, that is."

"They'd be cancelled if I did have other plans, but if that was your way of asking if I'm dating anyone else, the answer is no."

"I wasn't…I mean, that's nice to know, but I wasn't consciously attempting to pry." Deacon took a bite off his sandwich, trying to camouflage the fact he was grinning like an idiot.

"And you're welcome to lick anything you like," Steve added, "though I'm willing to offer suggestions should you require any."

"I doubt I will, but it's good to know you're there for me either way."

Steve let out a low rumbly laugh, attempting to keep himself in check. "I do have to work today and some tomorrow."

Deacon nodded, covering his mouth with his hand as he

talked with a full mouth. "I understand. I can find something to do while you're at work."

"Assuming I don't cuff your hot, naked ass to my bed tomorrow morning and leave you there till I get back home?" Steve asked, offering that up as one option.

Deacon coughed, trying to swallow his food. "You're a sick man."

Steve wiggled his eyebrows, looking at the spread Deacon had laid out across his desk. "This was really nice of you, by the way, thank you for lunch."

"You're welcome, it was my pleasure."

"You don't need to spend your hard-earned money on me, though."

"But it's okay for you spend yours on me?" Deacon said, his eyebrows cocked as if daring Steve to contradict him. He didn't, though he found Deacon's attempt at intimidation more amusing than anything else.

"Besides," Deacon added, "I get a good discount."

"You like working there?"

"Certainly grateful for the job, but yeah, beyond that, they've been really great to Ash and me. Mrs. Garibaldi is constantly sending food home with me. I've actually put on a few pounds as a result."

Steve watched as Deacon pooched out his belly and patted it. "I wasn't going to mention it before…"

Deacon's mouth fell open slightly and then tossed a pita triangle across the desk.

Steve laughed. "It looks good on you. You look good."

"Naw, need a haircut, kinda gotten scruffy, like a dog been left outside to play for too long."

"Been out playing, huh?"

"I meant like rolling around in the dirt, not offering my ass up to anyone and everyone. Haven't done too much of that lately. Got picked up by this sexy mother-fucker around Christmas time at a hotel bar who has proceeded to give me the best sex I've ever had several times over since then."

"That sort of statement doesn't mean as much when you're twenty-seven."

"It was mind-blowing," Deacon said, biting down seductively on his bottom lip.

Deacon turned slightly in his chair so no one could see from the wall of windows as he slipped his hand between his legs and rubbed his crotch.

Steve swallowed hard, finding it difficult to breathe all of a sudden.

"Really worked my ass out good," Deacon added.

Steve's face flushed. "You gonna date me or not, Deacon Miller?"

"You mean like going steady?" Deacon asked, apparently deciding he'd had enough fun since he went back to eating as opposed to taunting Steve.

"I'm serious, I'll even pay for a nanny if I need to, but I want to see more of you."

Deacon started to laugh. "Ashley's sixteen, not sure she needs a nanny."

"Even if I wanna keep you out all night?"

"I'm perfectly willing to go steady with you, Steven Actually Steele, but we have to take things slow to start out, you know? I'm still trying to figure things out, and Ashley and I are just beginning to fall into a comfortable rhythm. Her life has been turned upside down enough, and I made a promise to myself that I'd be there for her, you know?"

"You think going out with me might freak her out?" he asked.

"That's just it, I don't know. I'd like to think it wouldn't, but we've never talked much about it."

"Might help if I were to actually meet her," Steve offered.

Deacon started to fidget again.

"It was just a suggestion, buddy." Steve laughed under his

breath. "Whatever you need, Deacon. I'm perfectly willing to follow your lead. I just don't want you to drop off the face of the Earth again at some point and not see you for another two months. Now that I know you're here, I'll come looking for you. Won't be able to stop myself. You've been warned."

Deacon shook his head, though looked as if he might approve. "Never had a stalker before."

Steve chucked the pita back across the desk, smacking Deacon in the forehead with it.

"Ouch, dude." Deacon frowned. "I'll be noting that in my diary later. Possible abusive inclinations."

"You threw it at me first!" Steve reminded him before shoveling in a large forkful of potato salad.

"But I'm younger and therefore more prone to immature behavior. You're middle-aged, you should really know better."

Steve scowled. "Let's refrain from using the term middle-aged ever again, please."

"Yes, sir," Deacon said, trying not to laugh and failing miserably.

Steve shook his head, sighing. "Not even five minutes after officially agreeing to be boyfriends and already fighting."

"Terrible, isn't it," Deacon said, still grinning. "Our outlook isn't so good, huh?"

"Nope," Steve said, taking another bite of his sandwich.

Deacon was doing his best to appear all innocent, and it might have worked had Steve not fucked him enough times to know Deacon Miller was anything but. That was one of his favorite things about the man sitting across the desk from him. Looks were often times quite deceiving, and Deacon was no exception. In fact, he was quickly becoming the rule by which all others in the past would be measured and any others in the future would never live up to.

Of course, if Steve had anything to say about it, there wouldn't be anyone else in the future to live up to Deacon, because he would be the last.

CHAPTER EIGHT ~ APRIL

Biting down on his bottom lip, Deacon's brow furrowed as he attempted to avoid getting the steam coming off the hot skillet in his eyes. He'd never been very astute when it came to anything culinary, but he was determined to make Steve dinner, and Steve's favorite food was fajitas. It hadn't seemed like a difficult undertaking when reading the recipe, but his trial batch the night before hadn't ended well. He had the marinade down, so the flavor was right on, however there was apparently an art to keeping the onions and various types of peppers from becoming soggy while getting the beef cooked all the way through.

Pulling the pan off the stove, he dumped the contents into a glass casserole dish. He'd undercooked everything slightly, tossing the dish in the oven in an attempt to keep it warm.

Hearing the garage door begin to open, Deacon rushed to the sink and rinsed out the pan. He frantically went about cramming all the dirty dishes into the dishwasher and then wiped off the countertops. The man was a bit of a neat freak, and he didn't want any mess to take away from Steve being able to relax and enjoy the food.

Deacon heard a car door shut and glanced down to check himself only to find a grease stain had dribbled down the center of his T-shirt. He cussed under his breath and ripped it off as he listened to the garage door close. Steve walked through the door just as Deacon was heading out of the kitchen toward the bedroom to grab a fresh shirt.

"Hey," Steve said, with a hint of a grin, eyeing Deacon's naked torso. "Damn. Smells good in here."

Deacon paused long enough to plant a quick kiss on his boyfriend's lips, hesitating briefly since something seemed off. "I made you fajitas, but I trashed my shirt in the process. Be right back."

"Don't go to any extra trouble on my part," Steve called out as Deacon ran through the house, hopping over the corner of the coffee table before getting to the hallway. "You look good half naked!"

He was smiling over the compliment as he shoved the dirty shirt into his duffel, exchanging it for a clean one. By the time he made it back to the kitchen, Steve was munching on something while he pulled the glass casserole dish out of the oven.

"Smells amazing, baby," Steve mumbled.

"Stop right there, pal!" Deacon ordered.

Steve's eyes got wide, and he set the baking dish on the stovetop, visibly confused by what he might have done wrong.

Deacon took him by the hand and led Steve to the table where he forced the man into a chair. "You sit there and relax. I'll get you a beer." Deacon paused for a moment, taking a seat on Steve's lap and straddling him in the black leather-covered dining chair. "But first I'm gonna kiss you proper."

Steve chuckled as Deacon made good on his threat and planted another kiss on him. Steve's soft, full lips contrasting with the rough scrape of his perpetual five o'clock shadow was an intoxicating combination that had Deacon groaning softly in protest, forcing himself away and hopping up off his lap. Steve's grumbling tummy had rudely informed him that the man was hungry for more than sex.

Steve made a grab for his ass, but Deacon was too quick, padding across the tile floor to the fridge for the beer he'd promised moments before. The house was quiet, and Deacon could hear the cuffs of his jeans dragging across the floor.

Steve had gone silent, but Deacon could feel his eyes on him as he ran about, bringing all the food to the small table in the eat-in kitchen. He lit the candle sitting otherwise unadorned in the center of the table before grabbing Steve's phone, fumbling around, tapping on the screen until he pulled up one of the jazz playlists from his iTunes.

The room filled with music after he plugged the phone into the docking station.

"Eat, babe," Deacon said, coming back to the table.

Steve did as instructed, looking up when Deacon made a quick detour, hitting the dimmer switch that tempered the glow coming from the modest chandelier dangling above their heads.

He watched patiently while Steve went about filling a tortilla with various ingredients, then realized he was staring. Deacon forced himself to stop, reminding himself that his name wasn't Betty Crocker and he wasn't a housewife from the nineteen fifties. He berated himself for caring that much only to grin like an idiot when Steve finally took a bite and moaned his approval.

"You like?" Deacon asked.

Steve nodded, mumbling through another big bite. "So good."

Deacon shrugged, doing his best to now act like he didn't care one way or another. "Cool."

They both fell silent again as they went about eating, yet Deacon couldn't manage to shake the feeling that something was off with Steve. He had a pretty good nose for this sort of thing, something he developed growing up with an alcoholic mother that suffered from a wide range of mood swings. It had a tendency to make him super sensitive, a quality that used to drive Seth nuts.

Of course in retrospect, Seth dumped his ass a few months after Deacon began sensing all was not okay in their relationship, so annoying or not, he typically wasn't wrong. If Steve was unhappy with him or had grown tired of being with him, Deacon would rather know now—regardless of how disappointed he might be.

He sat with that for about sixty seconds, feeling sick over the thought Steve might want to end things before blurting out, "Are you upset with me?"

Steve looked across the table at him, visibly confused as to where that had come from, which made Deacon feel like an idiot.

"What kind of an asshole do you take me for?" Steve asked after swallowing his mouthful of food and looking over the spread laid out before him. "This was so nice of you."

"Right, sorry…you just seem…off?"

"Oh." Steve said. "Thought I was doing a better job hiding it. Just a rough couple of months at the dealership, but you, on the other hand, are the one bright spot in all of that, Deacon."

"Phew," Deacon said, as relief washed over him waves, before tempering himself. "Sorry, that was rude! I'm not relieved things are bad at work, just happy it's not me frustrating you."

"Oh, you definitely frustrate me, Deacon, though I don't mind that particular type of frustration."

Deacon laughed, smirking. "Happy to oblige then."

Steve winked, then sighed, taking another bite off his fajita. "Sales have been sluggish, that's all. A slump. Had to sell a few of my babies, no way around it. Needed the capital."

It took a few minutes before Deacon worked out what he meant by his babies. Then it dawned on him that Steve mentioned he and a few of his buddies at the dealership restored old cars—which he referred to as his babies.

"I'm sorry."

Steve grinned as he finished chewing his mouthful of food. "I know you think getting attached to a car is silly."

"Well, sure, but that's me. I know they're important to you, though." Deacon spooned a little more Spanish rice onto his plate. "I don't get why, but that's beside the point."

Deacon could tell by the look on his face Steve was disappointed that he didn't understand the whole old car thing.

"No other way around it?" Deacon asked.

Steve shook his head that there wasn't. "Things aren't bad, just tighter than I'd like, wanted a little extra cushion that's all."

Deacon wasn't sure what the right thing to say might be. He had no clue what went into operating a car lot. He was pretty clueless all the way around when it came to Steve's everyday life, and the sudden realization of that made him feel rotten.

He became aware that Steve was watching him from across the table.

"Where'd you just go?" Steve asked.

He felt his face flush. "Just figuring out how little I actually know about what you do all day, every day."

"I promise you aren't missing much," Steve said, sitting back in his chair. "The most important part of my job is that I have forty-eight people who work for me. That may not seem like a lot, but considering they all depend upon me keeping the lights on so they have a job to come to each morning, there are days when it can feel like millions."

He stopped when Deacon got up from the table.

Steve smiled a thank you when Deacon returned to the table with another beer.

"Don't stop, I'm listening."

Steve sighed, taking a swig off the bottle. "Of those forty-eight people, nearly all of them go home at the end of the day to a family, at the very least a spouse or partner, most have children, some have parents they care for in addition to their own kids."

"So forty-eight quickly multiplies, I can see that," Deacon said.

"And each one has a story, some hardship or a curveball life has thrown their way. One of my partners in the restoration shop, Mickey… he also manages the service department at the dealership. You haven't met him yet, right?"

"Don't think so." Deacon shrugged. "Only been there the one time."

"Right, right." Steve gave his head a quick shake like he might be attempting to free any cobwebs. "Mickey and his wife Anna have three kids, but his son, Alex is autistic—has all sorts of behavioral issues. It's been hard on them, and Anna used to be a nurse, but she had to quit her job to take care of Alex who requires round the clock care. She's constantly running him to and from different appointments. He has to have all types of therapy, and all of it costs a small fortune."

Deacon cringed.

"I know, it's sad." Steve sighed, stretching his back, which popped. "Mickey constantly worries his other two kids are suffering because so much of their time and attention gets diverted to Alex."

"I'm sorry to hear that."

"It doesn't stop there, Deacon, my secretary, Margaret—"

"I remember her!" Deacon interrupted, excited that there was some connection there, no matter how thin.

Steve laughed over the exuberance. "Margie and her husband were finally going to retire three years ago until her mother-in-law, Harriet, suffered a stroke. They now care for her full time, which is hard on Margie, considering Harriet has treated her like crap during their entire marriage. Pretty much made Margie's life miserable to the point she dreaded each and every holiday."

"That's shitty," Deacon said, as a sudden pang of terror ripped through his entire body. That had been a nightmare he'd feared his entire adult life. Afraid Patty would drunkenly injure herself and he'd be stuck having to care for her—stuck listening to her verbal abuse forever. The thought still made him sick to his stomach, and he pushed the plate away, signaling he was definitely done eating.

"Now poor Margie is forced to live under the same roof with the woman…has to wipe her ass and cook for her…clean for her. Any dreams of traveling they'd had were gone in an instant—had to use a good chunk of their savings to help cover medical bills. Knowing all of this kinda stuff is the price of owning a small business and working closely with the individuals you employ."

"You feel responsible for each of them?" Deacon asked.

"I *am* responsible for each of them, Deacon. They may not have to think about me when making decisions, but I don't have the same luxury. What I do affects all of their lives. I can't ever forget that."

"That's a lot for you to have to carry around, babe."

"That's small business versus big business. Think about the Garibaldi's. Why do you think that woman is always asking after you, sending food home for you and Ashley? I'm not saying every person out there who owns a business gives a shit about their employees to the extent that I do, but I see them all every day. It's a little more difficult to look through someone when they're forever standing in your path."

Deacon sighed then smiled and reached across the table to take Steve's hand. "Always knew you were a good guy, despite any insistence on your part to the contrary."

Steve smiled back as their fingers intertwined. Deacon's eyes bugged out when Steve yanked on his arm, pulling him out of his seat and around the small table. Moments later, he was once again straddling Steve who'd scooted his seat away from the table to make room for Deacon. They kissed, and Deacon went about kneading his fingers into the back of Steve's neck and shoulders.

"That feels nice," Steve whispered when Deacon pulled away.

"Hate seeing you all stressed out."

"I'm just being a baby. Sometimes you have to do things you may not want to in order to get by. It wasn't the first time I've had to do it, and it likely won't be the last time."

Steve took a deep breath and sighed, exhaling as he shrugged. Deacon could sense that Steve didn't want him to worry.

"Anything I can do to help?" Deacon asked, laughing when Steve's eyebrows arched up, like he might have one or two suggestions.

"Feel like taking a drive?" Steve asked.

"Not where I thought you going with that, but…sure."

Steve laughed. "We'll get to that eventually, never you fear. Go grab some shoes, and I'll toss the food in the fridge?"

Deacon nodded his willingness to go along with that plan, kissing Steve once more before bounding off through the house in search of his shoes.

* * * *

Steve pulled his Mustang into the parking lot outside the

brick warehouse. It was a simple rectangular shaped building with glass block windows, that sat six or seven feet up off ground level, allowing for filtered natural light without providing onlookers any easy way of seeing what went on inside. He could tell Deacon was nervous about the neighborhood, which did appear slightly post-apocalyptic on the weekends as little to no activity was going on in the area. Located at the southern edge of the city, Delray was pretty much a ghost town, nearly exclusively industrial at this point as most of the residential areas had been deserted over the years.

Placing the car in park, Steve hopped out, heading straight for the metal panel that concealed a keypad underneath, protecting it from the elements. He punched in the fifteen number code, and immediately, the large metal door to his right hummed to life—opening so slowly it gave one the impression of weighing a ton.

Steve ran back, slipped into the driver's seat, and slowly pulled the car inside the empty narrow spot, which could've potentially held three or four more cars. The area was otherwise empty, just brick walls on three sides and a long black folding partition sitting up on giant castors that stretched out nearly the entire width of the room on the forth side. The folding wall blocked any view of what lay upon the other side. He put the car in park and glanced over at Deacon who was now looking at him funny.

"What?" Steve asked, reaching across Deacon's lap to dig through the glove box for a garage door opener, which he tossed right back inside after pushing a button that started the slow process of closing them off from the outside world as the massive door shut behind them.

"If you've got the Ark of the Covenant back there, I'm outta here," Deacon said, sounding serious.

Steve laughed, giving him a quick kiss of reassurance. They'd watched *Raiders of the Lost Ark* the weekend before. He'd been shocked Deacon had never seen it before, and Steve found it sweet and a little funny that the film had managed to capture Deacon's imagination like that. It told him that perhaps much of Deacon's protests about not caring much about music or movies had more to do with the fact he'd not had much in the way of friends or family that bothered exposing him to it growing up.

He did his best not to focus on what Deacon had suffered without as a kid since it tended to piss Steve off to the point it could ruin an otherwise decent mood when he did ponder it for too long. Instead, he tried concentrating on what he could give him now to make up for that crummy past.

Right now, he intended to give his boyfriend a little glimpse into his own passion, in hopes a little of it might rub off.

"Come on, smart ass, it's time to take you to school," Steve said, getting out of the car.

Deacon followed suit, cussing under his breath after jamming his knee into the car door. "Unless you've got plans for some sort of Head Master slash Horny Student role playing scenario planned, this whole school thing sounds dreadful."

"While that's something we should definitely tuck away for some fun in the very near future, you're way off." Steve took him by the hand, leading him toward the opening in the partition wall. "Come on, pouty."

Deacon laughed under his breath, lumbering along and peering cautiously around the corner. Steve yanked him all the way into the dark space, letting go of his hand as he headed to the wall to their right, lifting a large lever that sent all the massive lighting fixtures humming to life.

Deacon's eyes squinted in the dim light as he surveyed the terrain.

"Takes the lights a bit to warm up all the way."

"Place is a lot bigger than it looked from the outside."

The open, expansive space was sectioned off into different areas. Immediately to their left was a row of cars that, judging by the snarl on Deacon's face as he looked them over, were diamonds-in-the-rust. Steve smiled, deciding that was likely a kinder description than Deacon would've offered. All throughout the remaining space sat different makes and models of cars in various states of repair, from bare-boned chassis to fully painted and nearly finished automobiles just waiting on interiors and shiny chrome trim.

He took Deacon by the hand and began walking him through the building. There was an area where they did bodywork and fabrication when they were unable to find original parts needed to finish a project. They were always careful to use only the same materials the original automaker would have utilized when they were forced to create replacement parts from scratch.

"We've currently got two chassis we're working on," Steve said.

Deacon nodded, his forehead crinkled up. "Weird seeing just the framework like that."

"We start off building a cart to stabilize the body, allows us to raise and lower it." Steve pointed at the cross bars inside the frame. "The X brace keeps the capsule from moving while we lift the body on and off of the chassis."

"So what kind is that one?" Deacon asked as they moved on.

"It's a '41 Willys," Steve said.

"Looks like a gangster car out of an old black and white movie."

"Yeah, considered more of a hot rod," Steve said. "Working on it for a guy in Texas."

"So you don't own all the cars you restore?"

"No, some are commissioned. Thanks to the quality of work JD, Willie and Mickey bring to the table, we're getting a decent rep. Good word of mouth in the right circles, you know? The ones we keep, those we pay for out of our own pockets, and we use them for shows. We'll rotate them in and out of the showroom at the dealership in the summer. They bring people in."

"More bodywork done over there," Steve pointed. "Mechanics and engine blocks just over there. Got a whole room in the back where we warehouse rare parts. Any leather and upholstery work gets farmed out. I know a few guys."

"Of course you do," Deacon said, pretending to be jealous as they stopped next to the body painting and sandblasting areas, which were separated with floor to ceiling thick plastic sheeting.

"Don't be cute," Steve said.

"And here I thought that was out of my control?"

"You're in rare form this evening," Steve said, eyeing him funny.

"Must be this place?" Deacon glanced around. "It's very… blue-collar-straight-dude."

"Turns you on, huh?" Steve grinned.

"Kinda does, yeah." Deacon poked Steve in the stomach. "Kinda want to get you naked and roll you around in some oil or grease or any other black-like lubey substance."

"We'll come back to that later," Steve said, enjoying the way Deacon was looking him over. "I'll cut to the chase since this is your first trip."

Steve led him past the washing and detailing areas.

"Cool, you can wash my car inside during the winter?" he asked.

"I would if you had a real car."

"So not funny. Lucky for you, I'll get over it long enough for us to have sex later."

"That is mighty big of you." Steve let go of Deacon's hand as they approached the five covered cars all parked neatly in a row next to one another. He patted the first covered car they passed by. "Underneath is a '72 Pontiac Firebird we brought back to life, but it's Mickey's baby, so I'll leave it be."

Deacon backed away from it slightly, putting a little more distance between he and Mickey's car, as if he feared his proximity to the vehicle might bring about some sort of calamitous event.

Steve pointed to the opposite side of the tarp. "Wanna grab that side and help me roll this back?"

Deacon did as instructed, moving cautiously and constantly looking behind him as if he feared being too close to anything old, rare or expensive.

Steve tried to ignore it as he was certain it was more behavior tied to some childhood trauma. "'69 Karmann Ghia—one of the first restorations we completed—a total rust bucket."

Deacon smiled, looking over the car from behind as he let go of the canvas tarp. "It's pretty."

"You can see the before and after picture on the wall behind you."

Deacon turned, and his mouth fell open as he got closer to the photograph. "That used to be this?"

"Pretty amazing stuff, huh?"

Deacon glanced at Steve, still wide-eyed, then at the car once again. "There aren't words. I'm…wow, Steve."

Steve tried to dial back his pride, which was swelling by the minute. "All we really did was preserve someone else's brilliance. Not like we created her or anything."

"But still." Deacon looked at the picture once more before he started walking around to look her from the front. "That you can do it in the first place. I've never been very useful."

Steve shot him a look that said he wasn't going to listen to Deacon berate himself.

"I didn't mean it the way you obviously took it." Deacon shrugged, looking back over the car with its pristine silver-gray paint and the chrome accents gleaming in the light of the overheads. "That you can do something useful with your hands. That's impressive."

"Mickey, JD and Willie do most of the impressive stuff. Jimmy and I are good with the basic mechanics, most of that we learned from Mickey when were kids. My father was in it for the money, but I loved the cars."

"Your dad died, right?" Deacon asked, helping Steve cover the car back up.

"Yeah, back when I was in college. He was a lot older than my mom, who he left his first family to be with."

"So you have step siblings too?" Deacon asked.

"Yeah, though my mom and I have never had a relationship

with them. They disowned my dad after he left them." Steve motioned to the next car, and Deacon hopped to attention, helping him uncover it. "Of course, my dad left my mother for a younger woman as well. Then he died a few years later. Heart attack."

"Sorry."

"It was a long time ago, though I don't think my mom ever forgave him or got over it for that matter. She basically dropped out of college to marry him. Then they had me pretty quickly so she never ended up going back to school."

"Beautiful," Deacon said, taking in the '63 Sting Ray, Riverside Red convertible Corvette.

"This is one I sold." Steve sighed his resignation over losing her. "She gets shipped off to California on Monday."

The top was down, and the black leather and brushed silver trim of the interior gleamed like it was brand new.

"Did you ever even drive it?" Deacon asked, tentatively reaching down to run his hand over the leather.

"Every now and then. They all get driven periodically. Not good for them to sit."

Steve showed him the '39 Cadillac Series 60 Special four-door sedan, which was the other car he'd been forced to sell, before moving on to his pride and joy, a fiery red '62 Jaguar XKE Series 1 Roadster.

"She's rare in this condition, Deacon, and a real beauty with sweeping lines and the aggressively sensual stance of the body? Many consider the XKE to be one of the most beautiful automotive designs ever."

Deacon's laughter snapped him out if his haze.

"What's so funny?"

"Let's just say I now know what Steve Steele in love looks like."

Steve burst out laughing as he rounded the car and gathered Deacon up in his arms. They stood there and kissed for a moment before Steve pulled away and opened the passenger side door of the Jag.

"Really?" Deacon asked, smiling. "Are we going for a ride?"

"Eventually," Steve said, shutting the door once Deacon was seated. "For me, cars are like moving sculpture, you know?"

He rolled his eyes as he walked around the front of the car, seeing Deacon staring up at him blankly.

"They're molded out of steel, chrome and leather, but they do so much more than get an individual from point A to point B."

"Okay," Deacon said as Steve slid behind the wooden steering wheel. "I see where you're headed."

"In its purest form, the automobile was a well-crafted piece of machinery, yet like a work of art, each one had a personality that was every bit as individual as the person who climbed behind the wheel. Like a brushstroke across a canvas or the polished curve created when a chisel is expertly used on a block of marble—a well-designed automobile should incite an emotional response, you know?" Steve stopped, able to see from the look on Deacon's face that he was getting carried away. "And now I'm just scaring you."

"No, not that." Deacon laughed, placing his hand on Steve's leg. "I'm a little jealous that you've found something you feel that passionate about."

"I promise to stop preaching all the same." Steve smirked. "I can be an idiot."

"An exceedingly hot idiot," Deacon added. "If that helps at all."

Steve clarified. "It doesn't hurt."

"Good to know," Deacon said as he leaned over and kissed Steve. He slipped Steve a little tongue before sucking on his bottom lip—a sure signal that Deacon was horny.

"You ready to fuck me yet?" Deacon asked boldly.

"You are excessively horny tonight."

"Dude, I cooked for you." Deacon nodded curtly. "You're gonna put out."

Steve burst out laughing once again. "You're great, Deacon."

Deacon wiggled his eyebrows. "Kiss me, stupid."

Steve shook his head, but he leaned over and did what was asked of him. The kissing quickly led to groping, and the groping led to awkwardly fumbling hands and open flies.

Steve slipped his hand up Deacon's shirt, fingers pressing into his warm, soft skin on his way to a nipple. He was addicted to the way Deacon's body reacted to his touch, always pushing into his hands as if begging for more. No one had ever made him feel like he might be the single best lover the world had ever known.

That's how Deacon made him feel each time.

Steve growled under his breath as Deacon freed his cock from the confines of his pants. The heat of Deacon's palm against the sensitive head of his dick made Steve's eyes roll back into his head.

As Deacon slowly jacked him off, Steve decided he could handle losing a car or two if it meant being able to hang onto the man currently shoving his tongue down his throat. Having Deacon whispering that he wanted Steve to come on him was all it took to shut off any other part of his brain.

The tour was officially over.

CHAPTER NINE

While the store itself looked dated in the worst possible sense, the dresses inside were mostly pretty. Deacon felt slightly out of place, sitting in a brass bamboo-shaped rail-back chair. The faded mauve and sea foam green fabric had held up well, but sitting next to the plate glass window had exposed it to decades of direct sunlight, which had taken its toll. He felt a sort of kinship to it in the sense he felt that way at times, like he'd been exposed to too much harshness during his childhood and it had drained Deacon in the same way.

Mel's mother, Trish, came around the corner, smiling from ear to ear. "They'll be right out."

Her excitement over shopping for prom dresses was borderline infectious, and Deacon couldn't help but long for some sort of inoculation to it.

This wasn't his bag.

Homosexual stereotypes aside, shopping for clothes had always been boring and tedious to him, even when the clothes were for him. His initial reaction had been to decline Trish's offer for him to tag along, but the instant he'd seen Ashley's eyes light up at the suggestion, he realized how badly she'd wanted him there.

The store was kinda sweet in an eighties teen-comedy sort of way. The dressing rooms were in the back, behind a stage and a long catwalk that allowed the girls to come out and strut their stuff for their mothers and friends. The endless loop of 'Material Girl' and 'Girls Just Wanna Have Fun' style pop music being piped in over the loud speakers was cute for about the first fifteen minutes, but Deacon was starting to get a headache from it. He'd never been an alt-hard rock kinda guy, but he'd begun to pray Marilyn Manson would enter stage right and vomit blood all over the store, forcing everyone inside to flee for their lives.

Trish took a seat next to him, giggling as she grabbed his arm and gave it a squeeze.

"Isn't this fun!" she squealed.

Deacon began to laugh as the woman looked like she might explode. "It is, indeed. Thank you for inviting me."

"I'm so glad I did, Deacon. Ashley is practically giddy that you're here, she's so proud. You should have heard her bragging to the other girls in the dressing room that her gay brother was here to help her pick out a dress."

He melted a little hearing that. He wasn't initially thrilled his sister was going with a senior, but Ashley was practically floating; he'd never seen her so happy so Deacon kept his mouth shut. He'd been socking back money for the past few months so he could afford to buy her a dress. Even so, he'd caught a glance at one or two price tags and felt his ass pucker over the amount. He'd tried giving her a rough idea of what he could afford to pay over the past few weeks by tossing out amounts during random prom-talk conversations. He'd felt awful having to do it, but they were on a budget.

Pushing back that sick feeling in the pit of his stomach over not being able to do everything he'd like to for Ashley, Deacon forced on a smile. The last thing he wanted was to ruin the experience by having her come out and see concern written all over his face. His sister was also an intuitive expert when it came to reading any sort of distress in others. Luckily, he was equally expert at masking his emotions, but Deacon had to work hard to keep her from suspecting anytime things weren't going well.

Trish took a sip off the lipstick-coated straw sticking out of the bottle of water she'd been carrying around with her after leaving her giant purse in Deacon's care.

"All the other girls were so jealous she had a gay brother! It was really sweet."

Deacon decided he might need to toss out a couple extra hawts and a fabulous or two as the girls came parading out in order to live up to his homo-hype. He knew most of Ashley's excitement revolved around the mere fact someone in her family actually cared enough to show up. This sort of thing had never been Patty's strong suit as she was typically either sleeping one off or tying one on.

The fact Ashley was bragging that he was here meant the world to him. Having her be proud that he was gay on top of that was a nice bonus.

"I can't thank you enough for agreeing to be the girls chaperone for this dance," Trish said, watching the stage opening with rapt attention. "We weren't at all happy with the idea of this after-party at the hotel, but knowing you and your boyfriend will be there meant a lot. Frank and I can finally have a night out for our anniversary and not have to worry."

Deacon's eyes bugged out slightly as this was the first he'd heard of any of this. He'd been told the girls had a midnight curfew and would be going home to Mel's after the prom.

"You guys know which hotel, right?" Deacon asked, making it sound as if he was merely concerned they were well informed.

"The Madison-Parker, yes," Trish said, nodding and beaming as the girls came out.

"I'll be sure to text you with our room number after we've checked in," Deacon said, smiling innocently as Ashley passed by, being silly and striking poses with Mel.

His sister looked quite grown up, in spite of the silly posing and antics. Dressed in a pale yellow spaghetti strap number that highlighted her pale skin and blonde locks, she all but shined. It made his heart ache a tiny bit as he decided to shake off his sarcasm and began to whoop and holler at them, catcalling and creating quite the disturbance, much to the girls delight.

"Thank you, I'd appreciate that!" Trish squealed again, apparently unable to contain herself, the woman was practically vibrating. Deacon was worried her head might pop right off her shoulders like a champagne cork.

Deacon was stunned that his supposedly sweet baby sister had used him and Steve for an alibi and then lied to his face about staying at Mel's. That stung a bit. Ashley hadn't even met Steve yet, the little deviant. He understood why, considering she knew he would've never allowed her to spend the night with some boy in a hotel room had she asked.

Deacon overheard Mel commenting to Ashley as they passed by how cool her brother was as he fished his cell phone out of his coat pocket.

He quickly typed out a text message to Steve, asking if he could please check for openings at the hotel for the date of the prom.

We'll see how cool she thinks I am once I drop the axe on all their evil-teen plans.

The prom was still about six weeks away, but he was afraid there wouldn't be any rooms left, and if that was the case, the girls were screwed because he'd be pulling the entire rug out from under them. As it was, Deacon didn't want to get the girls into trouble, and if anyone deserved a romantic night out, it was Frank and Trish. They'd done a lot over the years for Ash, more than he could ever repay, so not ruining their anniversary became objective number one.

He felt bad when Steve texted back that he'd booked them the *Gov ste*, which took a moment for him decipher as the Governor's Suite.

That sounded expensive, and Deacon texted back saying so.

Steve told him it was the only room the hotel had available, and he felt worse as Steve had understandably misunderstood the intent behind the evening as evidenced by a text that soon followed.

Will take $$ of rm out on ur ass soakn in pvt Jacuzzi.

That was followed by a fourth and fifth text that included several other suggestions he might consider performing for Steve.

Deacon could feel himself blushing in the middle of the dress shop as the girls came out in different dresses.

He didn't have the heart to burst Steve's elicit bubble just then, deciding an in-person blow job to follow up the bad news that they weren't there for a romantic evening might be in order. He replied with a simple smiley face and slipped his phone back in his coat, ignoring it when the phone chirped several more times announcing the arrival of what was sure to be more slutty texts.

"I liked the first dress on Ashley better, don't you think?" Trish asked, eyeing both girls like a fashionista-hawk ready to nitpick each and every seam.

He did agree with her, especially since the whore-red color of dress number two now made him uneasy, knowing the girls had been lying in order score a night out to do god-knows what. His phone chirped again, and he tried not to smile, thinking whatever nasty thing Steve was now texting was probably along the lines of what the girls had intended.

They might have time for dinner and sex if they started early enough. That would have to suffice.

He decided not to tell the girls he knew anything just yet. He'd wait to spring it on them last minute. That thought made him smile in a sick sort of way, but then he frowned, realizing he was probably officially old, considering ruining prom-night shenanigans now made him giddy.

By the time they'd gone through six more wardrobe changes, Deacon was no longer able to recall one dress from another. They'd all begun to bleed together, and his brain was fully fried from the girly perfumed pink interior and power-pop soundtrack pumping over the loud speakers. He decided to stand back, smiling away as the womenfolk debated each dress. He had the credit card in-hand, ready to pull the trigger while they huddled around the long counter by the cash register located to one side of the store.

"You have to have the yellow silk spaghetti strap one, Ash," Mel said, using a tone that intimated buying any other dress would be mind-numbingly ludicrous.

"I like it," Ashley said, glancing sideways at Deacon while chewing nervously on her bottom lip. "But I'm not sure it's right. The navy blue one looked nice, right?"

"It did look very smart on you, Ashley," Trish said. "But think of the entrance you two would make, Mel in her emerald green and you in that soft pale yellow?"

Deacon watched his sister gaze longingly at the yellow dress, and he knew it was the one she wanted, despite the fact she continued to leave her hand on the hanger for the blue one. The only thing Deacon could figure was that the yellow was expensive, and Ash was attempting to take one for the team.

"What do you think, Deacon?" Trish asked while nodding, subconsciously signaling that he should agree with her.

"No, it's almost five hundred dollars, that's just too much money to spend on a dress for prom," Ashley said.

Deacon was proud of the fact he maintained his composure, though he was sweating bullets on the inside. That was nearly his entire prom budget for her, including hair, nails, shoes, professional makeup, etc. He smiled calmly and sighed, buckling from the sad, disappointment lurking behind his sister's eyes.

He walked over, took the yellow dress off the rack and handed it to the salesclerk behind the counter. "I totally agree with Trish on this one. It *like* has to be the yellow one, right?"

Deacon stood there for several moments thinking perhaps he'd upped the gay a little too much by mocking the way Mel had said the same thing only moments before.

He nearly had a heart attack, physically startled when all three women began squealing simultaneously. Ashley jumped him with such a force it knocked the credit card right out of his hand. Deacon saw the greedy salesclerk scrambling to grab for the Visa as if the woman feared he might change his mind.

Ashley wrapped her arms so tightly around his waist that she nearly cut off the circulation to the lower half of his body as she hugged him with abandon.

Deacon tried to laugh, all the while secretly fearing for his life, deciding this was why straight men never went shopping with their wives and daughters.

This shit was dangerous.

When Ashley whispered that she loved him, Deacon felt his eyes begin to burn, welling up on him. He fought to keep himself from losing it. She'd sounded so earnest, almost like a prayer, like she was grateful to have him back in her life, and that crushed him on the inside. It wasn't the type of thing he or his sister had been used to hearing; they hadn't been raised in a family of I-love-you's.

When he finally got a hold of his senses, Deacon squeezed her back, cringing on the inside when he saw the lady swiping his card through the machine. "Love you too, Ash. You deserve that dress."

Mel and Trish were clinging to one another like refugees as they each cooed in harmony over the love-fest happening before them. Deacon was sweating and a little embarrassed, but he hugged his sister for just a little longer before finally letting her go, deciding that as foreign to him as it was, he didn't exactly hate hugging after all.

CHAPTER TEN

It was late Wednesday night, and Deacon was worn slap out as Steve pulled his Mustang into the driveway of Patty's house. He slowly drove along the side of the house and stopped in front of the detached one car garage that sat along the back of the property.

He apologized through a yawn, placing the apron from his Garibaldi work uniform in front of his mouth, fearing his breath was skanky. He'd spent the previous night at Steve's, who had picked him up the evening before at Patty's and then dropped him off at work earlier that day. Now he was playing carpool-Ken once again, having picked him up after his shift was finished.

"I feel bad, I could've called a cab or had Ash pick me up."

"Yes, but my way means I get to see you, even if only briefly before going home to an empty bed. Plus I get to do this." Steve leaned over, kissing Deacon, who'd been too taken back to object due to his questionable breath.

After several moments of a kiss like that, Deacon no longer gave a damn about things like gnarly breath.

"You sure you don't wanna let me come in?" Steve asked.

"Ashley's home." Deacon managed to get out before Steve kissed him again.

Deacon had begun to melt into the leather bucket seat, his entire body now flushed with heat.

"I can be real, *real* quiet." Steve added, pressing the palm of his hand firmly against Deacon's erection. "Feels like you want me to come in."

"I would love for you to come in, but it's not a good idea, baby."

Steve moved over to Deacon's ear, sucking gently on his ear lobe. "Fuck, I love it when you call me baby."

The heated breath brushing past his ear had Deacon panting slightly. "You know I have to be careful. Can't have anything gay getting back to Patty. I don't need her fighting with me about the guardian stuff."

"Have I told you how much I dislike your mother?" Steve asked, stopping the seduction long enough to look Deacon in the eye.

"Take a fucking number. I refuse to even see her at this point." Deacon sighed, patting Steve on the leg to reassure him they were on the same side with this one. "She was so hateful the last time I went with Ashley that I decided to wait in the car from now on. The bright side, she seems to be treating Ashley well. So that's something."

"I think it's about time we move past your mommy issues, and I meet your sister," Steve said. "Seriously, Deacon, how much trouble can she cause from prison? The fact that she's in there would likely temper any objections she made to you being Ashley's guardian. Top that off with her long and varied history of alcohol and all the abuse she's heaped on you and your sister?"

"She never really laid a finger on either of us, Steve."

"She verbally abused you and most likely your sister at times as well." Steve inhaled as if attempting to calm himself. "I'd like to strangle the very life out of her for that."

The vein in his temple was pulsing, and Deacon knew he was getting upset. He swallowed his own discomfort over the fact Steve had him painted as some sort of victim, and he smiled. "Then you'd be in prison, and I'd have no more mind-blowing sex."

Steve smiled slightly so Deacon could tell the distraction was working.

"Patty would win again!" Deacon yelped, his voice cracking, making him sound extra silly.

Steve laughed, running the pad of thumb over Deacon's bottom lip. "Damn, you're cute."

The sexual tension between them was coming back.

"I'll think about you and Ashley meeting, okay?" Deacon was still half hard, thrusting his pant-covered semi against the palm of Steve's hand.

Steve nodded, leaning in closer. "A dinner."

Refusing to commit until he spoke to Ashley, he said, "We'll see."

Steve kissed him again, his tongue quickly driving Deacon a little mad as he shoved it down his throat. He started to object when he felt Steve unzipping his fly, but Steve had him pinned to the seat with that heated kiss.

The truth was he didn't really want him to stop because it felt too good. The instant there was skin on skin contact, Deacon moaned, thinking he might come any second as Steve worked the pad of his thumb over the slick head of his cock. Steve pulled back, staring down into Deacon's lust-worn misty eyes.

Deacon was unable to focus clearly, and a sort of whimper escaped from within as Steve continued to tease his prick.

Steve smiled at the reaction and cleared his throat. "Just one last kiss and I'll let you go."

With that, Steve leaned over, taking Deacon's cock into his hot, wet mouth.

Deacon placed one hand on the roof of the car and the other on the back of Steve's head as his eyes rolled back into his head. He glanced nervously out the windows, praying none of the neighbors could see what they were doing while parked in the shaded darkness of the trees and detached garage.

He wasn't able to focus very long.

"Jesus," he whispered just before biting down on his bottom lip to keep from making any more noise.

Steve was cruelly taking his time, and Deacon was enjoying the torture, trying to force every last inch down his lover's throat.

"Gonna—" Deacon paused, taking in several short breaths. "—come."

Steve sucked him all the way down to the root, swallowing each load as Deacon shot his seed. Every muscle in his body tensed as he fought to keep quiet, seeing fractured hues of blacks and reds and gold flecks behind his closed eyes.

He was shaking by the time Steve finally released him.

Sitting up and settling back into the driver's seat, Deacon could see the big ass grin on his boyfriend's face.

"That was…"

Steve nodded his agreement as Deacon trailed off, not able to finish that statement. "I am talented."

Deacon laughed, hissing slightly as he shoved his still sensitive dick back inside his work pants. "Thank you."

"You're very welcome." Steve laughed. "You taste so damn sweet, and I won't see you for a few days, so you know, didn't seem right leaving without taking a piece of you with me."

"That's disturbing…yet I understand completely." Deacon shoved his hand between Steve's legs. "Now whip that big boy out so I can return the favor."

Steve glanced upward, mouthing the words, 'Thank You', as if saying a prayer while he leaned his seat back in order to provide easier access for Deacon who couldn't keep himself from laughing.

His mouth watered as Steve fumbled to free his cock, and silly as it sounded, a pang of sadness came over Deacon, wishing Steve was coming inside, knowing he would miss the man the instant he climbed into an empty bed. Deacon had been aware for some time that he was starting to fall, and that thought sent a chill down his spine. Love was never easy for him. It required trust, something he'd never been very good at giving.

His brain was buzzing, but the panic dissipated the instant Steve's erection was free, the bulbous head aimed right toward his lips.

He took more pleasure in the long, deep groan that Steve let out as Deacon took him all the way into the back of his throat than the fact he could get every last inch of Steve's thick cock in his mouth.

That was what he concentrated on, pushing any and all fears aside, working his lips and tongue along the shaft and sensitive head. Racing toward Steve's orgasm was all the distraction Deacon needed, getting easily lost in the rhythm as Steve grabbed him by the hair on the back of head and took over, slowly fucking his face.

He closed his eyes and allowed everything else to float away. Nothing else existed beyond the confines of the car, and Deacon would've been happy to never leave it.

* * * *

He could make out enough of his reflection from the glass pane in the back door of Patty's house to see that his hair was a complete mess, practically standing up on end. Deacon cursed under his breath but smiled as he furiously ran his fingers through his hair in an attempt to tame the mane. Steve had been using it as something to hold onto while forcing his dick down Deacon's throat only moments before.

He could still taste Steve, which left him floating along the edge of continued arousal. Steve had a habit of keeping Deacon there.

He waved goodbye to Steve who'd begun backing out of the drive when he saw Deacon had the back door opened. Entering the kitchen, which was dark apart from the ambient light coming from the living room, Deacon jumped, nearly dropping the single grocery bag and apron in his hand, letting out a horror movie worthy shriek when he noticed the shadowy figure lurking by the window above the sink.

His nerves began to settle when his sister jumped a mile off the floor, screaming as well since Deacon had scared the living daylights out of her.

He fumbled for the light switch and stared her down when they flicked on, flooding the room with light. "Damn it, Ash, give me a fucking heart attack, why don't you?"

She was already giggling, her hand clutching the cotton pajama top above her heart as she attempted to regain control over her faculties. "Never knew a boy could actually scream that high."

Deacon tossed the recyclable Garibaldi's bag onto the countertop. "Well, scare the shit out of a few more boys, and you'll see that it can happen."

"Sorry," she said through another whispered giggle.

"What the hell are you lurking around in the dark for anyway?"

She pointed toward the window. "Came to see why it was taking you so long to come inside the house."

His face immediately began to burn with heat so he turned away and began unpacking the grocery bag. "You shouldn't spy on people, it's rude."

"What were you two doin' out there, anyway?" she asked.

Deacon sighed, noticing the cheeky grin on her face as he passed by and tossed a few items into the fridge. It was obvious she had a pretty good idea, but he stopped long enough to peek out the window, ascertaining that thankfully she wouldn't have been able to see much from this vantage point.

He pointed at her when she opened her mouth and said, "Shut up, Ashley."

She started laughing again. "I know who to come to for pointers when—"

"Oh my god!" Deacon was now starting to sweat. "Seriously, never gonna go there with my baby sister!"

"Well, that's just stupid. What's the point of having a gay older brother then?"

"Um, go find yourself a gay bestie for BJ advice, Ashley. It's a system that has been in place for decades, and it works really, really well." He shoved a couple of cans of green beans at her and pointed toward the pantry.

"You never had a straight girl bestie," Ashley pointed out. "Never had any friends at all in high school."

"That's because I was paralyzed by the fear they'd end up meeting our mother." Deacon reminded her. "That and no one ever seemed all that interested in being my friend."

"Well, are you going to continue to hide your boyfriend from me?" Ashley smirked. "Are you ashamed of me?"

"What?" Deacon closed the cabinet door and turned to face her. "Absolutely not. I wasn't sure you'd want to meet him. I was trying to be respectful of your boundaries and stuff."

Ashley smiled. "Good, then I wanna meet him."

"Okay, fine, I'll set it up." Deacon placed his hands on his hips. "We could have dinner Saturday night?"

Ashley chewed on her bottom lip. "What time? Could it be early? I'm supposed to go to the movies with Mel."

"Sure." That sounded like a good plan actually, if they didn't end up liking one another, the dinner wouldn't go on for hours.

"Sweet!"

"But you can't talk to Patty about this kinda thing, you know that, right?" Deacon asked.

"Duh?" she said, fidgeting slightly as she toyed with the hem of her top.

"I'm serious, Ash. Patty will go ape-shit and start rethinking our current living situation. She could make things harder on us if she decided to."

"She wouldn't," Ashley said, her eyes bugging out when she saw the serious look on Deacon's face. "But I won't say anything."

"Okay then, I'll set it up."

She squealed, running over to give him a big hug before shoving him away and running back into the living room without another word.

"Teenage girls are frickin' weird," he mumbled as he fished his cell out his pocket. He tapped a text message to Steve, feeling bad that Ash had ever thought he might be ashamed of her.

"And for God's sake, don't go asking him for BJ advice either!" Deacon screamed at the top of lungs.

"Like I would!" Ashley yelled back. "Sheesh!"

"I wouldn't put it past you," he muttered, hitting send before putting the last of the groceries away.

Deacon sighed, leaning against the cabinet for support as he waited for word back from Steve. He certainly wasn't ashamed of Ashley, but he couldn't lie about the fact he was ashamed of Patty, this house of horrors and the neighborhood he grew up in—Vidale Heights came with a stigma, and it wasn't a good one.

If there was any area in Detroit that would be considered the wrong side of the tracks, it was Vidale Heights, which was located in the northern part of the city, adjacent to Hazel Park and Ferndale, where Steve lived. In high school, he'd made the choice to be invisible, to hide in the crowd as opposed to ever putting himself out there. Deacon never wanted to give anyone else the opportunity to reject him. It was bad enough his own mother had.

If he'd been able to keep Steve away from this house, Deacon would have, but the man could be terribly insistent when he wanted something, and Deacon wasn't very good with 'no' sometimes. To his credit, Steve never acted any different upon knowing Deacon was from this part of town. Still, the thought of Steve seeing the inside of this house made Deacon sick to his stomach. He was afraid of allowing something good inside some place so evil, like it might somehow spoil things.

At the same time, it might be good for Ashley to see that there were good, decent people in the world, so from that angle, meeting Steve could be a plus.

He laughed, closed his eyes and took a few deep breaths. Maybe now it was time to finally let go some of this baggage. It was all crap that Deacon couldn't change about himself, no matter how much he wished otherwise.

Have to stop worrying about shit I can't change.

New mission statement, he thought, hearing his phone chirp, signaling he had a text.

Deacon grabbed the phone off the counter and tapped the screen so he could read the whole text:

Awesome news!

Can't wait to meet her!
Dinner at ur place???

His smile began to fade, and his stomach got all crampy at the thought of Steve coming here for dinner.

"Maybe we could go out for dinner?" he asked to no one in particular, still staring at the phone in his hand. That annoyingly persistent new mission statement continued rumbling around inside his head.

He grumbled before yelling at himself. "Baby steps!"

He tapped out a new text to Steve.

"Baby what?" Ashley yelled back from the living room.

Deacon rolled his eyes. "Never mind!"

He reached over and turned off the kitchen light, then stood for a moment in the darkness, deciding he'd made an art form out of hiding from people. Seemed like a waste to just throw all that skill out the window now.

My future career as a secret agent is hanging in the balance!

With that flimsy justification tucked firmly into place, he decided to go to bed.

CHAPTER ELEVEN

Steve took them downtown to Birdy's, which was sort of an old fashioned diner and malt shop. The place had been there since the fifties and was pretty much an institution, yet Deacon had never actually eaten there before now.

The brightly painted white walls were covered in neon signs and fifties movie posters. White and silver speckled Formica tables with shiny chrome trim were scattered throughout, and the kitchen was viewable through an open cutout behind the long lunch counter that ran the length of the back wall. Deacon thought it might be fun to sit up there, but they decided on a booth along the front window so Ashley could keep an eye out for Mel, who was picking her up later.

It was a little chillier next to the window so Deacon decided to keep his jacket on, scooting in first and allowing Ashley to sit on the end. Steve sat across from them, already passing out the menus that had been crammed between the condiments at the far end of the table.

The glossy red, glittery vinyl covering the seats looked fairly new, but the small coin operated jukebox next to the condiments was original, and apparently still worked, though he didn't have any change on him so he couldn't test it out. They were playing that doo-wop style music that Deacon could only handle in short doses before it began driving him a little nutty. Despite the earlier hour, the restaurant was plenty busy due to the gray-haired early-bird-special set.

Deacon had been there once before, back when he was a kid. Patty was dating a new man named Gale, who eventually ended up being the first of many stepfathers, as well as the sperm donor that helped bring Ashley into the world. Gale had taken both him and Patty out for a burger and fries, an attempt to impress Deacon and suck up to Patty, no doubt. He was exceedingly charming and quite dashing, like an old-timey matinee idol. He ended up being the antithesis of all things fatherly. Gale was manipulative and played a mean game of emotional terrorism. Thankfully, he only lasted for a few years—long enough to leave Patty knocked up and penniless once more.

It ended up being a particularly dark period for Deacon, one that still left him feeling isolated and alone if he allowed himself to dwell on it for too long. Deacon was ashamed to admit it to himself now, but he'd been taken in by Gale. Of course, he'd been like eight or nine years old at the time, but still. It was an embarrassment he still carried with him. He learned exactly how duplicitous a person could be, thanks to Gale. It had been the last time anyone got the better of Deacon. He never again dropped his guard with any of Patty's men.

They didn't make it to the meal during that first visit because Patty managed to piss Gale off before the food arrived, and after a huge screaming match, they were not so politely asked to leave. Deacon had been humiliated and never returned, fearing they'd still remember him from that first time—like any of the same people would still be working there all these years later.

"Hope you guys are hungry," Steve said, patting his stomach, signaling he certainly was.

Deacon smiled, Steve's big toothy grin pulling him back from the shadows of the past.

"I'm not too hungry," Ashley began.

"Aka she's going out with a boy later and doesn't want to feel all bloated." Deacon snickered when she elbowed him.

"It's just a movie thing," she said nonchalantly, as if to intimate she was keeping her options open for the future.

"Good to know, Holly Golightly," Deacon said, happy he was able to work in something from one of the movies he'd watched with Steve.

"You realize that character is a prostitute," Ashley said matter-of-factly. "You just called your own sister a hooker."

"Nuh-uh," Deacon said, looking to Steve for backup.

Steve nodded that she was correct, smiling at the waitress who walked up to the table. "To be fair, the film suffers from a little too much censorship."

"Well, I'll be," Deacon said, impressed. "Totally missed that."

They went ahead and ordered dinner and drinks since they were on a tight timeline, thanks to Ashley's social calendar.

"Sorry I called you a hooker," Deacon said after the waitress was gone.

"No big." Ashley grabbed a straw and began the process of peeling off the paper wrapping.

"You see the good in people and overlook their flaws," Steve said, patting Deacon on the knee under the table.

They smiled at one another, then both looked over at Ashley who was grinning from ear to ear.

"So how is school?" Steve asked, then cringed slightly. "Christ, sorry. That's like every lame-ass old person's question to anyone in high school, isn't it?"

Deacon was trying not to laugh.

"You shut up." Steve pointed at Deacon as the waitress swung by, dropping off their drinks.

"I said nothing!" Deacon declared.

"You were thinking it," Steve added.

"You totally were," Ashley said, tossing in her two cents.

Deacon sneered. "So much for that whole blood is thicker than water thing."

"You have to love me," Ashley said, sucking down some of her soda. "Steve, on the other hand, needs to be wooed so when the two of you get married, he'll adopt me and give me a new car."

That had Deacon laughing, he couldn't help himself, aside from being mildly mortified.

"She's gonna go far in life," Steve said, wiping his watery eyes from laughing too hard. "You gotta deal, Ashley. If your brother ever marries me, I'll give you a new car."

"Sweet!" Ashley said.

"You'll do no such thing," Deacon said.

"He doesn't want me to have nice things," Ashley said, thumbing in the direction of her brother.

"I see that." Steve shook his head disapprovingly. "Shameful."

"Funny, you two," Deacon said.

Ashley shoved her hand across the table toward Steve. "Thankfully, we don't need him to sign off on this deal, do we?"

Steve shrugged, shaking her hand. "I don't think we do."

Deacon's mouth hung open slightly, watching the two of them go back and forth.

"Awesome," Ashley said, "consider him all yours, then."

"If I were to be completely honest, I kind of already did consider him all mine, Ashley," Steve said, wondering if he'd made a faux pas by overstepping. "But it's nice to make it all official-like."

"Aww, that's actually kinda sweet," Ashley said, taking Deacon's arm. "He's a keeper."

She looked across the table at Steve and wiggled her eyebrows. "See there, I'm already on the job."

"I see that," Steve said, as he and Ashley laughed with one another.

Deacon shot her the squinty-eyes of accusation. "I can't believe you're trying to work the man for an automobile."

"To be fair," Steve said, jumping in. "I partially agreed, out of the fear you'd force her into one of those toy cars like you drive."

Ashley laughed, mumbling something about a clown car under her breath. "Now he's going to start in about the great gas mileage."

"And only minutes ago you were complaining about a hooker reference, which was totally innocent on my part by the way, yet now you're working the poor man for a car."

The table went quiet, and Deacon sat back in the booth, feeling a little smug while Ashley tapped her chin with her index finger, no doubt working out some way to refute the insinuation.

"Mmm, no, your hooker theory doesn't really apply in this

situation," Ashley said, with a shrug.

Deacon showed no signs he was caving, sure he had her backed into a corner.

"As the pimp in this scenario, I hold all the power." Ashley smiled innocently. "Kinda makes you two my bitches, doesn't it?"

Steve burst out laughing, and she grinned sweetly, like a little angel. It was evident she was pleased with herself.

"How about we dial back the diabolical, for crying out loud?" Deacon reached across the table, grabbing Steve by arm. "She's usually very sweet."

"Ree-lax," Ashley said. "I'm just showing off a little."

"Oh goody, the food is here," Deacon said as the waitress plopped down a tray and began passing out the plates.

The food provided a much needed distraction, and Ashley seemed to understand that all the pimp/hooker references were making Deacon uncomfortable. She switched gears and went a little more wholesome-teen by discussing school, the upcoming prom and her plans for college. Unlike Deacon, Ashley made plans and had goals; she wanted to be a teacher first and foremost. Deacon envied her that.

Ashley's phone chirped and she scooped it up off the table, reading the text before glancing out the window. A less than savory looking vehicle was pulling up in front of the restaurant, and Ashley began waving as Mel rolled down the car window, thrusting her arm out and waving back.

"My ride's here," Ashley said, frowning for a moment as she looked across the table at Steve. "Sorry to eat and run, but I'm super-glad we finally got to meet."

"You've hardly eaten a thing," Deacon pointed out.

Steve thrust his hand across the table at her. "Thank you for spending a little of your Saturday evening with us, Ashley. I look forward to doing it again?"

"That would be awesome!" she said, patting Deacon on the shoulder. "I'll see you tomorrow morning?"

"Yeah, sure." Deacon was now eyeing the other people in the

car.

Her phone bleeped again.

"Says we're gonna be late for the movie." Ashley leaned forward and sucked down the last of her soda.

"Who are the boys?" Deacon asked, eyeing them suspiciously as Mel now hung out the car window, motioning for Ashley to hurry.

"I'll take some fries, okay?" She grabbed a fresh napkin and piled on the French fries.

Steve was laughing under his breath as she poked Deacon in the side in an attempt to make him laugh.

"I think I should come meet them." Deacon said, swatting her hand away.

"Dea, no, there's no time, plus you'll find some way to embarrass me."

Deacon scowled, trying not to take offence over the fact she was apparently too embarrassed for her friends to meet him.

Her eyes got all pleady, and she smiled sweetly.

"This is so not over."

She shoved a fry into her mouth. "Yummy dinner, guys!"

Deacon watched her slide out of the booth.

"I'll see if your brother can work out a weeknight next time, Ashley." Steve said, looking slightly uncomfortable like he wasn't sure whether he should get up or not.

"That would be perfect." Ashley was balancing the fries, her cell phone and her purse. "You'll make sure he gets home in one piece?"

Steve smiled at her attempt to turn the tables on them. "I will indeed."

"I approve," she declared before running for the door. "Be good, you two!"

Deacon laughed as he was about to yell the same orders out to her, but she beat him to it, already out the door.

They watched as she skidded to a halt on the sidewalk. Mel

got out of the car, allowing Ashley to crawl in the backseat.

"I really don't like those boys."

"Funny, 'cause it sounded before like you've never actually met them?" Steve asked.

"If this is going to work out between you and me," Deacon said, cringing when the car peeled out away from the curb. "You're going to have to start blindly agreeing to dislike anyone I do."

Steve rolled his eyes but decided to otherwise ignore Deacon's demand. "I like her, she's sweet."

"She's practically an extortionist."

Steve shook his head, picking up his burger to take another bite. "She's a good girl, Deacon."

He sighed, nodding that he was aware of that fact. "But good girls attract bad boys."

"Must be why you like me so much," Steve said through a mouth full of food.

"You're a good boy who *thinks* he's a bad boy." Deacon salted his fries before reaching for more ketchup. "Which means I get the sexy, cocky attitude with the sweet, someone-to-watch-over-me behavior. You're nearly perfect, actually."

Steve took another bite off his burger, but he was smiling like he might not mind that Deacon had his number.

"Plus you're great in the sack."

Steve swallowed, one eyebrow arching slightly. "Just great?"

"You can try working a better adjective out of me later." With that, Deacon took a huge bite out of his burger.

"The sex gauntlet has been officially thrown down," Steve whispered.

Deacon moaned in sheer ecstasy, pointing at his plate. "This is seriously the best burger I've ever had."

"Can't believe you're from here and haven't eaten one before." Steve smirked. "You sure you're not just trying to make me feel good for bringing you here?"

Steve's phone began to buzz and vibrate across the table. The screen lit up and a picture of a laughing little girl with long, curly black hair popped up. Even from his upside down vantage point, Deacon could see the word *Home* had come up on the caller ID.

"I should take this," Steve said, grabbing the phone and sliding out of the booth.

Deacon smiled, nodding when he made eye contact, making sure Steve understood he was cool being left alone.

"I'll make it quick, I promise."

"Take your time, Steve, I'm fine."

"Right." Steve shook his head as he answered the phone. "Hey, Clarissa, everything all right?"

Deacon chewed on another French fry, watching Steve step outside onto the sidewalk. He tried concentrating on the man's body language to clue him on what sort of a conversation it was, then realized he didn't actually know anything about people's body language or what it meant. For a split second, he found himself getting a teensy bit jealous as Steve paced back and forth outside the window talking to his ex. He didn't like to admit it to himself, but it bothered him—Steve having been with a women. For some odd reason, that aspect of who Steve was didn't sit well with Deacon, likely because he would not be able to fill that need should Steve ever decide he missed women.

Part of that uneasiness stemmed from his raging curiosity. He wanted to meet them at some point, but he didn't feel like he had a right to bring that up. The way things had typically gone in the past meant that Steve would likely end up being another something Deacon would have to get over at some point. That was part of the reason he hadn't wanted Ashley to meet Steve.

Steve stopped pacing on the other side of the glass long enough to wink at Deacon in that playful way, and Deacon laughed, instantly rescued from the bad thoughts and fears that had a tendency to plague him whenever he was left to his devices.

A huge smile spread across Steve's face, and it was as if someone had flipped on a light inside the man. Deacon felt his chest ache for the first time in a very long time, so long that he'd forgotten what it was and what it meant. The overly animated expression on Steve's face told Deacon he was talking to the little girl. He wasn't sure he would've even recognized Steve in that moment had he not witnessed the transformation for himself.

For the briefest moment, Deacon ached with a euphoric longing that he might someday inspire that same blissful happiness in Steve. Then reality came rearing its ugly head, and Deacon put that out his mind. Realistic expectations were difficult enough to procure, let alone the fantastical. No sense setting himself up for disappointment by wishing for more than he was ever going to get.

Watching Steve on the other side of the glass, unable to hear what he was saying…that felt closer to what he might manage to have with Steve. Not the whole man, mind you, only a piece of him. If Deacon didn't try to hold out for more, then this one time, he might finally be able to hang on to what he already had.

It bugged him that Steve had never really talked about them, but he quickly came to the realization he'd never actually asked about them either. Part of that was because he didn't want to upset Steve or make him feel bad. He still remembered how sad Steve became that first night. Once they were behind closed doors, locked away in that hotel room, Mr. Smiley faded away, replaced by another man. It was that guy Deacon had been crushing on ever since—the one who made love to him, almost worshipping him as opposed to just fucking him.

As he watched Steve now, looking so happy, Deacon understood it had been the sadness that had drawn him in initially. It appealed to him because he recognized it as something familiar. Something inside him had shifted in the last couple of minutes, though. He was so terrified of losing what they had that he hadn't dared push too hard for any details. The reality of the situation was, that Deacon would have settled for a lot less than what Steve was already giving him—so to a certain degree, he already felt lucky.

He absentmindedly shoved another fry into his mouth, and the self-doubt began to creep in. As much as he wanted to someday be the thing that made Steve light up that way, Deacon had serious reservations he ever could. It would require him being an entirely different kind of guy—the cheery, optimistic type he liked to poke fun at because it made him feel better about his own miserable self.

He took a sip from his soda and straightened up in his seat as Steve came back inside. He was still grinning as he slid back into the opposite side of the booth.

"Good call?" Deacon asked, hoping he didn't appear overly interested to the point he'd come off nosy. The sudden curiosity about Steve's previous life as a *straight* man was killing him.

"Yeah, thanks." Steve glanced down at his own plate as if trying to decide whether or not he should finish his own fries or spare himself the carb-overload.

"You never really talk about them," Deacon said.

Steve appeared slightly stunned. "I…had the impression you weren't all that interested. Don't take this the wrong way, but the few comments you've made in the past made me think you didn't find this particular part of my past very appealing."

Deacon sat there frozen, thinking back, trying to figure out what he'd said or done to make him feel that way. The fact that Steve wasn't wrong told him he must have. He didn't get the whole closeted thing, but he thought he'd been doing a better job at hiding those opinions.

Accepting the fact he was gay had been the life raft that helped Deacon understand that Patty's disdain for him wasn't truly about him as an individual. Yeah, Patty blamed him for certain things, like the fact his father abandoned her because of him, but his homosexuality was what she truly hated. It had been the thing that eventually freed him, and as a result, he'd always looked down upon others who felt trapped or disgusted by their own nature. He didn't like to admit that to anyone but himself.

Deacon was struggling to make sense of what he wanted to say without inadvertently making Steve feel crappy. "I won't pretend like you totally imagined that, though I guess I just don't get it."

"It's okay." Steve nodded. "I actually like that about you. Your intolerance for that aspect of my personality makes me think perhaps the world has changed more than I thought."

"You're so weird." Deacon smiled, indicating he was joking around. "But I don't mind you talking about them." He shrugged. "I'd like to know about all sides of you…but only if you wanted to share."

Steve was now grinning sheepishly. "You like me…right now, you *really* like me."

"Of course I do, why else would I be sleeping with you?"

"No, dummy, Sally Field? The Academy Awards?" Steve asked, rolling his eyes when it became apparent Deacon had no clue to what he was referring. "This is why I hate dating children."

Deacon sat back, folding his arms across his chest. "Spare me, Grandpa, like it's my fault you're too lazy to update your pop-culture references to something that happened this century?"

"Little asshole." Steve laughed, but his eyes got all squinty like he still disapproved of something. "What do you wanna know?"

"Um, everything? I don't know? Whatever you want to share? I'm ready to listen." Deacon nodded, deciding that was finally the right thing to say.

Steve sighed. "Once upon a time…"

Deacon reached across the table, trying to smack him, but Steve leaned back, dodging the intended assault.

"You need to settle it down over there."

"Or else?" Deacon asked.

"You are awfully wound up this evening."

"Too much caffeine?" Deacon pondered. "My bad. Please, talk to me, baby. Tell me what's going on inside that pretty little head of yours?"

"That's cute." Steve shook his head, not appreciating the sarcastic delivery. "I'm not sure what to tell you about that part of my life."

"Then tell me about Clarissa and Kylie." Deacon nodded.

"Tell me what they're like."

Steve sighed, staring down at the table. His fingers tapped in time to the music, and Deacon assumed he was trying to figure out where to start. "Think I already mentioned that Clarissa was a widow. Her husband, Kevin, had been a friend, more of an acquaintance, really, but he was a good-natured guy. Friendly. You know the type, able to pull a prank or rip on you in a way that never came across as mean or tinged with spite. Never heard anyone say anything bad about the guy."

Deacon nodded, then asked. "He wasn't a lover?"

"God no." Steve looked like he might be upset Deacon had thought he'd be capable of that sort of drama. "We shared a love of cars. I would run into them at shows, auctions, that type of thing. Clarissa is great. Easygoing, easy to be around. Beautiful, but like one of the guys. She fits in everywhere, you know?"

Deacon smiled. "You love her."

"I do," Steve admitted.

Deacon smiled, but his stomach dropped.

"Not the way a husband is supposed to, but I do love her." Steve poked at his now cold half-eaten burger. "I would've liked to have been the man she needed. Still hate myself for what I did to her. My intentions were good, I think. Genuine, if nothing else. It was still selfish of me, trying to hide behind her, but it doesn't change the fact that I did…do still love her."

"Can you not mend that relationship in some way?" Deacon asked.

"I don't know, Deacon, I can't see how."

Steve looked sad once again, and Deacon felt bad for dragging him back there.

"And the little girl?"

"Kylie?"

Steve was already grinning again, which had Deacon doing the same.

"Not sure I've ever met a sweeter creature, Deacon. She's

something else, a real girly-girl, tiaras and tea parties." Steve laughed a little. "Never met a stuffed animal she didn't like and worries about each of them as if they have their own feelings and personalities. She has obvious favorites but tries not to let the other stuffed animals know that. The first time I saw her fretting while attempting to decide which one to take to bed with her, I melted."

"That's nice." Deacon now felt sad, thinking it was wrong Steve would never be anyone's dad when he'd suffered through a revolving door of daddy-types growing up who shouldn't have been allowed anywhere near children. "Maybe she'll grow up and work with animals? Become a veterinarian?"

"I hate that I'm going to miss seeing her grow up."

"You don't get to see her at all?"

"Some, but not every day. I see her a couple of times a month. Clarissa will call and ask if I want to take her for a day, or I'll watch her when Clarissa has an appointment and her mom isn't able to keep Kylie. I had her for a whole weekend after Christmas."

"You should tell her you'd like to be a bigger part of Kylie's life, that you'd like to see her more often."

"You think?" Steve's brow creased, and he started to chew on his bottom lip. "I don't feel like I have the right to ask."

"But it sounds as if Clarissa is making an attempt to include you."

"She's not mine, legally speaking."

"If Kylie means that much to you, you should fight for her. I don't mean to tell you how to live your life, Steve, but just to give you another perspective, take it from someone who grew up with a long line of father figures who wanted me out of the way more than anything else. No child is going to complain about having too many people around who love them."

"God, I hate that you grew up like that. I don't wanna be a deadbeat dad on top of being a deadbeat husband."

"Then don't. It would be one thing if Clarissa was fighting or resisting the idea of having you involved in Kylie's life, but it sounds as if that isn't the case. It'll be different than before, and you may not be able to salvage your friendship with Clarissa, but you can't allow the possibility of getting turned away keep you from trying. You'd just be trading one closet for another, ruled by the fear of the unknown. I don't think that's who you are deep down, Steve, but even if you were that guy, Kylie deserves more. So do you."

"Damn." Steve stared blankly across the table.

"Sorry, I shouldn't have…it's none of my business, really." Deacon reached for another fry.

Steve grabbed his hand and held it there, hovering just above his plate.

"You don't ever have to apologize for telling me the truth, Deacon. And thank you. That was harsh, but I needed to hear it. I'm grateful to you for saying it."

They each sat there, staring at one another, Steve still holding his hand hostage as if letting go might break some connection.

"Can I take your plates?" the waitress tentatively asked.

Steve let go, looking down at his lap before smiling up at the waitress. "I'm all done."

"Me too," Deacon added, not quite able to take his eyes off Steve as he sat back, placing his hands in his lap. He could still feel the heat from Steve's hand on his skin.

As the waitress cleared the dishes, Deacon began to worry over his desire to touch and be touched by the man sitting across from him. It was so intense, tugging at his chest. It was like longing, which wasn't something Deacon had allowed himself to feel since he was little.

It struck him all of a sudden that he had no control over it—there was no switch he could go to inside to turn that off.

He began to panic until Steve smiled and winked at him, before asking their waitress for the check.

Like magic, his anxiety evaporated and all that was left was desire, a faint giddiness, and something else he didn't completely recognize. It felt dangerous but not necessarily in a bad way—at least not whenever Steve was around.

As they each got out of the booth and headed toward the cashier, the 'L' word was bouncing around inside his head, though he decided not to acknowledge the fact. It was too soon, and frankly, not something he had enough experience with to fully commit to—a working theory, perhaps, but nothing more at this point.

The instant they walked outside, they were greeted not too kindly by the sights and sounds of downtown, which was buzzing with people bustling along the sidewalks. The cool night air was refreshing, and the breeze carried with it the scent of food from all the restaurants and the music from all the nightlife and bars.

Finally, Deacon became distracted enough to let go of any misgivings about where things might or might not be headed—he could relax and just be.

* * * *

"You're kinda wonderful," Deacon mumbled drowsily.

The half-smile and flushed cheeks signaled the admission had embarrassed Deacon, making Steve think it hadn't been a pre-calculated comment. That fact made the sentiment seem more sincere.

"Thank you, Deacon." He grinned, but didn't return the compliment, even though he thought Deacon was pretty wonderful too. He decided to leave it for now as opposed to stealing his thunder by jumping onto the mutual admiration bandwagon.

Something told him Deacon wasn't the type to appreciate praise if it was given too often. That irritated Steve, but the last thing he wanted was to make him uncomfortable. It was apparent he'd suffered that emotion enough for one lifetime, and the one benefit of suffering the quiet desperation of remaining closeted for so many years was Steve had mastered the art of patience. He knew better than most that you can't force anyone into being ready—they either are or they aren't.

He just needed to decide if Deacon was going to be worth waiting around for.

Steve smiled, realizing that despite all the very enlightened mumbo-jumbo rolling around inside his head, his gut was informing him that it was already too late. He no longer had much choice in the matter. No declarations had been made by either one of them, but he certainly had feelings for Deacon.

Suddenly aware of the quiet that had fallen across the room, Steve glanced over to see Deacon had fallen asleep. He watched as the light from the full moon outside the window cast a glow across Deacon's torso, illuminating him as he mumbled something and kicked off the blankets Steve had tried to cover him up with. He shrugged, happier with the view this way.

Deacon's skin gleamed in the low, white light. He truly was beautiful to look at, a fact that didn't exactly suck for him, but Steve recognized something else was going on here—this was more than just getting his rocks off.

Not that I particularly hate the much appreciated added bonus.

It dawned on him that he needed to stop watching the man sleep, it was a bit creepy, at least he'd likely think so were the situation reversed.

Deacon stirred once again, muttering under his breath.

For the briefest moment, his entire body seemed agitated, only to fade once more into complete serenity. It was like watching an ocean, the ebb and flow as waves came rushing up onto the beach, only to retreat once more, before starting the cycle over again. It went on and on, and Steve found himself frustrated by it, that someone so young had been forced to deal with so much pain and stress that it literally continued to plague him while sleeping.

As if he subconsciously knew that Steve was worrying about him, Deacon moaned with seeming frustration, before rolling over onto his side and snuggling up against him. Steve rolled onto his back to better accommodate Deacon, whose arm slowly snaked across Steve's chest. Deacon's leg worked its way in between Steve's, so he wrapped the younger man up into his arms.

The real issue was going to be the age difference between them. He'd been out long enough that some of the guys at the dealership had begun commenting on his state of gay, and the age gap hadn't gone unnoticed. He understood it was a good thing—the fact that his friends were bringing it up meant they weren't as uncomfortable with the idea of Steve being gay as he'd assumed. But seventeen years was a lot, and he was going to look like the pervy older man chasing after twinks, which wasn't a particular stereotype he wanted to be saddled with.

Sadly, he still didn't see himself as old, not really. Though he was wiser now than he had been at Deacon's age, he didn't think of himself as being any different—despite the fact he knew it was a lie. One look at a photograph from back in his college days and the changes were quite evident.

Deacon twitched slightly, then sighed in his sleep before relaxing once again. His body was like a self-sustaining radiator, putting off a steady stream of heat.

Steve laughed quietly, thinking about all the money he'd save on heating having that in his bed each night. Would certainly be a welcome change from the cold sheets and array of pillows that normally kept him company at night.

Able to feel the burning want of sleep behind his eyes, Steve relaxed and allowed the warmth of Deacon's body to lull him into that quiet space in the back of his mind that allowed him to finally let everything go long enough to slip into unconsciousness.

His final thought was how much he enjoyed having Deacon in his arms, even though he thought he might not deserve him. Strangely enough, that didn't disturb him nearly as much as he'd expected, merely made Steve want to be more…to be better…to be that one thing Deacon never thought he'd ever be able to find.

CHAPTER TWELVE

The coffee house buzzed as if the very scent of the beans themselves had created a bit of a contact high that radiated off the patrons. It was pretty noisy between the conversations going on all around him and the loud hiss and gurgle of the espresso equipment being manned behind the glass and wood counter filled with a wide variety of pastries. Steve could feel the wood floors creak under his feet as he added a little cream to his coffee while waiting for the barista-babe to finish Clarissa's mocha-caramel cappuccino concoction.

Steve glanced over at their table to find Clarissa was staring out the large plate glass window people-watching. She looked great in jeans and a formfitting black sweater that hugged and accentuated her figure. Her long dark hair was bone straight and parted to the side. As usual, she didn't appear to be wearing much makeup, though he knew from experience that wasn't the case. When they'd first moved in together, it had shocked him how much time she spent getting ready. He'd have never guessed it, thinking she'd always looked very natural as opposed to a lot of the women he'd dated in the past.

Thinking back on it now, Steve understood the sluttier looking women that had been his 'type' over the years had been a subconscious choice on his part. The louder looking the girl, the more heterosexual he'd felt. It was all about the image. The fact his mother hated that type of woman had been a bonus. He knew there would be zero pressure for him to get married while dating that kind of girl. That kind of girl also had a tendency to respond well to the fact he respected them more than most men by not attempting to get into her panties right away.

His stomach cramped, thinking about how manipulative he'd been. It was pretty despicable.

The gal called out his name, signaling his order was ready. Steve tossed the stir stick into the trash and retrieved the tray from the pickup area. As he headed over toward the table, he couldn't help but think Clarissa appeared slightly anxious.

He could relate.

She smiled warmly as he took a seat across the table from her. Her smile turned into a lip curl when she noticed the chocolate drizzled buttery croissant.

"I'm trying to lose weight, asshole," she stated, snagging the giant mug off the tray.

"That's why we're going to split it." Steve winked. "Besides, you look incredible."

She made a pfft sound, dismissing the compliment. "That would've meant more a year ago."

"Should mean more now, I'm not trying to get into your pants anymore."

"Don't remind me," Clarissa said, her lip curling into a pout. "Of course in retrospect, you probably never were so I should get over it, right?"

"Don't do that," Steve said. "I fucked up, but don't ever think the attraction wasn't mutual. There was desire for you on my end, Clarissa."

"So hot I turned a gay man straight?" She sighed. "For a little while, at any rate."

Steve sighed, shutting his eyes for a moment as the guilt made its way through his gut. Her hand over his brought him back to the present.

Steve smiled at her. "I am sorry, don't think I could ever say that enough."

"No, I'm sorry, I'm trying to let it go, but it ain't easy, babe."

"I'm not asking that of you either. You should hate me. I'm a complete asshole. I stole six years from you. I'll never forgive myself for that."

"I don't look back at it that way, Steve, I just can't. You shouldn't either. If you truly cared for me the way I did you, then it wasn't wasted."

He nodded, taking a sip of coffee. "I hope you don't doubt

that I loved you, still do, in fact."

She smiled, finally relenting and tearing off a chuck of croissant to go with her swig of cappuccino. "The worst part isn't the betrayal so much. That still stings, I won't lie, even though I understand it to a degree. But losing the friendship…"

She'd drifted off, staring into her mug as if it might hold some sort of answer.

"We had a lot of laughs, you and I." Steve said, snapping her out of the haze.

"I have no one to torture with my reality television, which totally takes half the fun out of watching it, I'll have you know."

Steve laughed.

"The fact of the matter is, you helped put me back together at a time when…" She trailed off again, her eyes welling up slightly as she took a deep breath, fanning her face with her hands. "I was a fucking mess after Kevin died. You were there for me." She sighed and leaned back in her chair. "Do I wish you could've been honest with me? Yeah, definitely. You made me fall for you. That still hurts."

"I had myself every bit as fooled as I did you. I honestly entered into our marriage believing I was going to make you happy, thinking you were all I needed to fix what was wrong with me."

"There never was anything wrong with you." Clarissa stopped, took another drink and stared out the window once more, squinting from the light. "The truth is, on some level I think I knew. I ignored it because I knew you were safe. I didn't expect to fall in love again. I'd already had that once with Kevin. And you worshipped Kylie, so I knew you'd be a great dad. I knew more than I let on."

She looked back at him and shrugged. "I just didn't expect to fall in love like that again."

"Shit," Steve whispered, thinking a little piece of him just died all over again from the guilt. "I never wanted to hurt you."

She nodded but didn't say anything.

"What made you think I might be gay?" Steve finally asked.

"Kevin suspected. Said he caught you checking out guys in the locker room at the gym a little longer than he thought might be normal."

Steve winced.

"Said he caught you checking out his ass a couple of times as well."

"Not at all embarrassing."

"Not so much." Clarissa smiled sweetly. "Kevin had a really nice ass."

Steve snorted, choking on the mouthful of coffee.

"To hear him tell it, someone was always checking out his ass, though, so I often took what Kevin said with a grain a salt. The man had a ginormous ego on him."

"Rightfully so." Steve grinned, wiping his chin with a napkin. "He was a good guy. Probably watching over us right now, ready to kick my fucking ass, if I had to guess."

"So we both fucked up." Clarissa tore off another chunk of pastry and gobbled it down. "Now we try to make the best of it?"

"That's kinda why I asked you to meet me here. I would never presume to ask if we might ever be friends again, though I'll confess that I wish we could. But Kylie." Steve ran the tip of his finger along the hairline crack in the white porcelain coffee mug. "I don't want to be another thing she loses."

Clarissa nodded, a tear rolling down her cheek. "I don't want that either, Steve."

"I'll do whatever you think is best, but I would very much like to be involved, on a daily basis if you'd allow it. I'll totally follow your lead, but I want you to know I'm here and willing to be there for you both—as much or as little as you think best."

"I'm so happy to hear you say that. Kylie adores you, Steve, and she's really missed you—asks about you every day."

Steve sniffled, trying to keep his composure. He was solid until Clarissa reached over and took his hand. "I've missed her."

That's when they both lost it. Laughing and crying as their fingers intertwined.

"We'll work it out, right?" Clarissa asked.

He nodded, wiping his cheek with a napkin. "Thank you."

"Sure thing." She sniffled, dabbing at her nose with a paper napkin while staring down at the plate. "You gonna eat that? I'm starved."

They both cracked up, and he pushed the plate toward her.

She rolled her eyes as she ripped off another piece of flaky goodness.

Steve inhaled deeply before breathing a long sigh of relief. He was fairly certain he didn't deserve it but decided not to look the gift horse in the mouth. He wasn't going to take this second chance lightly. As she went off on a rant, bitching about her boss at work, he couldn't help but think everything would work itself out, that for the first time in a long time it was all going to be okay.

CHAPTER THIRTEEN ~ MAY

The metal screen door hadn't even had time to slam shut behind him before Deacon realized there was someone in the house. The hairs on the back of his neck were standing up on end, but before he had time to bolt back outside, he caught a glimpse of the interloper and time seemed to stop for a moment. His heart sank, and for a split second, he was once again transported back to that ten-year-old boy lost in hero-worship of the man standing before him—Deacon's stepfather and Ashley's birth daddy, Gale Grady.

"Hello, kiddo," Gale said, ripping Deacon out his thoughts and into the present.

His voice still had that amazingly disarming gravelly character. There had been a time when Deacon was every bit as entranced with Gale as Patty had been. The same cocky smile spread across Gale's face, though time hadn't been completely kind to the man. Much like Patty, age, along with alcohol and drug abuse, had taken its toll.

"What are you doing here?" Deacon asked, still frozen in place just inside the front door of the house. He was instantly sick to his stomach.

Gale was up off the sofa and taking some of the grocery bags Deacon had been clinging to like a shield. "Let me help you with these."

Before he could protest, Gale had turned and was headed toward the kitchen. It took a few more seconds before his feet began to propel him forward, following the man.

"Ashley will be home soon." Deacon finally found his voice once more. "I don't think you should be here when she does."

Gale placed the recyclable bags on the countertop with a tiny grunt. "She is my daughter."

"The daughter you deserted a very long time ago," Deacon reminded him. "I'll repeat myself once more, what are you doing here, Gale? What do you want? If it's money, we don't have any. We're barely scraping by as it is."

"I came because I heard about your momma, and I thought I might be able to help."

Deacon was impressed he'd actually managed to get that out with a straight face.

"Yes, but help yourself to what?"

Gale shook his head, then actually began taking the groceries out of the bags and placing them onto the countertop. "You haven't seen me in a very long time, kiddo. Don't you think I might have changed?"

"The thought never occurred to me," Deacon said flatly, tossing the remaining two bags onto the counter next to the sink. "And stop calling me kiddo."

It made him sad, like having his heart ripped out all over again, considering he had once worshipped the ground Gale walked on, as had his mother. For a while it had been like magic—their own personal version of Camelot. It had all been a lie of course, some rosy-eyed daydream that a very young and idealistic Deacon had managed to get lost in.

Both Patty and Gale drank and partied the entire time, but Gale initially somehow made it all seem less horrific than it really had been. It was what the man excelled at, getting you to look past the vomit, hangovers and the loud parties by convincing everyone they were having a great time.

Gale was the Pied Piper, and he used his powers for evil.

Eventually, he ran off with all their money, leaving Patty with two children to raise by herself. That was when the real darkness had set in. Without Gale there to make the tragicness of it all seem like grand good fun, the world became much bleaker than it had before.

Something in Deacon had died the day Gale left, Patty too, because the idealistic boyhood version of Deacon had been in love with Gale—his first love in the purest sense of the word. Seeing him again after all these years brought that emptiness back all over again. Deacon realized that there were apparently some holes in his heart that could never be filled.

"Deacon?" Gale asked.

He was startled out of his inner darkness and fought to regain control over himself, determined not to allow Gale to see how upset he really was.

"Can you please leave?" Deacon asked, surprised by how timid his own voice sounded.

"Look, kiddo," Gale said, oozing sincerity to the extent Deacon thought he might choke on it. "I didn't come here to cause problems or upset you, though I obviously have."

Deacon realized he'd failed to mask his own feelings. Gale placed the carton of eggs he'd been holding onto the counter and took a few steps closer to Deacon.

"How did you hear about Patty?" Deacon asked. Gale showing up now was too much of a coincidence.

"Oh you know, through the grapevine."

"Could you be a little less vague?" Deacon asked.

"It's not important, kiddo. But I am here to help, believe it or not."

"I'll go with no." Deacon felt the cabinets against his ass and realized he'd been backing away from Gale who was still advancing upon him.

Gale's hand on his arm sent crackles across his skin like electricity. Badness was the only sensation Deacon was getting from it as Gale now stood directly in front of him.

"The last thing I wanted was to show up here and make things more difficult for you. You know you were always my favorite little guy."

His other hand was now squeezing Deacon's shoulder.

"I can finally make things right by stepping up and taking over here. It'll be my chance to get to know my daughter again."

Gale was now massaging the back of Deacon's neck, and even though Deacon didn't want him to, he was powerless to stop it.

"You've got yourself that fancy new boyfriend so this could be your chance. You could move in together, start your new life without all this responsibility that you never asked for and frankly, isn't your burden to bear."

Deacon was slightly dizzy from the uneasiness washing over him, but he got stuck on two words, *new boyfriend*.

He twisted away, breaking from Gale's grasp, putting some distance between the two of them. "How the hell do you know that I'm gay, let alone have a new boyfriend?"

Gale laughed under his breath. "The way you used to look up at me all those years ago? Practically begging me to love you the way you did me? I knew then what sort of man you were going to be. Your mother and I used to laugh and laugh about it."

He could feel the bile at the back of his throat. "I was just a kid, I didn't even know what love meant. And again, how the fuck do you know I have a boyfriend, let alone a new one? Have you been…watching us?"

Gale just smiled, folding his arms across his chest, the cracks in his new and improved façade now showing the ugliness that lay underneath.

"Get the fuck out of my house, Gale, and so help me, do not ever show your face here again."

"This isn't really your house, though, is it, little man?"

"It sure as fuck isn't yours either, so get out before I call the cops."

His hands were up, signaling his surrender. "Whoa, calm down there, kiddo. I'll go…for now."

Deacon was close to losing his cool altogether when Gale turned, making a beeline for the front door. The words 'for now' were ringing in his ears, the veiled threat of more shit to come. He was covered in a cold sweat, freaked out over the fact Gale had been following him for God knows how long.

He raced over to the sink where he threw up, his stomach clenching as he fumbled for the faucet.

The sound of running water soon set his muscles at ease,

and he continued to spit in an attempt to get the taste out of his mouth. Deacon's mind raced as he went back over the entire altercation in his head, attempting to suss out clues as to why Gale was back and what he thought he might be able to get from them.

None of it had rung true.

The all-too-convenient timing of his return.

The bullshit about wanting to get to know the daughter he hadn't so much as sent a card or made a phone call to since the day he'd walked out the door and never come back.

That line about Gale and his mother laughing over the fact he was gay? Like Patty would have ever found that fact amusing.

They truly had nothing, aside from the paltry government aid check that Deacon placed into a separate account strictly for Ashley's expenses. There was the house, but the place wasn't worth much—though it looked ten times more presentable than it had back at Christmas.

But Gale wouldn't be able to sell it without Patty's…

Deacon stood back up and turned off the faucet. She'd promised him that she wouldn't interfere for Ashley's sake.

Why now?

He was so close to having permanent custody. Things were finally settling down and now this. It didn't make any sense. Unless…but how would Patty even know?

His phone chirped, and he glanced down to see the text from Ashley that she would be a little late getting home from school.

Either Ashley told Patty, or Gale had been visiting her. That was the only way she'd know anything about Steve. That she'd resort to trusting Gale, though? He knew his mother was an ignorant bigot, but this was too much—putting more faith in the man that ruined their lives?

What sort of angle was he working? If they were to get married while she was in prison, Deacon wouldn't be able to stop Gale. He'd own the house by default and could do whatever he wanted with it, and Ashley would be destroyed in the process…

collateral damage in Gale's attempt to get some quick cash.

There was only one way to stop this while still keeping his sister out of it. He'd have to choke down his own pride and go see Patty.

Just like that, his day went from horrific to sadistic.

* * * *

Deacon groaned hearing the knock at the front door, groaning because he knew exactly who was on the other side before even opening it. He got up off the sofa where he'd been holed up, clutching his cell phone, since Ashley had gone to bed. When he'd called earlier, he'd completely forgotten that Steve was babysitting Kylie so Clarissa could go out on a date. He'd just wanted to hear Steve's voice, figuring that might help calm his nerves after Gale's illegal search and seizure of what had finally begun to feel a little like home to him.

So much for safety and security.

All it had accomplished was upsetting Steve.

Deacon quietly unlocked and opened the door and as suspected found his exceedingly stubborn knight in shining armor waiting none-too-patiently on the front porch.

"I got here as soon as I could," Steve blurted out. "Clarissa was late getting home, and it took both of us to get Kylie down for the night."

"Dude, I told you I was fine."

"I didn't like the way you sounded over the phone. I know you well enough to know when something is wrong."

"That really sucks," Deacon said, attempting to shift the focus while being sincerely unnerved over the fact he was apparently unable to hide shit from his boyfriend.

Steve shot him that no mood for nonsense, stubborn-daddy look as he adjusted his stance slightly and folded his arms across his chest.

Deacon sighed, stepping aside so Steve could come inside. "Try to keep your berating of me down to a dull roar. Ashley's asleep, and I don't want her to know about Gale."

"That's nice, Deacon. You make me sound like an asshole for being worried."

Deacon secured the deadbolt and re-chained the door feeling like a shit-heel as he turned. "I'm sorry. It was kind of you to come check—*even though* I told you I was fine."

"You didn't sound fine," Steve said, heading to the sofa after Deacon signaled for him to take a seat. "And frankly, I don't give a damn if you're fine or not. I am most certainly not fine with this guy breaking in—"

"Technically, he has a key, so breaking in—"

"I don't care if he possesses magical powers that allow him to walk through walls, damn it," Steve's voice had gotten louder, but he forced the volume back down when Deacon began to look back toward the hallway where the bedrooms were located.

"You're right, he had no right to let himself in, key or no key."

"I'm pissed."

"Really?" Deacon asked sarcastically as Steve paced back and forth in front of the sofa. "I hadn't noticed."

With that, Steve finally smiled slightly, shaking the stress from his hands. He paused the pacing long enough to lean in for a kiss, which Deacon happily accepted, pulling a hug out of Steve as well. Deacon realized they weren't going to be taking a seat anytime soon as Steve was still too wired.

"Want something to drink?" Deacon asked, apparently still fidgety, which hadn't gone unnoticed by Steve either. "Gale isn't dangerous. He never hit us or Patty; he just stole money and ran off…twice."

"Please don't take this the wrong way, but is there any money for him to steal?" Steve asked.

Deacon winced, despite knowing Steve hadn't intended to insinuate they were poor white trash, he was still sensitive about the reputation that came from growing up on the wrong side of the tracks.

"You know damn well I don't give a shit about geography."

Deacon nodded that he understood. "There's the house, that's about it. If he managed to swindle Patty into signing it over to him, Gale could sell it out from under us. It's not much, but there's no mortgage."

"Let him have it," Steve said. "You could both move in with me."

Deacon wasn't expecting that. "It's home to Ashley. She doesn't hate this place like I do."

"But it's just a place, Deacon. She's a resilient kid, I think she'd adjust okay."

"And Patty's a royal bitch, but Gale has already taken from her twice, and this place is all she has left. Who knows where she'd end up without it, likely guilting Ashley into taking care of her for the rest of her miserable life, if I know Patty."

"You're a really good brother."

"You're a really good boyfriend."

"Glad you think so, 'cause I'm not leaving you tonight." Steve held up his hand when Deacon started to protest. "I don't give a damn what you say, this is not open for discussion. I'll sleep on the couch if that's what you want, but I'm not leaving you. You're still shaking, for Christ's sake."

Deacon was frustrated that Steve wasn't doing what he wanted him to do, but more importantly, he was relieved. He didn't want Steve to leave, he just wasn't sure him staying was very smart. For all he knew, Gale could be hiding in the bushes across the street watching—gathering intel to further ignite Patty.

Before he even realized he was doing it, Deacon threw his arms around Steve, who was forced to take a step back in order to keep them both upright. Deacon closed his eyes, listening to Steve laugh under his breath as he wrapped Deacon up in his arms.

"Glad you see it my way," Steve said, a hint of amusement in his voice.

"Thank you."

"For what?"

"For being the kind of guy who *occasionally* ignores the words coming out of my mouth and insists on doing the opposite."

"Everything's gonna be okay, Deacon."

"I don't believe that for one second, but I love you for saying it," Deacon said.

"I fucking hate that about you, damn it." Steve let out a frustrated sigh. "Things do work out, you know?"

"I don't know that, Steve." Deacon squeezed him tighter, glad Steve couldn't see his shame in admitting that. "I don't have any actual experience of things ever working out. I hope you're right, though. I pray that you are."

Deacon felt Steve's arms tighten around his shoulders, hugging him tighter. It was nice, but the beat of silence was about to kill him, now panicked that perhaps Steve wouldn't care for this darker side of his personality. It was ugly, and Deacon knew it, but it was part of who he was, and he didn't know how to rid himself of it.

"I'll have to believe enough for the both of us, then."

Deacon exhaled, not realizing that he'd been holding his breath.

"Take me to bed? Or am I sleeping on the couch?" Steve asked.

"Like I can sentence you to lumpy sofa time after that," Deacon said as they separated. "No sex, though."

"Whatever you say, babe."

"Unless you can be really, really quiet, that is."

Steve laughed again, reaching over and giving Deacon's shoulder a squeeze. He stared for a moment before shaking his head. "Like I'm the screamer between the two of us?"

Deacon frowned, punching Steve in the chest. He turned and headed for the hall, whispering back over his shoulder. "Don't dawdle…asshole."

CHAPTER FOURTEEN

Deacon had been smiling all morning long as he went about restoring the canned goods, glass jars, boxes and tins that lined the shelves of the international foods aisle. He pushed the shopping cart a few more steps down, tossing in a rogue box of pasta a customer had decided they no longer wanted—something that usually irritated him to no end.

Not today, though.

Today, customers could storm through and move anything they fucking wanted. Frozen peas in the chip aisle, bottled water with spices—Deacon didn't give a damn.

He was physically unable to force himself stop grinning, and such uncharacteristic behavior on his part had been noted by his coworkers. Elena, in fact, had been eyeing him like she suspected body snatching or alien abduction. Mr. Garibaldi had been watching him suspiciously as well, until Gilda whispered something into his ear, causing the man's eyes to widen as a frown passed across his face.

Deacon assumed he'd just been given too much information; the man now refused to look him in the eye.

Not even that could ruin him on this particular morning, which was saying something for the boy known to suffer more shifts in mood than a manic depressive off his meds. Instead of freaking, Deacon kept on about his work, bringing the product up to the edge of the shelf while ensuring the older stock was in front.

He noticed the time and realized they were just about to open. Deacon picked up the pace slightly as he still had about five feet left to go. Typically, he was more meticulous and usually the first one done, but today, he was bringing up the rear.

He snickered under his breath, as his own rear was sore in the best possible sense. Steve had fucked him for what felt like hours the night before. Deacon hadn't realized sex could even last that long, until now.

What made it even more unique was the fact it had taken place in his childhood bedroom and as such had officially become the single best memory Deacon had of being in that house. Steve being there with him, spending the night like that? Making love to him like that? It had been awesome, despite the crick in his back and the sore muscles in his thighs.

Moving to the endcap, he glanced up from his work when they announced over the intercom that the doors were being opened.

Surviving work today was going to be brutal because all he could think about was sex with Steve, which had a tendency to illicit inconvenient boners.

"Thank goodness for the apron," he muttered, straightening up the last of the product before glancing down at the contents of his cart.

A quick inventory and he'd worked out the most practical order he should use when restocking the unwanted items. His head was a bit fuzzy from lack of sleep and the sex haze, so a shot of caffeine was first on his to-do list once he was done with this.

Deacon glanced up just in time to keep from plowing down the woman and child currently standing before him.

"I'm so sorry!" Deacon said, trying not to laugh, having been as startled by them as they were him.

"It's fine, really," the woman insisted.

She sounded sincere, but she was keenly eyeing his name tag, which had him thinking he'd be in trouble later.

Deacon bent down, looking at the little girl with the long dark curls. She smiled sweetly, swaying back and forth as she clung to the small bright pink plastic shopping basket the store kept at the front door for kids to use while shopping with their parents.

"I hope I didn't scare you, young lady," Deacon said, praying that if he sucked up to the kid, the mother might decide not to report him after all.

"Nope," she said with a shrug. "I'm okay."

He stood back up, smiling at the mom while trying to figure out why the kid looked so familiar.

"Hi, Deacon," the lady thrust her hand out for him. "I apologize for the ambush, but Steve has been a little tight-lipped with details about you and curiosity got the better of me."

He fought to keep his mouth from falling open as the girl said, "My name's Kylie."

"Oh, shi—" Clarissa paused, cringing as she glanced down at her wide-eyed daughter. "I'm Clarissa by the way. Probably should have led with that, huh?"

He shook her hand, hoping his palm wasn't as sweaty as his armpits now were.

"Uh, no…it's fine, I'm sure."

"Really need to work on that whole, being patient thing, you know?"

His mind was racing with why she might be there, and he instantly felt sick to his stomach, thinking Clarissa was going to be that other shoe he'd been waiting to drop all this time.

"Crap, you look worried," Clarissa said. "Maybe I shouldn't have ambushed you."

"I'm sorry, no," Deacon said. "How can I help you?"

"Now I feel silly," Clarissa said, reaching down and using her fingers to brush her daughter's hair back off her forehead. "Honestly, I just wanted to meet you. Curiosity, I guess. Though maybe you think that's odd, I don't know how much Steve talks about us and—"

"A lot, actually," Deacon interrupted. "I mean, not so much in the beginning, but now he rambles on all the time about you both."

"Oh jeez, you probably wish he'd never started, huh?"

Deacon laughed nervously, thinking this was not going well. "Sorry, didn't mean that the way it sounded. And I've been curious to meet you as well."

"Oh thank gawd!" Clarissa said, startling Deacon and Kylie

who each jumped due to the outburst. "I swear I'm not usually this manic."

Kylie nodded, but Deacon wasn't sure it was nod of agreement with her mother's statement or a declaration that Clarissa was in fact a typically manic individual. He decided to go with option one, thinking children might not be all that sophisticated when it came to subtext.

"Not every day you meet your ex-husbands new gay boyfriend." Deacon shrugged, glancing down at Kylie who was staring up at him blankly, like he'd just fried her circuits with too much intel.

"Thank you, so glad you don't think I'm nuts," she exhaled dramatically. "We are like one more drama away from daytime television."

They certainly had an audience, he thought, noticing several of his coworkers were watching intently from afar. "They all probably think you're here to scratch my eyes out."

Clarissa glanced back, and Deacon watched everyone badly pretend to be doing anything else. "It is weird, right? Not bad, but…weird."

"I honestly can't begin to imagine what this must be like for either of you," Deacon said.

"We're okay, I think, right?" Clarissa glanced down at Kylie who smiled up her mother while keeping one eye on the bag of fudge-covered cookies Deacon had in his cart, waiting to get restocked. "But the reason I stopped by, aside from wanting to get a look at you, was to ask you to dinner, or lunch…hell, even breakfast if you're a morning person?"

"Um, I'm sure that would be fine?"

"We could do coffee if an entire meal is too much of a commitment at this point."

He was really more concerned with what Steve would think.

"If you're worried about Steve, don't be," she said, flipping her hand through the air. "He moves at a slower pace than the rest of us, so it's up to you and me to push him in the right direction."

She brushed her long dark hair back behind an ear. "I would love for him and Kylie to spend more time together, and I got the impression you were at least partially responsible for Steve finally reaching out when he did."

Deacon smiled, deciding that was one thing he'd done right.

"I want him to be happy, but I also want that for my girl, and having Steve in her life is going to accomplish that."

"That's right," Kylie piped in before pointing at the cookies. "Can I have those, Mommy?"

Deacon went to grab the bag so he could give them to her.

"No, sweetie, those are very bad for you."

Deacon froze, not sure what to do at that point. There'd been times for him growing up when he and Ashley made meals out bags of cookies because Patty was either too drunk or passed out and in no condition to fix them anything proper to eat.

"Then how come they taste so good?" Kylie asked.

"Because the manufacturer loads them up with addictive preservatives that taste good, but they turn into poison after you eat them," Clarissa said matter-of-factly to her daughter.

Kylie's eyes were now wide as saucers. "That's mean."

"She went to a sleepover at a friend's house, and they let the girls eat that kind of stuff," Clarissa said, looking at Deacon.

He hadn't asked for an explanation. "The monsters."

"Now she's like a crack addict," Clarissa added, shaking her head as if dealing with the withdrawal of processed sugar and preservatives had nearly been enough to push her off the deep end.

"Dinner would be great," Deacon said, hoping to steer the conversation back around to the original reason she'd stopped by before he ended up getting fired for doing more talking than working.

"Oh super!" Relief seemed to sweep across her entire body as she wiped the back of her hand across her forehead. "Guess I'll get out of your hair then. I'll handle Steve, so no worries there and…I'll let him get back to you with the details?"

"Okay, sure," Deacon said, unnerved by the way Kylie was still eyeing the bag of cookies. "Bye, Kylie."

She smiled as if on cue, waving as Clarissa took her by the hand and led her back down the aisle toward the front of the store.

"You should bring your sister, too," Clarissa called back. "Nice meeting you!"

"Okay!"

He brushed his hands across his apron as an elderly lady passed by, eyeing him funny like she feared he might try snatching her purse.

He smacked himself upside the head. "Nice meeting you!"

He realized she was already gone. "Too."

"I don't know you!" the old lady snapped.

Deacon jumped, startled by her outburst, which in turn startled her right back. They stared at one another before each turning to head in opposite directions.

CHAPTER FIFTEEN

The first time he'd prepared to come to visit Patty with Ashley, he'd been slightly overwhelmed by the process. There was a reason television shows and movies cut to the chase, showing the visitor and prisoner already seated and ready to chat. The procedures and the applications that had to be filled out and approved ahead of time were annoying. He'd made a promise to Patty that he would bring Ashley to visit at least once a month so he'd suffered through all of it because he'd given his word.

Of course Patty had been so nasty to him when he'd accompanied Ashley the first couple of times that, in order to hang onto his sanity, he'd stopped going in with her. The fact Ashley had never brought up the fact Deacon didn't go in with her anymore, told him Patty wasn't sorry he stayed away. Today would be his first time back inside the visiting room in two months.

The most surprising thing about visiting people in prison had been the list of shit you weren't allowed to wear. It was about as long as his arm and basically could have been summed up with a simple, don't wear anything slutty.

"I'll have to save my spandex mini slash tube top combo for some other occasion," he mumbled, placing his braided leather bracelet and glass-beaded necklace into the locker next to his wallet and keys.

Clipping his visitor pass onto his shirt, he shut his eyes for moment and said a little prayer that he'd be able to get through to her.

By the time he'd made it to the visitation room, Patty and her fellow roomies were already seated throughout the room at the white, round metal tables. The inmates wore khaki colored scrub-like uniforms, and there were guards standing about, keeping a watchful eye and ensuring everyone obeyed the rules.

Deacon wasn't the first visitor through the door as evidenced by the hugging and smiling faces, which felt unauthentic considering where they were. What was there to smile about in this place with its institutional concrete floors and light gray walls?

It was depressing.

There were, at least, thin slit-like windows that allowed for some natural light to go along with the florescent tube lighting set throughout the ceiling.

The stools were not moveable, attached instead to the table itself, making it one large piece, which was bolted to the floor. Deacon initially assumed this was to prevent anyone from going ape-shit and tossing them at one another during a riot. He quickly recognized that was a slightly melodramatic scenario brought about by having watched too much trashy television during his formative years. There was a lone stool located on one side of the table where the inmates sat, and there were three others clustered closer together on the opposite side for visitors—probably designed to prevent family members from being able to slip anything under the table to their loved one.

There was very specific etiquette involved. No talking to anyone at neighboring tables other than brief greetings—Ms. Manners wouldn't have it any other way.

Only one kiss and hug allowed per visitor, unless posing for pictures. Like it's fucking Disneyland or something? Let's go take a ride on the Penal System Plunge! Why anyone wanted to create a photographic memory of this hell, he couldn't understand.

A flash went off, temporarily blinding him, and he rolled his eyes.

Great, now I'm photo-bombing Petty-Theft Penelope and the people who love her.

Deacon forced a smile as he reached the table, noticing Patty was looking around him, hoping to see Ashley.

"Just me this trip, Patty." Deacon took a seat across from her, and that familiar sadness came over him, seeing the disappointment on her face.

She actually looked decent, even without the makeup that she typically enjoyed caking on to cover up the wear and tear from all the hard living. Her black hair was streaked with gray, more so right around her face, but it was clean and had an attractive natural wave to it that made it appear styled even though it wasn't. Her face looked tired, but her eyes seemed bright.

It took a few moments for him to figure out why, before Deacon cleared his throat, recognizing they weren't bloodshot all to hell for once.

"Before we waste each other's time going through your whole I-can't-understand-why-you're-here dance, I've already seen Gale, and I know without a shadow of a doubt that you are responsible for his skanky, fresh out of the woodwork resurgence."

"He's got a right to see his daughter if he wants to," Patty spat out, not bothering to deny it. "Certainly a better role model than you are. I don't want Ashley exposed to your sickness, boy. I can't control what you do, you've made that clear, but the good Lord will take care of you and your kind. That I know. I can, however, do something about you infecting my baby girl with your lifestyle."

Deacon sighed, so frustrated with her ignorant religious bullshit he wanted to scream.

"You really are hopeless," he said, rubbing the palm of his hand over his face. "I used to tell myself it was just the booze. That if you were ever actually sober long enough to form a coherent thought, you'd come around to understanding that there is nothing wrong with me—at least nothing that wasn't your doing."

"I didn't make you this way," Patty snapped.

"Technically, you did, Patty," Deacon snapped back. "It's genetic, you nitwit. You had sex with a married man, who knocked you up before deserting you, and nine months later, little gay me came along—fresh out of the oven and already programmed to like other boys."

Pifft, Patty spat, indicating he was full of it.

"You can ignore the science if you want, but it was you who

made me who I am. You made me, and I ended up gay. You spent years verbally berating and beating me down till there was nothing left because you fucked up your life by getting pregnant, and instead of taking responsibility for that fact, you blamed me."

"I never beat on you," Patty said, the look on her face visibly indicating she felt she deserved a medal for that fact.

"Beat on me? True, you weren't what I would consider physically abusive, though you did slap the crap out of me the time or two I made the mistake of getting between you and the bottle." Deacon shook his head, not sure if the repetitive muscle twitch in Patty's temple signified her indignation or guilt. "Wonder what the good Lord does to people who hit children."

"I didn't mean to do that," she said, glancing down at the table. "That was the liquor that made me sick."

"Do you honestly believe Gale loves you?" Deacon asked, watching Patty intently, who said nothing. "Or is it truly just me that you loathe to the extent you'd prefer ruining the little happiness and security Ashley has found?"

"You don't know Gale like I do," Patty muttered.

"You're sure as shit right on that one," Deacon said. "He screwed you over twice in the past, so why would you expect a different result this time around? He will marry you, sell that house out from under you, and then he'll run. You'll never see him again because you'll have nothing left that he can take."

The muscles in her jaw were tightening, and he knew she wanted to say something, but for whatever reason, didn't.

"So let me recap things for you, in case you've somehow forgotten where you stand in the big bad world, huh?" Deacon held up his hand, sticking up one finger. "We've already established Gale isn't going to be there for you when you get out of jail."

She once again said nothing as Deacon flipped finger number two up in front of her face. He laughed out of frustration as she'd clearly decided to shut down and at the very least was going to pretend to ignore anything else he had to say. "Both your parents are gone, though they'd pretty much disowned you when they were alive due to the drinking and extramarital affairs."

Deacon added finger number three. "The latest in a long line of loser-druggie boyfriends deserted you back at Christmas—which led to your fourth DUI, providing you with this lovely holiday in prison."

He added two other fingers making four and five. "You've completely alienated Aunt Sara, who washed her hands of you years ago, and you've most definitely lost me—I will never forgive you, Patty. Not *ever*. I wouldn't touch you to scratch you at this point."

He wiggled all five fingers in front of Patty's face as she stared blankly back across the table at him.

Deacon let his hand fall.

"All you have left is Ashley, who for whatever reason still loves and defends you despite the fact you've pretty much been drunk throughout her entire childhood. And what she gets in return for her loyalty is you, siccing her good-for-nothing, two-time-deserting, con-man of a father on her?"

He could see Patty's eyes beginning to well up.

"The one selfless thing you've ever done for her was letting go of all your own bullshit and backing me when it came to becoming her legal guardian. And now you want to ruin that because you refuse to see me happy?"

She wiped off the tear that ran down her cheek, but said nothing.

"I don't actually expect my coming here to make any difference, but I swallowed my own bullshit and came on the off chance you aren't the monster I believe you to be. Either way, Patty, please understand that I will fight you tooth and nail over this. I have a feeling it won't take long for any decent private investigator to discover whether or not Gale has a record or any outstanding warrants. And I have zero issues taking the stand and telling the judge about every rotten-ass thing you have ever done to us. I have letters of support from Mel's parents and my employers. Letters from Ash's school and her teachers attesting to the bump in her grades and overall improvement in attitude since your ass was locked away in this place. All in all, I like my chances with or without your support."

Patty exhaled, her lip quivering and her gaze set firmly on Deacon. He could tell she was pissed off and close to cracking, but there was no bottle for her to turn to in this place.

"The only thing you threaten by moving forward with this is your relationship with Ashley. You know deep down Gale has no interest in being a part of her life." He made sure to make eye contact with her in hopes it would knock that point through her thick skull. "I promise you, Patty, if you ruin things for her now, she will hate you, maybe not the way that I do, but you *will* lose her. And you won't win in the process, so it'll all be for nothing."

With that, Deacon took a deep cleansing breath before getting up from the table and walking away. He never wanted to come back here, and after the things he'd just said to Patty, he seriously doubted she'd welcome seeing him again even if he did.

He'd done the only thing he could do at this point, and he'd done it for the right reasons. There was no part of him that believed Patty wouldn't eventually self-destruct and ruin her relationship with Ashley in the process. Deacon didn't want his baby sister to have to experience that just yet.

He said a little prayer as he left that the drive down had been worth it. With Patty, you never knew what she might do, but he was ready to pin all his hopes on her this one last time for his sister's sake.

CHAPTER SIXTEEN

Deacon was chewing on his bottom lip, watching intently as Steve slowly and seductively removed his clothes one piece at a time. The man knew how to work a tease, no one could suggest otherwise. It wasn't a good sign that seeing the man with his shirt off was enough to get him hard, but Steve was built just like Deacon liked 'em. He was solid without being overly bulky, and the hairy chest and tight waist made his mouth water.

Steve knew it too, and that made it even worse. Deacon walked around feeling off-center most of the time. He'd never manage to win an argument because that blue collar, high school coach look Steve possessed made Deacon long to do very, *very* bad things.

He was fairly certain Steve knew that, too.

"You need to hurry up and make your call, Deacon," Steve said standing in the doorway to the main bedroom of the hotel room while unzipping his suit pants. "We only have a few hours before the giggling school girls descend upon us, and I have a lot of plans for you between now and then."

Deacon felt his face burn hot watching Steve rubbing his cock through his trousers. He reached for his cell phone, thinking he had one or two ideas himself.

The Governor's Suite was humongous, like something out of a movie. The architecture was old-timey, but the room felt opulent, plus it had modern conveniences like wifi and stuff, which he thought was kinda cool.

He'd only stayed in one or two hotel rooms his whole life, and none of them had ever been anything like this.

The large living area had two sets of French doors on either side of a fireplace that led outside to small balcony that hailed a beautiful view of the Detroit skyline. The Renaissance Center could be seen to the left, with a clear view of the water, front and center, and finally One Detroit Center and the rest of the business area partially viewable to the right. He'd spent a good ten minutes out there gawking, not caring much that he likely came off looking like a goober straight off the farm.

The room even came with something called concierge service, which from what Deacon understood was sort of like having a butler, but he had zero intentions of making use of it. Three's a crowd after all, and he wanted Steve all to himself for as long as possible.

Despite the fact Steve offered to pay for the hotel room, Deacon had decided he'd have to pay the man back. It was likely going to take him several paychecks to do it, but they were only here because of him so it didn't feel right letting him pay.

"Phone," Steve commanded, snapping him out of his own thoughts. "Now."

While the view from the balcony was undeniably amazing, the sight of his naked boyfriend was much more appealing.

Deacon swallowed hard, watching Steve loitering in the doorway to the bedroom slowly jacking himself off.

"Fuck," he whispered.

"I'd like to, if you'd hurry the hell up."

"Right." Deacon shook his head to try and clear the sex from his thoughts as he dialed Ashley's cell number. "You need to go away, baby. I can't concentrate with you standing there doing that."

Steve laughed and disappeared back into the bedroom. Deacon put the phone up to his ear just in time for Ash to answer.

"Hello," she said, shushing whoever was giggling in the background. "Everything all right, Deacon?"

He could tell she was doing her best to sound extra innocent. "I'm great, Ash, but can you put me on speaker phone? I wanna wish both you and Mel a good night."

Deacon glanced down, feeling a little silly getting ready to rag on his sister wearing nothing but the neon blue jockstrap Steve had purchased for him, requesting he wear it this evening.

"You're on speaker," she announced.

He couldn't believe how quiet it now was on the other end.

"Hi, Mel," Deacon said cheerfully.

"Hi, Deacon," Mel said.

She sounded a bit more hesitant.

"I just wanted to wish you both a great time tonight, and to be careful."

"We will," they each said in unison.

"I want you and your dates to stop by my room the instant you make it to the hotel tonight. We're in the Governor's Suite, that's on the twelfth floor."

"What?" they both asked in unison.

"Yeah, Trish told me about the party, and she thanked me and Steve both for agreeing to chaperone."

"Oh shit," Mel mumbled in the background.

"I know, right?" Deacon asked. "I was sure it must have just slipped your mind, what with all the prom plans and such, which is why I didn't bother Mr. and Mrs. Williams by telling them you forgot to mention it."

"Totally slipped our mind," Ashley said, sounding a lot less chipper suddenly.

"I figured," Deacon said flatly. "I knew there was no way you'd risk getting into any kind of trouble since the judge still hasn't officially awarded me custody."

"No." Ash said softly.

"Never, Deacon, I swear it," Mel said with a little more conviction, which actually put him more at ease. True or not, she certainly sold that last bit.

"Great to hear," Deacon continued. "We have an adjoining room all ready for the two of you, so after your curfew of midnight…" He paused, hearing the groans, then added using a tone that said this was the final word on the matter, "I mean one a.m., you girls can come straight upstairs. I have bags here all packed for each of you."

"Okay, Deacon," Ashley said, sounding deflated.

"Now that that's all settled, have an awesome time! I'm really looking forward to meeting your dates."

"Thanks, Deacon," Mel said. "You know, for not telling my parents."

"Shouldn't have any reason to ever mention it so long as everyone plays by my rules."

Ashley sighed. "Message received."

"Lovely," Deacon said, grinning from ear to ear. "Feel free to text me when you're leaving the dance."

"Okay, see you later," Ashley said, disconnecting the call.

Deacon snickered, imagining that the mood inside the limousine those boys had rented just took a nosedive. He knew they were probably cussing him, certainly their dates if not the girls. Mel was probably sighing in relief that he hadn't ratted her out, and she should've been, her parents were mega-strict. She'd be grounded till their senior prom had they found out.

"You enjoyed that entirely too much," Steve said, naked and still hard as he stood in the doorway to the bedroom.

"I really did," Deacon admitted. "Nobody will be violating my little sister on my watch, damn it."

Steve laughed and took a nice long look up and down Deacon's nearly naked frame. "Now that you've had your fun, it's time for me to have mine, so get in here and suck my cock."

"'Kay," Deacon said, tapping out one last text to Mel's parents, letting them know what room they were staying in.

Steve shook his head and sighed. "You could try to sound a little less chipper when agreeing to my demands so easily, sorta ruins the fantasy a bit."

"Pretend *not* to wanna suck your dick, check." He tossed the cell onto the coffee table and then hopped up the two steps, following Steve into the bedroom.

"You really suck at this whole role playing thing."

Deacon shrugged, dropping to his knees in the middle of the room. He crooked his finger, signaling he wanted Steve to come to him. "Can't you just be glad I really suck?"

Steve laughed under his breath, sauntering over all cocky-like as he took the few steps required to close the distance between them.

Deacon moaned softly, his mouth watering, now lip to tip with the cock in question. He glanced up at Steve who looked so sexy it took Deacon's breath away. "Is it wrong that I want you to hose me down with your jiz so badly?"

"I'm gonna go out on a limb and say, hell no," Steve said, grabbing the base of his dick and running the head of it across Deacon's lips.

He groaned when Deacon sucked the precome off his bottom lip.

"So damn sexy," Steve muttered.

Deacon smiled sweetly, and just when Steve began to smile back, Deacon sucked him down to the root. The spicy musky scent he inhaled through his nose, now buried in Steve's pubes, was all the motivation Deacon required. He wrapped his fingers tightly above Steve's nuts and tugged gently, eliciting a grunt of approval followed by those big hands on the back of his head.

Deacon was home.

CHAPTER SEVENTEEN ~ JULY

Deacon smiled, shaking his head as Ashley continually changed the radio station in his car, attempting to find a song she liked. It was one of his sister's habits that drove him slightly mental, but he bit his tongue and forced himself to concentrate on driving. They were only a few more blocks away from Steve's neighborhood, and Deacon was nervous, so any distraction was a good one at the moment—even an annoying one.

The last five weeks had been like some sort of dream. Deacon and Steve began spending more time with one another, time that included Ashley, who genuinely seemed to appreciate the kind of man Steve was. Deacon and Steve had also met Clarissa and Kylie for dinner.

He hadn't been thrilled they'd had that dinner in the house that Steve had once shared with Clarissa, but she'd made lasagna. Deacon decided that meant something to Steve, judging by the tone and reverence he'd used when announcing that they had no choice because of it. Deacon didn't quite see it, especially since Mrs. Garibaldi made lasagna all the damn time—no one threw a hissy over that.

However, Deacon swallowed his pride and went along with it, a smile on his face. In all honesty, he'd gotten wiggy over a whole lot of nothing. While he couldn't say it hadn't been awkward, watching Steve help out in the kitchen, knowing exactly where to go to find the cheese grater. It was odd, and Deacon wasn't fond of the way it made him feel, having his nose rubbed in their marriage.

All objections aside, Clarissa had been exceedingly open and very sweet with him. Deacon found no animosity aimed his direction by her, and that had surprised him. He'd have wanted to scratch her eyes out were their roles reversed. As it was, he found himself falling for her in a sense. Clarissa turned out to be exactly as Steve had described her.

Even Kylie had won him over, which was saying something

considering Deacon had never been great with kids. He couldn't claim to have completely won her over, but they'd shared a moment after dinner, when she allowed Deacon to hold one of her stuffed animals. It had been sweet and kind of funny, as Kylie kept one eye on him at all times after entrusting Deacon with her favorite penguin, who was named Blinky—Deacon assumed this was due to the missing right eye.

The pirate eye patch he'd purchased a week later at a party decoration store for Blinky cemented Kylie's seal of approval. She'd giggled and laughed after Deacon tied it onto the penguin's head, clapping her approval and renaming the animal Captain Blinky.

Deacon was 'in' from that point forward. As far as Kylie was concerned, he could do no wrong. Deacon suspected Steve was a little miffed about that, jealous no doubt. He managed to get over it, either way.

Now he was about to face yet another test of nerves as he and Ashley exited his car and began making the block and half trek to Steve's house. It was a Thursday afternoon, and even though school was out for the summer, the elementary school parking lot had been packed.

Twice a year Steve played host to the people who worked for him, these were traditions he'd adopted from his father. Once at Christmas, he'd rent out a restaurant or a banquet hall and have food catered, and then again in the summer for a Fourth of July BBQ that he hosted from his home. The school solved the issue of where the forty-some-odd people who worked at Steele Automotive were able to park in the middle of a residential neighborhood.

Neither one of them had said much as they walked slowly along the sidewalk, enjoying the mild temperature outside. He was just thinking how nice the quiet was when Ashley took it upon herself to ruin the moment.

"You're awfully quiet," she said as they headed up the driveway toward Steve's house.

Deacon slowed, noticing a handful of people hanging out on

the porch, waiting to get inside. "Sorry, don't mean to be."

"You seem…nervous?" she asked, sounding unsure of herself.

"No, I mean…maybe, yeah…but that's normal, right?"

The expression on her face got all pinched and tortured, like she'd become suddenly constipated. "Hell if I know."

He laughed, thinking it was borderline pathetic that neither one of them were exactly experts on what was normal. "I really need to find some friends my own age."

Ashley shoved him as they started climbing the steps.

Deacon plastered on a smile as they passed through the front door of Steve's home, and he made a mental note to not let go of it again until they left.

Ashley looked at him funny as if she could tell something was off.

Deacon knew it was the smile that was foreign to his sister. It felt odd on his face, even to him, but it seemed like the best expression to stick with while interacting with Steve's people.

Deacon was painfully aware this was his equivalent to a Debutante Ball. He was being presented to all of them—the first gay steady of their fresh-from-the-closet car salesman employer.

Steve still had that new-gay-smell people love so much, fresh from the closet and still sparkly. Deacon was more of a secondhand-gay—he'd been out since his early teens so he was slightly used and a little soured, which meant he'd have to work harder at being liked.

He definitely had a case of the nerves, but Deacon figured his was nothing compared to what he imagined Steve was experiencing. That's what he continually reminded himself each time the urge to flee came over him. He'd always been a loner, so this whole expecting the approval of others was new to him. He didn't particularly care for it, but Deacon desperately wanted to fit in for Steve's sake—the man was very much a social beast.

Shocking behavior for someone working in the sales industry, he thought, rolling his eyes over that brilliant deduction.

Move over, Sherlock, there's a new sheriff in town.

He sighed, irritated by the fact his feelings for Steve made his acceptance by these people more important than it would have otherwise been. It was death by socialization, but what truly irked him was that being with a man like Steve had placed a spotlight on him. Deep down, Deacon was terrified that being the focus of so much attention would only serve to highlight the very long list of shit that was wrong with him—all the things Deacon tried to hide from himself, the stuff that Steve had yet to notice about Deacon because they were still new and under the blinding spell of love and lust.

Just as the waves of panic threatened to completely take him over, Ashley grabbed his hand, giving it a squeeze of reassurance.

He was suddenly quite grateful to his sister for coming with him.

Deacon commanded himself to stop whining, swallow his discomfort and soldier on.

It's one afternoon, asshole, you can do this.

Oddly, the fact that Clarissa and Kylie were coming managed to put him a little more at ease. The real problem stemmed from the fact Deacon believed he had nothing in common with any of these people.

He wasn't a fun guy.

He was dark and gloomy and from the wrong side of the tracks.

Not like he was ever going to win anyone over with the heartwarming tales of growing up with a raging alcoholic for a mother.

Of course, that philosophy wasn't mutually exclusive to Steve's peeps. Deacon felt that way about most people, even the Garibaldi's, who'd been nothing but kind and supportive.

He felt at home with Steve and his sister, and that was about it.

As he and Ashley approached Steve's mother, Elizabeth Steele-Baker, Deacon's palms began sweating, so he quickly attempted to shake the nerves out of hands.

He'd met her briefly once before, she was leaving just as he'd made it to Steve's one evening. She looked like a mom, in the good way, unlike Patty. Elizabeth was understated, but well put-together in khaki capris and a peach-colored long sleeve cotton shirt paired with flats and pearls.

The only real difference he noted between now and the first time they'd met was the absence of gray peppered throughout her dark hair. She'd recently been to the salon, and today, nothing looked out of place—if only she felt the same about him.

Elizabeth had been pleasant enough when Deacon initially met her, and she'd certainly not mistreated him in any way, however Deacon couldn't shake the feeling that she didn't approve of him and Steve as a couple. He assumed it was the age difference that concerned her, but she was older, almost twenty years older than Patty, so it could've been the gay thing—different generations and all. She'd also been born and raised in Detroit, and while much of the stigma of where he'd grown up had waned over the years, especially considering the current economic climate, she was likely old-school. The fact Deacon was Vidale Heights might've still meant something to her.

There was the cautiously warm smile he remembered as she took his hand in hers.

"Hello, Deacon," Elizabeth said, holding court in the living room like she was the official greeter for all who passed over the threshold.

"Hello, Mrs. Steele," Deacon said, introducing Elizabeth to Ashley.

The smile remained, but the quiet inspection of Deacon soon followed, like she might be attempting to find any and all defects that could be used to prove him unworthy of her one and only child.

"Quite a gathering."

"Yes, indeed," Elizabeth agreed, momentarily staring intently into Deacon's eyes. "Well, you two go get yourselves some iced tea or fresh lemonade. I look forward to chatting with you later, Deacon."

"Yes, ma'am," Deacon said, nudging Ashley toward the back of the house. "I'll make sure to find you."

Elizabeth moved on, cheerfully greeting the next group coming through the front door.

He and Ashley patiently made their way through the house full of people and onto the patio, where they each grabbed a red Solo cup full of tea before heading down the steps into the yard.

Deacon was able to breathe once more. He'd never been comfortable amongst large groups of people. In high school, he'd always been more comfortable on the outskirts, hanging in the back. He was experiencing a *déjà vu* moment, once again feeling like a stranger in Steve's home—despite the fact he now slept there a couple of nights a week. The presence of all these strangers had altered what had taken months to become a safe harbor for him.

"Are you sure you're okay?" Ashley asked.

Deacon sighed, rolling his eyes. "I'm fine, just being an idiot."

"So nothing out of the ordinary then?" Ashley asked.

Deacon smiled, realizing his sister had just rescued him from himself again. "Zip it, child. Time to be seen and not heard."

She grinned, visibly pleased with herself.

The house sat on an oversized lot, just over an acre, which was more than enough room for the large white tent covering the rows of rented eight foot tables and folding chairs. Deacon closed his eyes, taking a moment to recall how much he enjoyed watching a shirtless and sweaty Steve mow the lawn.

"This is American's new favorite pastime," he muttered under his breath.

The sound of screaming children drew his attention to the two large blow-up contraptions Steve had rented—one was a giant gorilla whose thick meaty arms wrapped around making a deep pool filled with plastic balls. The other was more of a bouncy house shaped like a castle. Each was surrounded with netting and fabric to prevent escape or injury or perhaps both.

That particular decibel of squealing was not something

Deacon was used to, imagining his head might actually explode were he to venture too close. A small herd of momma bears were hanging out between the two air-filled structures, chattering away and coming and going in groups of ones and twos, taking turns so there were always a handful of adults on hand in case of fighting or an emergency.

He waved at Clarissa, who was currently on guard duty, and he turned in time to see Ashley gravitate toward a group of other teens her age—one of whom she apparently knew from school, judging by the way she hugged the girl.

So much for solidarity, he thought, realizing he'd been left to his own devices. Deacon began scanning the crowd, looking for Steve. People he'd never seen before were smiling his direction, which was odd.

It was almost like they were happy to see him?

A few even waved so he waved back.

"Hi, Deacon," one woman said as she passed by, heading for the house.

"Hey," he said, turning awkwardly and doing a three-sixty. He recognized her from the one time he'd visited Steve at the dealership, but he didn't know her name, and it unnerved him slightly that she knew his.

Everywhere his gaze landed, someone was staring back, and they all appeared to be glad to see him.

It was like he'd stepped into an alternate universe or one of those eighties teen comedies staring Molly Whatserface—where the unpopular kid gets noticed by the quarterback and suddenly they're no longer one of the invisa-kids.

Deacon could feel the sweat beginning to run down his side, not comfortable with his sudden popularity. With great desirability comes a whole lot of nosy-ass people who want to know all your business, which would inevitably lead nowhere good.

"This has disaster written all over it," he muttered, forcing himself to stop fidgeting.

As if by sheer power of will, his attention was pulled out toward the back of the yard where a group of guys had gathered around the massive grill Steve had delivered for the party. Steve was there, smiling, a beer in one hand and waving at Deacon with the other while holding an enormous spatula—a sight that lent him an extra punch of whimsy.

Deacon laughed, waving back, and for the briefest of moments, all the angst and stress melted away, replaced by an overwhelming sensation of safety and security—like he'd found his way back home. Steve's attention was pulled away and with it went whatever spell Deacon had been under. The ick slowly crept back in, and he didn't know what to do with himself, but he quickly decided standing there like an idiot wasn't going to help.

He needed to distract himself.

He needed something to do.

With that shocking revelation firmly in hand, he turned, heading back inside the house, making a beeline for the kitchen.

Standing there, momentarily unsure what to do or who to talk to, Deacon started chewing his bottom lip. It didn't take long to figure out that the nice Margie lady who sat out front at the dealership was in charge, nor did it take long for her to take notice of Deacon.

"You need something, sweetie?" Margie asked, her smile as warm and genuine as he remembered.

All the other women stopped what they were doing and turned his direction. Immediately, he regretted the decision to come looking for something to do as he stood there, smiling weakly.

There were six ladies in all, including Margie, who somehow managed to exude a no-nonsense yet jovial vibe that momentarily threatened to put him at ease—sort of an Alice from the *Brady Bunch* type. Three of the other gals were middle-aged types, maybe late thirties or forties and the final two were younger, likely closer to Deacon's age or a little older.

"Is there anything I can do to help?" Deacon asked, forcing

himself to stop fidgeting, again.

Margie opened her mouth to speak, but no words came out.

Deacon could tell she was trying to figure out what his real issue was so she could deal with it and move on with her day. He didn't get the feeling she was put-out over the fact, it was merely an inherent instinct. From what Steve had shared about her, Deacon knew her to be the fixer. She was the person everyone went to with problems at the dealership. Steve worshipped the ground she walked on.

He decided to try her out by coming clean. "I need something to do, *anything*. I'm no good just standing around idle and stuff."

"Words you seldom hear coming from a man's mouth," one of the ladies said, sarcastically.

"Maybe all the good ones really are gay?" the younger gal next to her muttered.

"Please, anything at all?" Deacon asked, deciding to just let that one go the way of the wind.

Margie smiled, pointing to a large bin of corn sitting on the table. "You could help me finish the corn. A little butter and seasoning before wrapping it in foil?"

"Awesome," Deacon said, heading straight for the sink to wash his hands before joining her at the table. "Thanks."

He was aware she'd watched him long enough to ensure he knew what he was doing before going back to concentrating strictly on her own stack.

As he went about his work, he quickly discerned that all but Margie were wives of men who worked at the dealership. The two Kathys he'd met at the sink, they were rinsing and slicing fresh strawberries to go on top of the shortcake for dessert. One had dark red hair and the other, dirty blonde but were otherwise the exact same height and build—sort of round and pear-shaped. They worked very well in unison with one another, which made him think they were longtime compadres.

The fourth and final gal from the more mature lot was Rachel. She had long red hair and was quite curvaceous—tall, even without the strappy heels. Deacon sensed she was the type that never stepped outside her front door undone. Yet aside from the rich, red lipstick and smoky eyes, she didn't seem overdone. Her outfit was heavily concealed by multiple aprons as she oversaw the large foil pans of baked beans in the oven, further insinuating she gave a damn about her clothes and overall appearance.

The two younger girls, Jessica and Luna were scooping out the gallon jugs of potato salad into large plastic serving bowls.

He quickly determined Jessica was kind of snotty, based upon the few times she popped into the conversation with a negative dig at the expense of someone Deacon didn't know. She was pretty enough with long straight dark hair, but her attitude turned him off. She wore her unhappiness on her tongue, and Deacon watched Margie biting her own tongue anytime Jessica opened her mouth.

Luna, he liked immediately. A spicy little Latina-diva, she was definitely a smart ass who was in no way shy with her opinions—the exact opposite of himself. But she didn't come off mean-spirited as her snark was directed mainly toward herself, her husband or in most cases her husband's family.

The woman did not like her mother-in-law, who she continually referred to as a *puta*.

The Spanish he'd had in high school was pretty much forgotten at this point, but he was fairly certain puta wasn't a term of endearment. He liked that she looked him in the eye when she spoke to him, unlike some of the other ladies.

"It's weird for you, right?" Luna asked, smiling evilly. "With the ex-wife here?"

And apparently a bit of a gossip-hound, he thought, as several of the other women chastised her for being so rude and nosy, while staring at him to see if he was actually going to answer.

When he didn't immediately jump in to clarify one way or the other, Margie piped in. "I apologize for her, Deacon."

"What?" Luna asked, trying to appear innocent of any perceived wrongdoing. "I'm from Mexico, we like our *telenovela* extra spicy, so sue me."

"Clarissa has been very kind," Deacon said, hoping that would kill any further discussion.

Luna's lips pursed, and Deacon grinned, able to tell she was disappointed.

"Exactly how old are you?" Jessica asked.

"I'll be twenty-eight…soon," Deacon said, hoping that adding on the extra year a few months early might somehow help things.

"Sometimes I really hate men," one of the Kathy's said. "No offense, dear."

"They do seem to love chasing their youth with their penis," Rachel said matter-of-factly, creating a ripple effect of giggles throughout the room.

Deacon laughed but a bit more nervously, once again rethinking his brilliant idea to help out in the kitchen. He couldn't really pull off indignant, since their age difference was yet another log on the insecurity fire burning steadily in the back of his mind.

The instant Luna began dancing around the topic of how good or bad the sex might be, Margie put her foot down, quashing the topic. Much to Jessica's delight, considering the topic of man-on-man action turned her face pale.

"That is quite enough, Luna," Margie said with an arched brow.

Luna didn't seem all that fazed, winking at Deacon while whispering she'd come find him later for a little chat.

"Something to look forward to," Deacon said, only moderately freaked, figuring he should be able to avoid that nightmare easily enough with this big of a crowd.

"You're on Kaminski," Steve yelled back at some unknown individual as he slipped into the kitchen. "There you are, hiding out with this lot, I see."

"Thought I'd try making myself useful," Deacon said, happy to see Steve up close and personal.

He caught the scent of burnt charcoal, lighter fluid and a slight hint of sweat coming off Steve, and he didn't exactly hate the combination. He wanted to kiss Steve, but that was one of the reasons he'd decided against venturing out to the grilling area earlier—no awkward bumbling as he tried to guess what was or wasn't acceptable.

Surely no kissing, right?

That had ended up feeling awkward the one time he'd decided to show up at the dealership unannounced.

So if not a kiss hello, a handshake, perhaps? Maybe a hug?

It was already making his head hurt when Steve reached over and gave his shoulder a squeeze of reassurance before relocating to the back Deacon's neck for an impromptu, quickie massage. The effect of a simple touch from Steve never ceased to amaze Deacon. He was instantly at ease, any hint of stress was gone, baby, gone.

"The grill is ready, ladies," Steve announced. "So what first, the corn, right?"

"Yes, and it's almost ready to go," Margie announced as she and Deacon worked on wrapping the last five or six cob's on the table.

Steve kicked one bin of corn on the floor while continuing to massage Deacon's neck. "I can grab this one, Deacon, would you mind following me back out with the second bin when you're done?"

"Happy to," Deacon said, looking up at Steve who winked at him, that flirty smile staring back.

Steve glanced up at the women working away. "Might I also say how absolutely stunning you ladies look this fine Fourth of July?"

Deacon was less than shocked by his boyfriend's inability to turn off the flirt monster forever lurking inside. The woman all protested, quite pathetically, as to how wrong he was and how utterly awful they must look after slaving away in the kitchen all day.

"Nearly good enough to turn me straight again," Steve insisted, laughing when Deacon fumbled, dropping the last ear of corn on the floor.

It seemed out of character for Steve, but Deacon was proud of him. He knew being out had always been difficult for Steve, the fact he was making light of it now meant he was coming to terms with it and accepting who he was.

Margie elbowed Deacon playfully. "Perhaps you should go ahead and help Casanova with that corn before he spreads the shit on so thick we can't get out from under it anymore."

"Yes, ma'am," Deacon said, getting up from the table while shaking his head at Steve who was now hunched over and clutching his stomach, laughing over Margie's colorful use of language. Deacon kneed him in the butt. "Let's go…*honey.*"

With that, Steve saluted his obedience before picking up the first bin and waiting politely for Deacon to follow suit—as if he feared Deacon might get lost were he not there to lead the way.

* * * *

By the time they got outside and were walking side by side toward the giant grill, Steve had settled himself down but was still grinning from ear to ear. "You sure look awfully cute today."

Deacon shook his head. "You just can't turn it off, can you?"

"'Fraid not, 'specially not after a couple of beers." Steve laughed, slowing down just enough to steal a nice glimpse of Deacon's tight bubble butt in the dark khaki cargo shorts. "Can't wait to get you alone later tonight."

He watched as Deacon's face flushed, something that Steve found incredibly satisfying.

"What makes you think I'll be hanging around long enough for you to molest later?" Deacon asked.

"The fact you're blushing for one." Steve chuckled, watching the smirk appear across Deacon's face. "You find me irresistible, I know."

And that finally did it, Steve thought, watching as Deacon began laughing. He'd been waiting entirely too long to see that as it was. Making Deacon smile or laugh uncontrollably had become his drug of choice. Nothing made Steve feel better than that—except making Deacon come while he was fucking him. That was pretty goddamn awesome, too.

"I love you," Steve said, just before getting to the BBQ area where his boys were all standing around holding court over the massive grill, drinking beers.

Watching Deacon's eyes bug out of his head as he fumbled, dropping the container on the ground and then nearly tripping over it were all clues confirming that Steve had actually just said that out loud.

Nice move, asshole. He cursed himself for being so stupid. Saying those words now...for the very first time, no less. *Could you have picked a less romantic moment?*

The panicked expression on Deacon's face was answer enough.

All that was missing was the siren and flashing red light floating above his head. Deacon was ready to bolt. Steve had his friends and the threat of social awkwardness to thank for the fact Deacon wasn't hightailing it off into the sunset. All the whooping and hollering as they welcomed Deacon into the inner man-sanctum of fire kept Deacon's feet firmly planted.

"Have a beer," Jimmy said, expertly fishing a cold one out of the giant bucket with one fluid scoop of his hand before tossing it to Deacon.

Jimmy nodded at Steve, letting him know he and the boys had this.

Deacon managed to awkwardly catch the bottle, thanking Jimmy while doing his best to avoid making eye contact with Steve.

This group of guys had been Steve's best buds for years, as well as his partners in the restoration business.

Mickey managed the service department at the dealership

and was the oldest. The man had never met a bowling shirt he didn't like and was a living, breathing Encyclopedia Britannica when it came to automobiles. Like Margie, he was a holdover from when Steve's father had run the business. Hardheaded and old-school Irish, he was the closest thing Steve had left to a father figure. He'd been the one Steve had most worried about accepting his homosexuality, but in spite of his adversity toward anything resembling politically correctness, Mickey had been great.

"What you do with your Johnson doesn't change who you are to me, kid," Mickey had said the night Steve got wasted enough to tell him the truth about the reason behind his divorce.

It made Steve believe that in another life, where his dad hadn't died while he was too young and too chicken shit to be completely honest with himself, that perhaps his father would have been able to accept him as well.

"Let's get those cobs on the grill, boys," Mickey said, heartily slapping Deacon on the shoulder as he grabbed the bin off the ground in front of him.

They all jumped in to help, including Deacon, who paused just long enough to watch how everyone else was doing it. Steve was dying inside, ready to slap the crap out of himself for being such a bonehead. There was no way to spin this. He'd have to bite the bullet and cop to being carried away in the moment—apologize for the timing while emphasizing the positive.

I do love him, Steve thought, feeling himself begin to smile as they lined up the last few pieces of corn. *So there is that.*

JD caught his eye, and Steve could tell he'd been able to sense something was off.

Despite the macho posturing and hunky, well-muscled physique, JD was the most intuitive and sensitive of the bunch. Granted that wasn't saying a whole lot, but he was a guru of the *why fight when we can fuck* philosophy. Raised in a strict catholic household, JD enjoyed anything considered a taboo, though he'd deny it if you accused him of that. With his too-tight shirts and dark, classically Italian good looks, he had a tendency to melt panties, which created a lot of unnecessary drama with his wife,

Luna.

It took several of them to pull the massive lid to the grill down, and Steve noted the time before glancing over at Deacon who was watching him. He still had that deer-in-the-headlights look to him, and Steve grinned, hoping to diffuse the bomb he'd inadvertently dropped.

Willie was grinning like an idiot, staring back and forth between Steve and Deacon. Every bit as clueless as usual, and like most of the clueless people in the world, Willie had a big mouth that he never knew when to keep shut. He was Mickey's nephew and had inherited the mechanic genes, as well as the dark red hair. They called him Patch, which was short for Patch'n'Match because nobody was better with bodywork—Willie was a magician.

"So, Deacon—" Jimmy began.

"Yeah, I'll go check on them burger patties," Deacon blurted out, cutting Jimmy off before turning to head back to the house.

The five of them all stood there awkwardly, and everyone but Steve appeared to be rightfully confused.

"He always like that?" Willie asked.

"No, he's not." Steve hung his head and sighed. "I kinda fucked up."

Jimmy laughed under his breath. "Of course you did."

Steve flipped him off.

"I'm almost afraid to ask," Mickey said, cocking his head slightly. "But what the hell did you do?"

"It's fine, guys," Steve said. "We really don't have to talk about this."

"Don't be a pussy." JD cracked open another beer. "I can drink the memory of this conversation away."

Steve snickered, shaking his head. "Seriously, this isn't the kinda stuff you guys—"

"For fuck sake, Stevie, do not turn into one of those drama queens." Jimmy patted JD's shoulder. "Having one in the group is enough."

Mickey laughed, his beer gut jiggling up and down as JD shrugged Jimmy's hand off his shoulder.

"Go to hell, Jimmy."

"Honestly, it's nothing, really," Steve finally said. "I used the 'L' word for the first time, like a few minutes ago while we were carrying the stupid corn."

They all stared back at him, straight faced, showing no emotion.

"I'm sure it'll be fine." Steve shrugged.

"You told him you love him?" Mickey asked.

"Over a bin of fucking corn?" Jimmy asked, straining to maintain a straight face.

"You're screwed," JD said.

"Sorry, I don't know the homo-protocol for this shit," Mickey said. "Flowers?"

Steve rolled his eyes, as did Jimmy and JD.

"What? That's what I do for the wife." Mickey snorted. "Get him a bushel of forget-me-nots."

"They're gay, not girls," JD said, wiping his chin and smiling. "Get him a cock ring."

Steve shook his head no, and Willie's face snarled up like he wished he hadn't heard that.

"What the hell is a cock ring?" Mickey asked, sounding pissed off that his suggestion wasn't getting more traction.

"Never mind, old man, we wouldn't wanna give you a heart attack," JD said. "The things you don't know are astounding."

"What were you thinking?" Jimmy asked, looking at Steve.

"Apparently, I wasn't."

"On the bright side, you apparently love the dude, right?" Mickey asked.

Steve felt his face flush with heat. "Seriously, guys, I thank you for making the attempt, but we're cool here, honestly. I do not expect you to start taking an interest in my new gay life, okay?"

JD wiped his brow. "Phew!"

"Thank gawd!" Mickey added.

"That's a relief." Willie said.

Steve sighed, also relieved, considering he was less than comfortable talking about this shit with his friends.

"It is weird seeing you with another dude though, boss," JD said.

"I get it, JD, and I'm sorry about that, but that's the way it's gonna be from now on," Steve said, checking the time so they didn't forget to flip the corn.

"I hear ya, and I didn't really mean it like a bad thing, just different, you know?"

"Yeah, Stevie," Jimmy piped in. "Nothing personal but I still kinda have to do a double take every now and again, myself."

"It pisses me off," Willie said, his expression showing no sign that he might be joking.

It got very quiet around the grill as the men all eyed one another.

"We used to all be in the same boat, you know. But now, you're a gay dude. I'm a dude, and I'm fucking horny all the damn time, so two dudes... together? You gotta be bustin' a nut all night, every goddamn night." Willie kicked at the grass, expending some of his frustration. "I practically have to dip my dick in chocolate to get Jessica to blow me."

Mickey shook his head over his nephew's little rant, but then turned to Steve along with the rest of the guys. Steve could tell they were waiting for an answer, some sort of confirmation that it wasn't that easy. While he didn't get to spend every night with Deacon, they always made the most of their time whenever they did get a night alone.

Steve grinned without commenting and quietly took a swig off his beer.

They all started yelling and screaming in protest simultaneously, causing Steve to bust out laughing.

"That's bullshit!" Willie said, placing a hand on his forehead.

"Asshole!" Jimmy added.

"You fucking suck!" JD said.

Mickey rolled his eyes. "He's queer now, of course he sucks, you moron."

Steve flinched over the use of the Q-word, on top of being completely embarrassed. He definitely didn't want to discuss his gay *sex* life with these guys, but when he stopped to really think about it, for years it was nearly all they'd ever talked about—sex or sports. It was ingrained behavior that now felt odd, considering the player in his bedroom had changed.

"I don't think you're supposed to use the queer word, Mickey," JD said, shaking his head.

"Save it for Dr. Phil, asshole, Stevie knows I didn't mean anything by it."

"Jesus, can't take you anywhere, old man," Jimmy said.

"What?" Mickey threw his hands in the air. "He's the only homo I know. Sue me if I don't know the lingo."

"I can promise you Steve ain't the only gay dude you know," Jimmy said.

Mickey brushed that suggestion off by dismissing him with a wave of his hand.

"You tryin' to tell us something, Jimmy?" Willie asked.

Jimmy flipped him off, and Willie shot him back an exaggerated air kiss to let him know he wasn't fazed.

JD grabbed at his crotch and hunched over, lowering his voice. "I could let a dude suck me off, you know, if it were like life or death. But that up-the-ass biddness? No fucking way, shoot me now."

"God, why'd you have to go there?" Mickey asked.

Jimmy smirked. "Exactly what sort of a life or death scenario could be cured by getting head?"

"I'm just sayin'." JD straightened back up. "I'm talking stranded on an island, no other options."

"Life or death, my ass." Mickey said, shaking his head. "A six pack of beer and any warm wet hole would do for you, you freak."

Steve started laughing as did Jimmy who barely stopped himself from spewing his mouthful of beer.

Mickey added. "How that gorgeous wife of yours puts up with you, JD, I'll never understand."

"She's a freaky-deak just like me, old man," JD said, striking a pimp-pose. "And I keep my woman sa-tis-fied. Turn that shit out."

Mickey sneered, visibly disgusted.

Steve was grateful they'd seemed to gravitate off the subject of him, despite the fact he understood and appreciated they were only trying to make it seem like nothing had really changed between them. None of them were truly asking for details so much as dancing around the issue of his new lifestyle.

"Tell me you don't do any of that asshole stuff, Stevie?" Willie asked, his face all pinched up in disgust. "I can take anything but that."

Then again perhaps I'm wrong?

They all got quiet again, waiting intently for an answer.

Mortified, his face burned beet red, and he started laughing nervously deciding to avoid once again by taking another swig from his beer.

They all began screaming and yelling in protest.

Willie's entire body writhed in protest. "Dude, that's messed up!"

"Not the back door, man!" JD said using an 'Oh the humanity' tone.

Mickey had covered his ears. "Just say no to the tushie pushie!"

They all stopped and looked at Mickey like he was nuts.

"Tushie whatie?" JD asked, trying not to laugh.

"What are you, like twelve?" Jimmy asked.

"I'm trying to keep it G-rated, assholes. There's kids around, damn it," Mickey snapped.

He wasn't wrong, but most of the women folk knew to keep the younguns away from the BBQ pit at these shindigs since the language was typically of the more colorful variety.

"It's not a big deal, guys, Jesus. I've fucked girls up the ass before," Jimmy said matter-of-factly, while eyeing JD like he suspected he wasn't the only one.

"It's different with girls!" JD said.

This revelation had Mickey's mouth hanging open.

"It was nice...*tight*," Jimmy clarified.

"That's *sick*!" Mickey declared, before holding his hands up. "Not that I judge."

"Oh no, you're practically a saint," Willie said with a deadpan expression.

"Real tight," Jimmy added, smiling as he reached down into the cooler and snagged another cold one, which he passed to Steve, able to ascertain that he might need one at this point.

"Jesus, Mary and Joseph," Mickey muttered.

"I think the gays leave it at, Jesus Mary," JD said, elbowing Steve as Jimmy and Willie snickered.

Steve burst out laughing as he tossed his empty and announced it was time to start flipping the corn. The rest of the guys hopped to, grabbing a set of tongs so they could help. Steve silently prayed the distraction would lead to a much needed change in subject matter.

* * * *

Deacon was completely embarrassed, running off like that. He still couldn't believe Steve had actually said it. *Of course, his friends now think I'm a freak.* He smacked himself on the hip while making his way back toward the house.

On the plus side, he was a freak that Steve said he loved.

Deacon was aware he was grinning like an idiot, but he couldn't seem to stop himself. Granted, the timing was odd, but the only time Seth had ever uttered those words had been while he was climaxing, and in retrospect, Deacon was fairly certain Seth had likely been talking to himself when he had uttered I love you.

By comparison, this was a giant leap forward as far as Deacon was concerned.

It was spontaneous, in the moment, and during one where any agenda beyond the pure was highly unlikely.

He was now practically floating on air.

"Hey there!" Clarissa said, bringing him back down to earth as she sidled up to him, taking his arm in hers. "How you holding up?"

Deacon shrugged. "I'm not entirely convinced I am. Feel like everyone is watching me."

"Oh they are, sweetie," she confirmed.

"That's not helping," Deacon said as she giggled it off. "The least you could do is lie to me."

"Not really something I'm very good at," Clarissa said, squeezing his arm.

His mind drifted back to Luna and her disappointment over the fact there was no drama between him and Clarissa. It hadn't occurred to him before then, which now made him feel somewhat naïve.

"How come you don't hate me?" he asked. "You know that's what half of these people are wondering."

She slowed to a stop, pulling Deacon to one in the process, and seemed to be pondering that for a moment while glancing down at her snazzy, silver-beaded sandals. "I can't honestly say that it doesn't sting sometimes, and in those moments, I find myself less than thrilled by your existence. But allowing myself to succumb to that sort of madness doesn't do me any favors, you know?"

He nodded, able to recognize how destructive that particular rabbit hole might be.

"Don't allow my overall attitude of acceptance fool you into thinking this is easy for me, though. I like you, Deacon, I truly do. You're very sweet and kind, and you have this slightly wounded quality that I'm particularly drawn to. It took me a very long time to stop being angry, to stop myself from wanting to jump in my car and run Steve down in a homicidal rage. He hurt me."

She stopped, her face squishing up as if having admitted that to him had been painful.

Deacon cringed. "I'm sorry, I shouldn't have asked."

"No, I mean," she paused as if trying to collect her thoughts. "It's fine, I get why you'd want to know, and I'll be honest and say that even though logically, I understand that the end of our marriage wasn't my fault—what was wrong with us was Steve's issue. I'd entered into our marriage honestly even though he did not."

"How do you get over something like that?" Deacon asked. "It's a pretty big betrayal, intentions be damned."

"It is, Deacon, and you're right, I believe Steve had good intentions when he married me. I have to believe that." She nodded as if reaffirming that for herself. "But I also have a child who worships the ground he walks on. Kylie is a daddy's girl, and Steve has always been incredible with her, and he's the only daddy she's ever known. When my first husband passed away, she was barely more than a year old. At the time, I wasn't able to imagine that anyone other than her real dad would be able to love her so completely. But Steve would step in front of a bullet for her."

She glanced around to make sure no one was close enough to eavesdrop on their conversation as she wiped her eyes, having gotten a little worked up. Deacon squeezed her arm this time, which put a little smile on her face.

"I'm sorry for bringing this up here," Deacon said, frustrated with himself.

She shrugged, folding her arms. "It means something to me that you did, strangely enough. That you acknowledge Steve meant something to me, that he still does."

Deacon nodded, a little guilty that he hadn't really gotten there on his own—it had taken Luna's nosy question to make him truly look at things from Clarissa's perspective.

"I can't in good conscience deprive my baby girl from experiencing that relationship with Steve—it's magical, really—the bond they share."

"I get that," Deacon said. "And you're right, Steve talks about Kylie all the time, and when he does, his eyes light up like nothing I've ever seen. That's partly what I love about him, I think. I never had that growing up, and I'd have given anything for it. The fact he's capable of it is…"

Clarissa nodded. "That right there is why I'm simply not capable of hating you."

Deacon wasn't sure exactly what she was referring to, and it must have shown.

"You're likely to take this the wrong way, so I apologize in advance," she said, greasing the wheels before dropping the axe. "But you have to be one of the single, saddest people I've ever met, sweetie."

And there it was, the uncomfortable *ick* that came over him whenever anyone else shoveled a heaping helping of pity his way.

"I know, and I'm sorry," Clarissa said with a sigh. "I really am, but I just can't help it. It makes me so angry when I think about all the crap your mother has put you and your sister through. Honestly, I could just spit. It makes me that enraged."

He said nothing but was aware she was watching him intently.

"I knew I should've kept my mouth shut, it's none of my business, Deacon, and don't be mad at Steve for telling me. I think he just needed to vent to someone and didn't want to lay all that on you."

Deacon swallowed his discomfort over the fact Steve had said anything to anyone about his personal business, yet he understood it to a degree. Most normal people likely needed to talk to someone about stuff like that in order to process it. Just because Deacon was able to bottle it all up and stuff it deep down inside didn't mean Steve should have to.

He'd had decades in which to hone that skill.

"I'm glad he has you to talk to, I guess," Deacon finally said, trying to ignore the sense of betrayal that washed over him. "We don't have to talk about all this right now, though. I apologize for sticking my fat nose into your business to begin with."

"I'm glad you did, actually, kind of confirms what I've always suspected, that you're a good guy who gives a damn about other people's feelings."

He nodded, shocked by that revelation and happier for hearing it. He'd long confused not caring what others thought of him as being the same as not caring about others, and that wasn't an accurate accounting of who he was or wanted to be.

That gave him a tiny boost as they continued arm in arm toward the house. He was surprised by how much more he liked Clarissa with each and every visit. It was a reminder that he needed to take more chances—there were good people out there, kind people, who didn't only want something from him.

The world had much more to offer than bad people like Patty and Gale—who he'd thankfully not seen nor heard from since his visit with Patty last month. Deacon prayed that it meant he'd actually been able to get through to her. For once, she'd made the decision to think about someone other than herself, and that meant good riddance to Gale, who no longer had any reason to bother him or Ashley. They had nothing he could take from them.

As he and Clarissa passed through the back door of the house, Deacon began to feel his spirits lift. There was a man out there who appeared to actually care for him, a handful of new friends and his sister who Deacon had managed to actually do right by for once. He was on a bit of a roll, and in spite of the initial urges that it would all turn to shit, Deacon tried to make a small change by focusing on what was going right instead of what could possibly go wrong.

****

"I could never marry a girl who let me fuck her up the poop shoot," JD said, the instant they finished flipping all the corn.

Steve started to laugh, shaking his head and doing his best to not scream for mercy—which would've been a dick move considering they were going out of their way to make him feel included. The fact he was exceedingly uncomfortable, Steve decided to keep to himself while praying that any number of the hot women currently scattered throughout his backyard would pass by, distracting the guys from all things anal.

"I'm being serious," JD went on. "I don't think I could introduce my mother to an up-the-ass-girl."

"This coming from the man who'd let a dude blow him?" Jimmy asked.

"You can blow me, Jimmy."

"Fuck you, bitch," Jimmy said.

JD smirked. "You'd like that, Mr. Tight Hole."

"What the hell are you boys talking about?" Luna asked, giving each of them the evil eye, before settling on her husband.

Deacon was standing just behind her, along with Rachel, holding coolers filled with burger patties and hotdogs.

"Meat, ladies," Mickey finally said, puffing his chest out as if daring anyone to say anything to the contrary. "We're talkin' about meat."

Jimmy was snickering, desperately trying to keep from busting out laughing, and anyone would have thought Willie had died, his face had gone stone-cold sober.

Steve and JD took the coolers from the two ladies, and Deacon followed them over to the far side of the grill, placing his on the grass next the others.

"Why do you men get so excitable over an open flame?" Luna asked, causing Steve to choke on his beer.

It was quite clear that Luna wasn't buying what they were

selling, yet it was obvious she didn't have a clue what was actually going on. Jimmy began slapping Steve on the back, and Deacon was visibly beginning to suspect something odd was up as well. Steve shook his head just enough to send him a signal not to ask. The one raised eyebrow told him that Deacon had received the message loud and clear.

"Go away, woman," JD said, smiling slyly at his wife, something she obviously took pleasure from witnessing. "The grilling of meat is a man's job, but never fear, baby, we'll yell if we require any input from you."

Rachel scoffed, obviously less affected by JD's swagger than Luna. Even still, Luna rolled her eyes. "Like we could tell the difference, all you do is yell."

With that, the two women spun on their heels and headed back toward the house, each one yacking it up as they walked away.

The instant they were far enough away, Willie turned to Deacon and said, "So Steve is being stingy with the deets, but you gay guys are doing it all the time, right?"

Deacon's face went blood red, and his mouth fell open, allowing some sort of odd squeaking noise to escape. Steve reached over, smacking Willie upside the back of the head, followed quickly by Jimmy, Mickey and JD all taking a turn at abusing the back of Willie's skull.

"I'm-uh, gonna go grabba…something. Kitchen?" Deacon managed to get out before speed walking away, grabbing a bottle of beer out of the tub as he passed by.

"What'd I say?" Willie asked.

"Why you gotta be such an asshole, Patch." Jimmy asked.

"Dumb ass," Mickey added.

Willie shook off all the insults. "I'm sorry, sheesh, it was just a question."

"So, how old is he anyway?" JD asked, squinting at Deacon as he disappeared into the crowd.

Steve felt his face flush with heat, and he rolled his eyes, choosing to not dignify the answer.

"Gotta little man-lolita action going on?" Jimmy asked.

"Christ, he's twenty-seven…nearly twenty-eight, you guys are sick."

JD held up his hands in surrender. "He looks young for his age, sue me."

"But you're the dude, right?" Willie asked.

"What?" Steve asked.

"In the bedroom, you know, you're the dude, and he's the chick?"

Mickey smacked Willie upside the back of the head again. "They're both dudes, you moron, that's what makes it queer."

"Gay, boss, he meant gay," Jimmy clarified, smiling innocently, though Steve could tell he was doing his best to keep the torture going.

He knew Jimmy well enough to know his best friend was thoroughly enjoying Steve's squirming. The bastard had been egging this shit on the entire time.

"You're a rat bastard, Jimmy." Steve rolled his eyes. "Get me another beer, asshole."

Jimmy was now laughing too hard to be of any use to anyone so JD grabbed one for him.

"Shut it, Willie," Steve added, seeing that Willie was about to ask yet another mind-numbingly mortifying question. "I think we've covered enough gay for one day, don't you?"

Willie sort of slunk back down, sitting on one of the coolers, probably realizing he'd been a little more interested than he should have been. JD and Jimmy were snickering over that fact.

Mickey pointed them toward the grill. "Mind the meat, assholes. We end up burning dinner, you three are paying for the pizza we'll have to order to feed this greedy lot."

Steve nodded a thank you to Mickey who, true to his nature, shrugged it off as nothing. As the four of them went about flipping patties and turning the dogs, with Mickey supervising each and every move, Steve found himself grinning. All in all, this first hurdle with the guys had been brutally embarrassing, but his best buds had just met his first official out-and-proud-ish boyfriend, and no one had stormed off swearing never to speak to him again. That was huge, as it was pretty much the worst thing he'd been able to imagine happening.

End of the day, they were still gonna be his best friends. For Steve, that was pretty fucking awesome, and for the first time in a very long time, he began to believe that perhaps he just might be able to have it all. It felt wrong in a way, even just thinking it. Decadent—like something no man should be able to attain.

Steve nodded, flipping another row of patties, sweat pouring down his face and the smoke and heat burning at his eyes. He'd never been happier than he was in that moment.

Bring on the fucking decadence.

* * * *

Steve walked into the small bedroom that he used as his home office to grab a pair of scissors so they could cut the rope and string up the piñatas. Something he meant to get done before everyone arrived.

His mother was sitting on the edge of the wooden desk, flipping through one of the photo albums Steve had unpacked over a year and half before—haphazardly tossing them onto a bookshelf. She didn't notice him at first, and the light pouring in through the window cast her in a pool of angelic white hazy light. He was momentarily transported back to his childhood when he'd sit playing quietly on the floor at her feet as she sat in her favorite chair reading.

That's how he most liked to remember her, happy and content, laid back—the way she'd been before his father left her. She was never quite the same after the divorce. She'd dated and even remarried once, but it was like she never truly trusted anyone again.

Her second husband, Harry, had been a kind man. Steve had

actually liked him, but he never got the sense that his mother really loved the man. Harry had felt it too, he'd said as much to Steve one time. He'd passed away several years ago, and Elizabeth had been alone ever since. That worried Steve, but as far as he could tell, she had little interest in looking for husband number three.

The sound of her turning a page in the album brought him back to the present, and she glanced up hearing the floor creak as he took another step into the room.

"Oh, sorry, son," Elizabeth said, closing the cover and smiling sweetly. "I wasn't trying to snoop, just taking a trip back in time through your eyes."

"It's fine, I don't mind, Mom."

She shrugged, getting up off the desk, and placed the album back on the shelf. "I must say, even looking through those pictures, I don't see anything that helps me with this whole gay thing, Steve."

He smiled. "Looking for evidence of the things you missed?"

"I suppose so." Her forehead crinkled up like she might be thinking too hard. "You know, I honest to God never once suspected."

Steve sighed, scratching the back of his head. "I pushed a lot of it back, Mom, for a good many years. It wasn't something I was able or willing to deal with, so I kept pretending."

She walked back and sat on the edge of the desk once more.

He knew she wanted to ask for more, but he had a house full of guests. That being said, Steve could tell she was genuinely confused, and he didn't want her wasting time on what-ifs and might've beens.

"In all honesty, Mom, I think I'm probably bisexual to a degree, apparently a person's sexuality can be somewhat fluid. But had I been honest with myself fifteen or twenty years ago—really explored all of who I am? I don't know, things might have been different. I might have still met and married Clarissa and been able to live happily ever after. As it is, I wasn't able to suppress the overwhelming sense that I was missing something—not so much experiences, mind you, more like a piece of my soul."

She nodded, though visibly still didn't quite get it. Steve was aware it could very likely be something she never understood. His mother had always been a black and white type of individual. Shades of gray and malleable sexuality weren't something she'd been built to withstand.

"Just please know that what I did, ending things with Clarissa—as difficult and heart-wrenching as it was to do? I knew, deep down, it was the right thing to do. She's got time to go out there and try to find something special as opposed to the something ordinary she would have had with me."

"Is that what you think you've found with Deacon?" she asked. "Something special?"

He could tell that there was no animosity in the tone of her words, no judgments, only concern.

"I do, Mom." Steve reached over to give her hand a squeeze of reassurance.

"I'll be honest with you as well and say that I have my doubts and concerns." She paused for a moment, like she might be afraid he'd get angry with her. "There's the age difference, which may not be a problem now, but take it from someone who knows, it very likely will someday."

"I'm not completely ignorant of that possibility, Mom." Steve shrugged. "I just think he's worth the risk."

Elizabeth nodded that she understood, but he could tell there was something else she wasn't saying.

"It's okay, Mom, whatever it is, let's get it out there so we can deal with it and hopefully move on."

"Okay," she said with a long sigh. "My biggest concern is that there seems to be something inherently sad about him, Steve. Perhaps I'm imagining it—"

"No, you're not," Steve interrupted. "He and his sister haven't had the easiest of upbringings. I don't feel as if it's my place to delve into all the details with you, as it's not my story to tell." He felt bad enough about the fact he'd broken down and discussed it with Clarissa. "It's taken a toll on him, for sure. His entire life, it's as if the world has done nothing but make Deacon feel small and insignificant—"

"You want to fix him," Elizabeth interrupted.

Steve smiled. "Not the way you think. There's nothing I could ever do to erase all that's been done to him, but I can affect what happens to him in the future. And I'm going to do everything within my power to make sure he knows happiness from this point forward."

"I can see how much you care for him."

"There's a lot to love. He's kind to the point of being selfless when it comes to his sister, like he wants to make it up to her—their upbringing, the fact their mother was never much of a mother." Steve stopped, seeing that worried expression taking over her face. "You don't like him?"

"I'm worried for you, that's all. There are times, dear, when a person can become so beaten down that no amount of love and support will ever be enough. I fear Deacon will never be able to see beyond those experiences of his past. It terrifies me that he'll drag you down into the darkness where I fear he spends so much of his time."

"You don't like him for me?"

She smiled, then sighed, looking out the window for a moment. "I worry what will happen if you can't fully break through that armor Deacon carries around to protect himself from further emotional tragedy."

"I'll just have to show him there's another way then, huh?"

"And if you're unsuccessful?"

"I wasn't raised to be a quitter."

"I'm well aware, if only your father had been blessed with the same sense of commitment."

Steve sighed, sorry to see his mother still carried that disappointment around with her all these years later.

"Just be careful with your own heart, dear. You can give too much of it away."

Steve reached over and squeezed her knee. "You can't let your personal history cloud what I have with Deacon, Mom."

She nodded, though concern was still coming off of her in waves. "You've been waiting to be happy for so long, Steven. But as you say, you aren't the type of man who's going to stop fighting, and if you're able to lift Deacon up into the light, make him see what you see in him…"

He smiled, able to see that she was getting a little worked up.

"I'll be so very happy for you both. Just knowing you were loved and appreciated." She smiled at the thought.

Steve sat next to her on the desk, sliding an arm around her. "Having you for a mother, I've never *not* felt loved and appreciated. Something I recognize and appreciate all the more because of Deacon. I truly hope that someday, you'll see all that I see in him. When that day comes, you'll love him the way I do."

"I don't dislike him, son," she said. "He's been nothing but kind, mind you."

"I know." Steve gave her shoulder a squeeze, hugging her. "You worry about me, I get it."

"Something like that," she said, reaching up to give his face a couple of light slaps. "We should get back to the party, I suppose."

He nodded. "How about I come pick you up one night this week and take you out for dinner? Just the two of us?"

"That would be lovely, dear," Elizabeth said, getting up from the desk and heading for the door. "You're paying, right?"

Steve laughed, able to hear the return of the teasing tone in her voice. "It would be my pleasure."

He followed after her before stopping at the door and rolling his eyes, heading back to the desk in order to grab the scissors from the drawer.

* * * *

Deacon had walked quietly out the front door of Steve's house, head down, careful not to make eye contact with anyone. It was as if someone had knocked the wind out of his chest, and those same words were now running over and over on a loop inside his head.

It terrifies me that he'll drag you down into the darkness where I fear he spends so much of his time.

He winced, fishing his cell out of his pocket. He hadn't intended on eavesdropping. He knew it was wrong, but it had taken hearing those words to make him stop, to force him away from the door to Steve's office in retreat, before he heard anymore gut-wrenching observations from Steve's mother. He knew she wasn't a fan, but he hadn't realized she disliked him quite that much.

"She thinks I'm going to ruin his life," Deacon muttered, tapping a text to Ashley that he wasn't feeling well and wanted to leave. She was still at the party, which was just now really kicking into high gear.

Deacon was all but running now, desperate to get as far away as he could in an attempt to get to his car, which was parked at the school down the block.

She came back with a text saying her friend could give her a ride home later, unless he needed her. He let her know he was okay to get home by himself and then did something he really hated himself for, he asked her to let Steve know he'd left.

As soon as that was done, he turned off his phone and kept moving. He didn't want to lie to Steve, but he apparently had no problem allowing his sister lie for him. That realization did little to ease his conscience.

The last thing he wanted to do was drag Steve down.

The thought that he might terrified Deacon to his core. It literally made him sick to his stomach, which seemed a fitting punishment, considering his cowardly lie to his sister only moments before.

What he needed was time, to take a beat and really consider

Elizabeth's concerns. If he was being completely honest, as great as Steve had been and as happy as he'd made Deacon—the relationship hadn't been a cure-all for what ailed him.

Realistically, Deacon knew it never could be.

So was Elizabeth right, after all?

Did the fact that he was sad most of the time mean his relationship with Steve was merely a Band-Aid—one that would very likely break with too much pressure?

"No," Deacon said, rushing to get inside his car as if he feared being stopped should he dare to turn around and look back. "Can't do that to Steve."

The heat inside his car combined with the quiet that came over him once he shut the door on the outside world was calming.

"You're a time bomb," he said, looking at his reflection in the rearview mirror.

One that was going to explode eventually. Maybe not tomorrow or next month—it could be years—but eventually, it would happen.

"You can't do that to him, damn it."

He backed out of the parking space, his heart breaking, pounding, aching as if it were being violently ripped from his chest. He cried out and gripped the steering wheel as he drove away from Steve, still hearing those words as if already haunted by them.

He'll drag you down into the darkness...

The farther away he got, the more he knew it. Believed it. Understood that if he truly cared about Steve, there was only one thing he could do to ensure that he'd never hurt him.

He'd have to leave Steve alone.

CHAPTER EIGHTEEN

It had been two days since the BBQ, and thus far, he'd managed to avoid speaking to Steve. He'd called in sick to work and mostly remained within the confines of his bedroom, telling Ashley and texting Steve that he didn't feel well. He knew this tactic wasn't going to work for long, but Deacon didn't want to do what he knew he needed to. He wasn't sure he actually possessed the strength it would take to look Steve in the eye and walk away. He'd come to believe it was likely what he should do if he truly cared about Steve.

He turned up the stereo in his car, hoping Lady Gaga could drown out all the inner voices in head. They were each screaming different things at him, and Deacon was rightfully confused and sad, and suffering from an overwhelming sense of hopelessness. He'd driven a couple blocks over to the nearest quickie-mart for chocolate and Red Bull, the breakfast of champions—at least for the depressed kind of champions.

Deacon tapped the brakes as he drove along the street, getting closer to Patty's house. He could see there was someone on the porch as his car continued to roll. He thought for sure it was Steve at first, thinking his attempts to put off the inevitable had just crashed and burned.

Closing in on the driveway, he sighed a momentary bit of relief, able to tell it wasn't Steve. However, a different sort of sickness crept into the pit of his stomach once he realized it was Gale attempting to let himself back into the house with a key that no longer worked. Steve had sent a locksmith out to re-key all the locks after Gale let himself in the last time.

Seeing the frustrated look on Gale's face as he pulled into the driveway, Deacon couldn't help but smile. His ex-stepdad was not happy, and that made Deacon feel better, more in control after the emotional roller coaster of the past few days.

He'd been wrestling with himself about whether or not he should talk to Steve about the things his mother had said.

Of course, in doing so, he'd have to admit that he'd been eavesdropping, which wasn't exactly stellar behavior on his part.

Opening the car door, Deacon hopped out, heading straight for Gale who was smirking at him from the front porch.

"You changed the locks, I see," Gale commented, his voice flat and cold despite the grin on his face.

"My boyfriend did that, actually," Deacon corrected. "He wasn't very happy to hear you broke into the house the last time."

"It's not breaking and entering if you have a key and permission from the home owner." Gale smiled coolly. "Of course, you probably told your *boyfriend* I molested you as a child or something."

"You're sick, Gale, honestly." Deacon hopped up the three steps and shoved past the man before unlocking the door. "Sounds more like your type of manipulation."

Deacon opened the door and stepped inside, turning and blocking Gale from entering the house. "God only knows what sort of lies you've been telling Patty."

Gale was looking past him into the house, like he might be attempting to figure out a way to get past him.

"It would seem that you somehow managed to get to your mother," Gale said, taking a step back before leaning against the porch railing. "She's refusing to see me all of a sudden."

"Perhaps like the rest of the free world, Patty has finally come to the conclusion you're a snake, all on her own?"

"No, I don't think so." Gale looked him up and down in a way that made him uncomfortable. "It was you, something you said—always were a pain in my ass."

"Awesome," Deacon said. "Thanks for sharing, however, it seems there's no longer anything here for you, so perhaps you could do us all a favor and fuck off…forever."

"Look at you," Gale said, taking a few steps closer to Deacon. "Got yourself a fancy, rich boyfriend, and now you think you're too good for the likes of me."

Deacon found it difficult to swallow as Gale took another step forward, the expression on his face no longer that of amusement but darker, more sinister.

"You used to worship the ground I walked on," Gale said, his gaze piercing right through Deacon. "There was a time when you'd have spread those legs and begged me to fuck your faggoty little teenage ass."

"You're disgusting," Deacon said, his voice sounding a little less confident.

"Probably still want it, don't you?" Gale asked, reaching out to touch Deacon.

Deacon slapped his hand away. "Go away, Gale, before I call the police."

"Why don't you call your fancy new boyfriend instead?" Gale asked. "Beg him to come rescue you? Allow me to demonstrate for him that you're only good for one thing."

Deacon was getting sick to his stomach, thinking the last thing he ever wanted was for Steve to meet Gale. Even now, he felt an overwhelming amount of shame because there was a nugget of truth to the things Gale was saying. It's how he reeled people in, glomming onto the tiniest shred of reality and twisting it to convince you that he alone held the answer to all your prayers.

There'd been a time when Deacon had worshipped Gale, who had charmed him every bit as much as he had Patty. That's what he did, though. He was a con man, and the version of Gale that Deacon had fallen in love with hadn't been real. The man was like a mirror—showing you only what he wanted you to see as opposed to the soulless excuse of a human being that lay underneath.

"You think he actually loves you, don't you?" Gale laughed, the entire aura around him darkening even more. It had Deacon backing away, struggling to catch his breath as if all the oxygen was being sucked out of the room.

"You think I'd hurt you?" Gale asked with a smirk. "You aren't worth the effort, kiddo. This Steele guy knows it, too. He doesn't love *you*. That tight little ass, which you seem all too willing to offer up, perhaps, but you're just a thing to him."

Gale stopped just on the other side of the threshold.

"Meat."

A wicked grin formed just before he added.

"A warm hole."

"You're disgusting," Deacon said again, doing his best to put up a good front.

"Eventually, he'll get tired of you. Trade you in for a younger, tighter piece of ass, and you'll be right back where you started. Right back here where you belong." Gale looked around the room and shook his head. "You can clean it up and slap a coat of paint on it, but it's still Vidale Heights and you're still nothing but trash. Your own momma saw that, it's why she didn't want you, kiddo. Eventually, your new boyfriend will come to the same conclusion."

"Go away." Deacon said, now shaking he was so angry. "Before I decide you are worth it."

Gale sneered until Deacon reached for the baseball bat Patty kept in the dinged up brass umbrella stand next to the front door. Gale pretended he wasn't afraid, but Deacon could see he wasn't quite so confidant anymore. The scum bag must have been intuitive enough to see that Deacon was close to snapping.

"Get out before I take this bat and beat you to death with it, you sick, sadistic mother fucker."

One more nasty comment would've been enough. Deep down, Deacon was frightened of himself in that moment. He was viciously angry, and he could taste the blood in the back of his mouth from where he'd bitten the inside of his cheek in attempt to regain control over himself.

All he could see was red.

As Gale slowly backed away from the door, Deacon added one last warning. "If I ever catch you anywhere near Ashley, I'll kill you with my bare hands, Gale. You understand me?"

Deacon could see the hatred in his eyes, but Gale nodded that the message had been received as he went scrambling down the porch steps, making a beeline for the sidewalk.

Deacon exhaled, his breath shaky as he glanced down at his white-knuckled grip on the handle of the bat. He forced himself to drop it, fingers cramping as he watched it fall to the floor in what seemed like slow motion.

The noise that came from the bat making contact with the hardwood floors was the sound that snapped him back into real time.

He shut the door, turned the deadbolt then latched the chain, before leaning against it for support. His entire body was shaking as he slid down, collapsing into a heap on the floor.

His eyes burned as the tears began to flow.

It was as if someone had taken a sledge hammer to the wall he'd meticulously constructed inside his head—the one that held all his ghosts and inner demons at bay, making him fit to walk amongst the rest of society.

"Not true, not true," he muttered over and over again as his body convulsed from uncontrollable sobbing. "Not worthless."

He could hear his own words, but deep down, he didn't actually believe them.

It didn't matter what he did, how good he was or how worthy he might try to be, there had to be a reason no one had been able to love him his entire life. Gale hadn't been wrong about that, and even though Steve seemed to be the one exception, what if Deacon was wrong about Steve as well?

Perhaps it would be just a matter of time before Steve tired of him?

Steve's own mother didn't believe Deacon was good enough for him, so who was he to argue with that?

Deacon wrapped his arms around his stomach, which now ached. He let go of everything in that moment, including Steve.

As he lay there and continued to cry, Deacon allowed another tiny piece of who he so desperately wanted to be, to fall away.

Then another.

And another.

Letting go of any hope for happiness was the sensation he'd become accustomed to over the years, but it cut straight through him this time—deeper into his core like a surgeon using a scalpel to remove a tumor.

Deacon wished he could cut out his own heart because nothing had ever felt this bad before. He knew deep down he was no good for Steve. He feared he might die from his own disappointment. But better to run now and save everyone the heartache.

He'd have to cut Steve off, stop seeing him altogether, and next year, after Ashley had graduated from high school, Deacon would leave this place again, and this time, he'd never return.

CHAPTER NINETEEN

Running seemed like the most appropriate activity for Deacon, considering it was what he was doing to Steve. Running away. He was convinced cutting things off was the right thing to do, but that fact wasn't making staying away any easier. It was for the best. If he left the man alone once and for all, Steve would have a shot at finding the right kind of guy—one that wouldn't inevitably make him miserable due to all the negativity, which followed Deacon like some sort of a hex or curse.

And this was the only way, completely cutting any and all ties. Easier said than done, which was what had led him to River Rouge Park.

It was hotter than hell, even this early in the morning, but he needed to be outside in the fresh air. The open space was better for him than staying holed up in Patty's house, feeling oppressively guilty for not having had the balls to face Steve in person as opposed to leaving him a freaking voicemail, saying they couldn't see each other anymore.

He was no better than Seth, it would seem. He still couldn't quite accept the fact that he'd been capable of ending their relationship that way. It was low and cowardly, but he couldn't bear to see the look on Steve's face. He just couldn't do it.

There was no way Steve would understand, which meant there'd be lots of screaming, and Deacon was desperate to prevent that from being his final memory of Steve. He didn't want their relationship to go out like that.

It was maddening, and he needed a distraction, a break from the war going on inside his head. Going for a run was exactly what the doctor ordered, and he liked running here in particular. The grass had been cut the day before, and the scent of it was strong in the air from the fresh layer of dew on the ground.

The smell made him think about Steve mowing the lawn all sweaty.

How turned on Deacon would get while watching him.

The blazingly hot sex they'd have once Steve finished, the smell of his sweat-drenched body, those thick, long fingers digging into Deacon's skin.

All of that flashed through his mind as he ran and that just made him run faster.

If Deacon ran fast enough and long enough, eventually everything else would fall away and all he'd be left with was controlling his breathing, maintaining his pulse and keeping a steady pace. There would also hopefully be the added benefit that some exercise might wear him out to the extent he could manage to get a little sleep for a change. Deacon wasn't laying any bets, but this felt proactive, which was the only positive thing he'd managed thus far this week.

That feeling of empowerment quickly evaporated as he rounded the bend, slowing to a full stop. There weren't many other cars in the parking lot between the pool and the tennis courts. Not this early on a weekday, which made Steve's Mustang stand out like a beacon of doom. Deacon's chest was heaving, attempting to get his wind back as he stretched his legs, watching Steve get out of his car—making any fantasies about running for cover under the trees moot.

He'd definitely been spotted, and realistically, he'd been aware this confrontation was going to happen sooner or later. Asking Steve to not come looking for him was never going to fly, but it had been worth a shot.

Deacon made his way across the parking lot, trying to bury any and all thoughts of how good it was to see the man—even though Steve appeared stiff and apprehensive, perhaps even a little pissed.

Filled with a curious mix of dread and excitement, Deacon stopped at his car, getting a towel and his bottle of water from the passenger seat before turning to face Steve.

"What are you doing here?" Deacon asked, before taking several large gulps of water.

"What the fuck do you think I'm doing here?" Steve asked. "You won't answer my phone calls, completely ignore my texts, so I'm left with this." Steve's arms flailed dramatically through the air. "Stalking you like some sort of schmuck."

Deacon opened his mouth to say sorry, but that seemed too simple for this particular situation so he said nothing.

"Mind explaining to me what the hell is going on?" Steve asked. "I think you owe me that much."

"This isn't easy for me, either." Deacon's voice was quiet.

"Then why are you doing it?" Steve was definitely pissed.

"There's no part of me that doesn't want to be with you, Steve, honestly. I…I've never been so happy. You did that. But the sad fact of the matter is, I'm no good for you."

"What the hell are you talking about?" Steve looked rightfully confused.

Deacon wiped his sweaty face with the towel once more, not really wanting to admit that he'd eavesdropped on Steve's conversation with his mother. It had been entirely unintentional. He'd been sneaking back to Steve's bedroom to use the bathroom when he'd heard his name. He knew it was wrong, that he should have immediately walked away, but he found himself quietly creeping closer to the doorway to Steve's office instead.

In retrospect, he wished he'd never overheard that conversation, hearing Steve's mother saying what a sad, pathetic harbinger of unhappiness that Deacon was…that was tough to hear, even though he'd suspected that she didn't like him.

"I overheard you, at the party, talking to your mom?"

He waited until the recognition came over Steve's face.

"Is that what this is about?" Steve asked, looking momentarily relieved. "That wasn't, you weren't meant to hear that for one, and honestly, it was nothing more than a mother worrying for her son, Deacon."

"Just because I don't have a mother who gives a damn about what happens to me doesn't mean I'm too simple to understand what that looks like when I see it."

"Don't do that, Deacon," Steve said. "You know damn well that isn't how I meant it."

"You're missing the point, babe."

"Which is?" Steve asked with an exaggerated sigh.

"That I'm no good for you!" Deacon bent over, momentarily resting his hands on his knees while he took several deep breaths in an attempt to maintain control over himself. "Your mom isn't wrong about that. Doesn't matter where I go or what I do, misery fucking loves my company, and you don't deserve to be saddled with that."

Steve shook his head, not at all pleased with what he was hearing.

Deacon glanced down at the ground for a moment, concentrating on the frayed laces of his running shoes. "I can't think of anyone else who's done so much while requiring so little in return."

"I do that because I love you."

"And please know that I am so proud of that fact. That you could love someone like me. But the sad fact is I have these demons inside—all the self-doubt, the self-loathing and incessant fears of never being good enough."

"But that's all bullshit, Deacon. You're a wonderful person, did you miss the part where my mom also said that?"

He hadn't heard anything like that, of course he hadn't stuck around long after the whole *Deacon is a sad, unhappy man who will drag you down* part. He flinched, hearing Gale's words floating around in the back of his head that he was nothing but trash.

"I may never be whole, even with you attempting to fill up all the emptiness inside of me...trying to make up for everything that isn't there could very well be pointless and impossible. As wonderful as you've been, there still hasn't been a day that's gone by where I haven't felt like crap. Being with you has been amazing, and I truly have experienced moments of happiness, probably for the first time in my whole life. But even on my best day, the bad stuff never completely goes away. You can't love it out of me, and you deserve better."

Steve just stood there, his confusion apparent from the

emotions playing out across his face. It killed Deacon to be the source of that pain, but in the back of his mind, he was aware that either way he'd eventually end up driving Steve away. Like the Declaration of Independence, Deacon believed these truths about himself to be self-evident.

Deacon wiped at the tear running down his cheek. "You deserve to have it all. A whole man, one who can love you back with the same wild abandon that you so freely give to me. I'm *never* gonna be that guy, Steve. And I refuse to be the thing that prevents you from finding it."

Steve's breathing had deepened, and his hands were shaking slightly. He was so quiet, and that had begun to frighten Deacon, who'd already blathered on longer than intended due to his frayed nerves.

The fact he wanted to be selfish, that every fiber of his being was screaming for him to jump into Steve's arms and never let him go wasn't helping.

"This is best. It hurts…badly, but letting you go is the best thing I can do for you. My one selfless act where you're concerned. I'm afraid I won't be able to if I wait, Steve."

Steve still stood there saying nothing, just staring at Deacon in disbelief.

"I so want to be strong for you."

"Fuck you, Deacon," Steve finally said. "Fuck you for not believing in me. In us. Fuck you for being able to walk away so easily." Steve's voice cracked, and his lip quivered for a moment before he managed to regain control over himself. "I wish you had a little more faith in me…more faith in yourself."

Deacon stood there, feeling empty and lost with nowhere left to run. "Faith isn't a luxury I'm able to afford, never has been. Faith is dangerous for people like me…leads to silly dreams and unrealistic expectations." Deacon rubbed at his chest like it ached. "Faith can cut so deep that it kills, Steve."

He could no longer tell what Steve was thinking. All the color had drained away from his face, the man was a blank slate.

Deacon took a deep breath as Steve walked up to him and placed the palm of his hand over Deacon's heart. "Don't toss away what could be because you're scared, Deacon."

He could've stayed right there forever, hypnotized by Steve's gaze for all eternity and been perfectly happy. He didn't want to end things, but it was the right thing to do, wasn't it?

He doesn't love you.

…you're only good for one thing.

…you're just a thing to him.

…nothing but trash.

Deacon stepped back, shaking his head as he wiped the back of his hand across his cheek. He took another step, then another and another, finally whispered, "I can't."

Steve stood there for a moment, stoically, and then without another word, he turned and quietly walked back to his car.

He stopped briefly, not looking Deacon in the eye as he opened his car door. "Fuck you for not loving me enough to stay and fight for me the way that I would've fought for you."

Deacon jumped slightly when the car door slammed shut.

A million doubts began to creep in, and he wanted to call out for him to stop, but it was too late. Steve was already driving away, leaving Deacon behind.

It was what he'd wanted, but standing there in the parking lot, desperation and loneliness washed over him in waves. This had been what he'd tried in vain to avoid—the finality of a confrontation. There was no going back now. Steve hated him, would never take him back after that. It was what had to be, but the hole in his chest felt endless and infinite. A drop of rain hit his forehead as he stood there crying. He'd just let go of the only good thing that had ever come his way, and it was now unequivocally over.

Two more drops fell before the sky opened up, drowning Deacon's regret and despair, washing it away as he went about reconstructing the walls around his heart, stone by imaginary stone, determined to never again allow anyone else inside.

CHAPTER TWENTY ~ AUGUST

Sitting on the twin bed in the bedroom he'd grown up in, Deacon stared at the brown pressed wood seventies style paneling as a nasty bout of *déjà vu* came over him. For the first time in a very long time, that same desolate sense of isolation had taken hold inside his chest, making it difficult to breathe.

Frozen in a state of undress, his finger poked through the hole he'd discovered after removing the white ribbed tank before allowing the garment to slip from his hand, falling to the floor next to the work shirt that lay at his feet. He had one shoe on, one off and his belt was unbuckled—the sound of the metal clinking whenever he moved reminding him where he was.

Staring at the smart phone in his other hand, he tapped the screen with his thumb and replayed the message Steve had left him weeks before, after Deacon snuck out of the BBQ. He could no longer count how many times he'd listened to it, and Deacon closed his eyes as fresh tears ran down his cheeks before falling onto his lap.

The sound of Steve's voice filled his bedroom once again.

"Hey Deacon, shit, baby, I totally freaked you out, right? I mean, I got the message you weren't feeling good, but the way you slipped away from the party? It was the corn-I-love-you, I know it, which was really ill-timed, baby, I get that, I do. But I can't in all honesty deny that it isn't true, D. I do love you. So you're just gonna have to deal with that, 'cause it isn't ever going to change. So please, call me back, and we can put our heads together and come up with a way for me to make that whole corn-declaration up to you, okay? Love you. Call me."

He couldn't seem to make himself stop listening to the message, couldn't delete it. It was like some sort of sick time loop he was trapped inside. It was over, and he needed to move on, but Deacon couldn't make himself do it. This message was all he had left, the only proof that someone had loved him—at least for a little while.

It hurt like hell, and now that he'd finally started once again, he couldn't seem to make himself stop crying. The level of desperation seemed exponentially endless, like some sort of worm boring deeper and deeper into his soul, rooting itself so far down that he'd never manage to rid himself of it.

Nothing had ever felt as bad as this did. The fact he had done it to himself only seemed to make it worse. As good as Steve was for him, Deacon loved him too much to shackle himself to the man—like some sort of albatross bringing nothing but bad luck and frustration.

That's all Deacon would ever bring anyone.

A lifetime of disappointment had taught him that. It's all he'd ever known. It was to Steve's credit that he'd made Deacon believe his life could actually become anything else.

Steve's mother had seen the disaster written all over him, and as if to prove her forecast true, Gale came along, punctuating the point. Born out of desperation and the misery of others, Deacon's entire existence had been tainted by it.

Replaying the message again, Deacon's entire body ached at the sound of Steve's voice. It hurt so badly he began to understand why Patty might have turned to alcohol. If the pain cut deep enough and lingered for months or even years? It would take a stronger person than him to trudge along carrying that weight.

The door to his bedroom burst open, and he jumped, dropping the phone. Ashley took one look at him and shook her head as she scrambled to pick up the phone. He screamed in protest, standing up just as she deleted the message.

He'd been so lost in his own thoughts he hadn't heard her come home.

His heart stopped, and the entire world went still and quiet as he crumpled back onto the bed. Even his tears stopped flowing as the realization that his last little piece of Steve was gone forever.

He went numb.

Ashley stood there, breathing heavily, and he could tell by the look on her face she was able to see the effect her actions had on him. She started to say something, but no words came out, and then she started to cry.

"I'm so sorry," she finally said in a whisper. "I…could hear you crying. You kept listening to it, over and over."

He tried taking a deep breath and felt a fresh tear run down his cheek. He'd been so careful, keeping her away from all of this. She'd asked him several times what had happened. Why they had broken up? Each time he'd smile, making sure to put her at ease before giving her the same line he'd given everyone at work—that he and Steve just weren't right for one another.

She'd caught him off guard, and Deacon hadn't been able to downshift that quickly—the emotional equivalent of being caught with his pants down.

"Please say something," Ashley said. "You're scaring me."

He shook his head that he couldn't.

"I thought you were okay." She sat on the bed next to him.

"I'm not," Deacon yelled, startling her with the outburst as he jumped up off the bed and began pacing. "This is killing me, Ash. It hurts…so badly…" He stopped, placing a hand over his chest. "I can't fucking breathe."

He could see that he'd frightened her, but Deacon couldn't help it. It took him a good ten to twenty minutes each morning to ready himself, getting the mask in place so he could interact with her and the rest of the world. There was a whole routine that consisted of breathing slowly and lying to himself that everything would be okay with time. He didn't believe that deep down, but Deacon was somehow able to cling to that lie long enough to get through the day, not breaking down again until he crawled into bed.

"How am I supposed to know what's going on with you, Deacon? You never open up and tell me what you feel."

"Of course, I wanted to keep all this from you. I'm supposed to take care of you, Ashley, not the other way around."

"Well, that's just stupid." Ashley folded her arms, her forehead creased. "I'm not a child."

"But you should be, damn it. You should be carefree, going out and having fun with your friends. You should have that, and I wanted to give it to you."

"That ship has sailed, big brother. You've helped me feel safe for the first time in as long as I can remember, but we grew up in the same house. You think I'm going to magically be able to forget all of that?"

"That's depressing." Deacon sighed.

"What's depressing is that you refuse to let me in. You refuse to confide in me, so I walk around like some idiot, giggling and laughing while you're doing this…emotional cutting behind closed doors?"

"I'm sorry, Ash, I never meant—"

"It's kinda sick to discover you loved Steve this much yet I never knew it," she said, cutting him off. "Probably never would have known, had I not come home early, I suspect."

"I don't talk about the good things Ashley. I never have. I inevitably somehow manage to lose the things I love the most whenever I do talk about them. A person can only be broken so many times." He reached out and took her arm, making sure she understood. "I'm getting to the point where I'd rather never have it if I'm only going to lose it."

"Maybe you don't have to lose it this time, Deacon."

"That's not the way my world works."

Ashley stopped, looking frustrated. "That's disappointing to hear. I mean, according to your logic, our entire future is going to be dictated by our past? Since you and I share the same past, that means all I have to look forward to in the future is misery and disappointment?"

"God, of course not, that isn't—"

"It's either true or it isn't, Deacon, so which is it?"

"I see what you're doing, but—"

"Are we damned or not?"

"Of course not, I mean, you can't go around thinking like that."

Ashley pointed at him. "You are."

"That's different, Ash, it just is."

"That's bullshit." She got up from the bed and walked out into the hall before turning around. "As awesome of a brother as you've been, you're kind of a shitty role model, Deacon."

He stood there, speechless as she stormed off, jumping when the front door slammed, announcing she had left the house.

Never had he considered she might gauge her own opportunities in life by what he was able to accomplish. Thus far, he hadn't given her much to pin her hopes on, and that tore him up even more. She deserved to have all that life could offer, even if Deacon couldn't see that for himself.

Part of him knew it was cowardice, that hoping or yearning for more had only ever managed to break him in two. That's why he'd stopped expecting anything. If he never wished for something more, he was never disappointed.

The thought of his sister learning that lesson from him made him nauseous.

That couldn't be his legacy to her.

He didn't know how, but Deacon knew he'd have to fix it. Not with Steve, he knew that ship had sailed. Steve had made it crystal clear that he never wanted to see Deacon again, and Deacon couldn't blame the man for that. Nor did he want to gamble with wrecking Steve's life, the stakes were too high and he loved Steve too much.

But moving forward from this point, he could change.

He owed his sister that much.

There was still time for him to pick up the pieces and begin again, he thought, wiping his face dry, doing his best to bury his misery.

Doing his best to put Steve out his mind.

It would take time, but he understood that he needed to make some changes.

"For Ash," he muttered, nodding his head. "I can do that for Ash."

CHAPTER TWENTY-ONE

Steve glanced up from his computer screen, hearing the intercom buzz from the phone on his desk. He was about to rip Margie a new one for interrupting him after he'd implicitly left instructions that he was not to be disturbed. His mouth was open, but no words came out, seeing Ashley standing out at the front desk.

She looked slightly distressed and disheveled, with her hair pulled back into a loose ponytail. She forced a smile and waved at him, cautiously.

"You have a visitor," Margie said, her tone flat, letting Steve know she'd been able to tell he was irritated with her. She waved Ashley to go on back, waiting until she'd stepped away before muttering into the phone, "You better be nice to that little girl or so help me—"

"Yeah, yeah." He cut her off. "Never you mind."

He sneered back at Margie, getting up out of his seat when Ashley peered sheepishly around the doorway into Steve's office.

"This a bad time?" Ashley asked, fidgeting in that same way that Deacon did, which sent a slicing pain through Steve's chest.

"No, it's fine, Ashley." Steve motioned to the chairs on the other side of his desk. "Everything okay?"

"Yes and no," she said, taking a seat, frowning slightly from Steve's reaction to her cryptic vagueness. "No emergency or anything like that."

Steve sighed a little in relief, sitting on the edge of his desk, but he was mad at himself for still giving a damn. He didn't want to care anymore because it hurt too badly, yet he couldn't seem to turn it off.

"I suspect you know why I'm here," Ashley said quietly.

"The fact that it's you and not Deacon, doesn't exactly fill me with—"

"I get that," she said, interrupting him this time.

"I suppose he's blaming me for us breaking up?" Steve asked, already livid before she even responded.

"He's not said much of anything, aside from some vague rambling about him not being good for you."

Steve felt his jaw tighten, teeth clenched in an attempt to keep himself in check. He wanted to explode, but it wouldn't be fair to Ashley for him to unload his aggression and frustrations onto her.

"He made his decision, Ashley." Steve shrugged.

"I get it...at least, I think I do." Her brow furrowed as if perhaps she didn't really.

That makes one of us, Steve thought to himself. All that bullshit about not being good enough. It was ludicrous, a pathetic excuse.

"I've seen my brother sad before. Many, many times, in fact. But this time is different. This time he's...gone." Ashley waved her hand in front of her face, the way you would attempting to get someone to look at you. "I hear him crying at night, so I know he's hurting, but the rest of the time it's like Deacon has left the building. The lights are on, he's moving and breathing, but there's nobody home inside."

"I'm very sorry, Ashley, but I'm not sure what you'd like me to do."

She glanced down at the floor, and Steve could tell that wasn't the response she'd been hoping for.

"I love your brother," Steve said, praying she wouldn't start crying. He couldn't deal with the crying. "But I can't force him to be with me. I'm not going to beg or plead with him, Ashley. I need Deacon to want to be with me, to act as if I'm worth fighting for. Not this lame-ass, supposed self-sacrificing bullshit. What it all boils down to, is Deacon doesn't truly want to be with me. He's using this as his excuse to cut and run. If he loved me, he'd never roll over this easily."

"Growing up the way we did," Ashley began, reaching up and placing her hand onto Steve's when he sighed, looking up at the ceiling.

"You can't blame this on your mom," Steve said. "She's no longer in the picture."

"Funny, you'd think that would be enough, right?" Ashley asked, smiling awkwardly. "Doesn't quite work that way, though."

Steve instantly felt like shit for intimating that he truly knew what it had been like for either of them. He knew better, but he was still pissed at Deacon for quitting on him. He'd been in high school when his dad left his mother for a much a younger woman, but it had affected Steve profoundly. He never completely forgave his father, and to this day, it still felt like a betrayal. That was only a fraction of what Patty had put her children through.

"We blamed ourselves, you know?" Ashley said, her voice sounding smaller. "We believed the threats that we'd get into trouble for telling our teachers or anyone else about the things that went on at home. Deacon took the brunt of that on, his attempt at sparing me, though I still experienced the guilt. I still get so angry at times."

"I am sorry," Steve said quietly. "That doesn't excuse him walking away. I love him. All I wanted to do was make him happy."

"He doesn't believe he deserves it, Steve." Ashley finally looked him in the eye. "We aren't equipped to recognize love when we see it, you understand?"

Steve didn't really, mainly because it didn't seem fathomable to him. Both his parents had loved him, even after they split. He'd never known anyone who grew up the way they did.

"It's messed up, I know. Even now I feel guilty over the fact that the longer Patty is away, the better I feel. The freer I feel. These past eight months, I've started to allow myself to believe that my future might hold possibilities. I never had that before, and part of it is because of Deacon. He got out, you know?"

Steve nodded.

"But despite leaving, Deacon was never free. He still doesn't believe he deserves or will ever find happiness. Despite leaving Patty behind, she's still in there, drunkenly berating and quashing anything good and decent. That's what feels familiar to us. Happiness wasn't something we were brought up to believe in. But I'd like to think we can find it. Seeing you and Deacon together?"

She smiled, wiping at the tear that ran down her cheek. Steve went and grabbed the box of tissues sitting on the small table in the corner next to the small, black leather sofa.

"You with my brother," Ashley said, taking the box from him and using a tissue to wipe her nose. "I started to believe that I might be able to find that myself, you know? I realize we're damaged, broken even, but we need you to help put us back together again."

She reached over, taking his hand again, squeezing it tightly, as if she were afraid he might say no.

"I know it's a lot to ask, but I believe you love my brother. I think you love him in that soul mate, meant-to-be kind of way. I understand that it's not my place to ask, but I'm doing it anyway, because Deacon never will. Not because he doesn't love you with his whole heart, Steve. I believe with every fiber of my being that you are his whole life's happiness."

Steve took in a deep breath, doing his best to hold his shit together as she continued to cry, making him feel like a massively huge asshole.

"So it has to be you, you see? Deacon isn't capable of the grand gesture. You can't ask for something if you don't believe you deserve it, but he does deserve it, damn it, so you need to ask yourself what's more important. Getting the guy or getting your way?"

With that she stood, ripped a few more tissues from the box and nodded as she wiped her face dry.

"Just think about it, please."

She placed the box on the desk and quietly slipped out the door.

He started to call after her, but nothing came out when his mouth opened.

His mind was racing, and on some base level, Steve knew everything she had said was on the money. He was already sweating the fact that he'd dropped the ball—had allowed his own ego to get in the way of his happiness and had inadvertently done the one thing he'd promised himself months ago that he would never do.

"Damn it."

Steve practically leapt off the table, startled hearing Margie's voice over the intercom.

"Are you gonna sit there like a dumb ass, or are you gonna go after that sweet little girl?"

He realized he hadn't disconnected her earlier when she first buzzed him. "Were you listening the entire—"

"Of course I was, you big lummox," Margie snapped. "Now stop worrying about me and get your butt over to that boy's house and make things right."

"This is none of your damn business, Margie," Steve said, his voice getting a little louder than normal. "You had no ri—"

"Do not raise your voice to me, Steven Anthony Steele," she snapped back. "I have been working here since before your bony butt was even born, so you will not sass me, you hear?"

He stood up a little straighter, still pissed off but deciding to keep his mouth shut considering she was the glue that held this place together.

"You have been an absolute bear since you ended things with that man, and everyone here has put up with it, but that ends right now."

His eyebrows arched, seeing she'd gotten up out of her chair behind the long desk out in the showroom and was clutching the handle of her phone so tightly it threatened to snap clear in two.

"You love that boy, so take your keys out of your desk, march your stubborn ass out to your car, and do not come back until you have fixed your shit!"

In all the years he'd known Margie, he'd rarely ever heard her use foul language, and he was stunned into silence—and apparently obedience as he found himself taking his keys out of his desk and grabbing his suit coat off the back of his chair.

As he came out of his office, he saw Jimmy leaning against the wall, his arms crossed and a shit-eating grin across his face. He wanted to smack it right off his face, but before he got a word out, Jimmy pointed down the hall toward the service entrance doors in the back where all the employees parked.

"You heard the woman," Jimmy said, enjoying his humiliation a little too much—the way Steve most likely would have, had Jimmy been on the receiving end of Margie's scorn.

"No respect for anyone's privacy around here," Steve muttered.

He began gritting his teeth, resisting the strong desire to deck the asshole as he passed by, listening to Jimmy snickering the way he used to back when they were teenagers and getting into trouble for one thing or another.

The thing that pissed him off most was that this time, it wasn't Jimmy that got him into trouble.

He had no one to blame but himself.

CHAPTER TWENTY-TWO

Steve got out of his car, taking a beat to gather his thoughts. It was unseasonably warm, and the midday sun was beating down upon him. He yanked on his tie, taking it off altogether, and tossed it onto the passenger side seat on top of his suit jacket. He unbuttoned the top few buttons of his shirt, able to breathe a little easier and set his mind on the task at hand before locking and closing the car door and crossing the lawn.

He'd already been to the grocery store, only to be informed that Deacon had left early because he wasn't feeling well. That news had been accompanied by a none-too-friendly glare from Gilda Garibaldi, making it quite clear she'd expected more from him. He refrained from informing her that this breakup hadn't been his doing and took it on the chin. He was a big boy; he could handle it.

"Just one more unhappy person to add to an ever-growing list," he said under his breath as he quickly hopped up the few steps onto the porch and knocked on the front door.

It took his breath away when Deacon finally opened the door, visibly surprised to find Steve standing there. All Steve wanted to do was take him in his arms and kiss him. Part of him had feared that some of that passion might have waned after the past couple of weeks apart combined with the disappointment, chaos and pain Deacon had created, but that was not the case. Steve wanted him every bit as much as he had the first time he'd spotted Deacon sitting at that damn bar out by the airport.

"Hey," Deacon said, his toes wiggling as he began to fidget from his bare feet on up. "What are you doing here?"

"Can I come in?" Steve asked.

"Um...sure, I guess." Deacon stepped aside, allowing Steve to enter the house.

"Look, I've been a total asshole and a fucking idiot," Steve began, turning to see Deacon hovering next to the now closed door.

"What is this?" Deacon asked.

"This is me, trying to get you back," Steve said matter-of-factly.

Deacon opened his mouth to respond, but Steve beat him to the punch.

"Just shut the hell up, Deacon," Steve said, not bothering to leave the irritation out of his voice. "I know what you're gonna say. We're better apart. You're no good for me, blah, blah, bullshit."

"Don't strain anything trying to sugarcoat it for me," Deacon said, using that smart ass tone that drove Steve mental.

"I'm not going to, damn it. We're both idiots, and neither one of us deserves the other, considering we each walked away so easily."

"Do you want something to drink?" Deacon asked, noticeably uncomfortable and straining to change the subject.

"No," Steve said flatly and sternly.

"Okay, *sheesh*." Deacon's entire upper body wriggled as he moved past Steve and headed for the sofa. "Forget I offered."

"Why are you home today, are you sick?" Steve asked.

"No, just don't feel good." Deacon flopped down onto the sofa.

"You're miserable, I'm miserable—"

"Who said I was miserable?"

"Your sister." Steve shook his head.

"Well, Ashley doesn't know what she's talking about. I'm fine, Steve. You don't need to worry about me."

"Well, I'm not fine and thanks for asking by the way, asshole."

"Oh. I'm sorry." Deacon glanced down at the floor, refusing to look Steve in the eye.

"Do you love me?" Steve asked, ready to cut past all the bullshit.

"That's irrelevant."

"Answer the goddamn question, Deacon."

A pained look came over his face, and he squirmed around on the sofa. "You know I do."

"I know you do what?"

Deacon sighed, popping his knuckles, finally looking back up at Steve. "Yes, I love you, but—"

"No buts." Steve cut him off, finally sitting next to Deacon on the sofa. "We're back together, and I don't wanna hear anything else about it."

Deacon's eyes widened slightly, but he didn't protest, which Steve took as a good sign that he'd won the battle. He understood the war was going to take a hell of a lot longer and would most likely require a shit load of therapy—probably one or two prescriptions for himself, if he intended to maintain his own sanity.

"I'm still no good for you," Deacon said softly.

"I don't need you to worry about what is or isn't good for me, Deacon. I'm a grown-ass man, I can figure that out for myself, thank you very much."

"'Scuse me," Deacon said, the hint of a grin forming.

Steve sighed, relaxing back into the sofa, and wiped his face with the palm of his hand. "I've never met anyone like you, Deacon, you're so tragically resilient. So much awful has happened to you and at such a young age, yet each time the smoke clears, there you are, standing tall…if not exactly proudly."

"I don't need your pity." Deacon folded his arms across his chest as he puffed himself up slightly.

"You have to hear this, or I need to say it, not really sure which anymore. Either way, I can't stand by on the sidelines and watch helplessly while you suffer. You're like air to me, Deacon. If I could hold you and keep you safe forever and always, I would."

"But you can't do that, as nice as it sounds and as much as I love to hear you say it, you can't be that for me."

"I can try, damn it." Steve took Deacon's hand, their fingers intertwining. "I've waited my whole life to find someone who makes me feel the way you do. I'm not even sure how to describe it. Strong, yet in a completely treacherous way, weak with a need to be near you…to be inside you. Terrified you'll look at me one day and realize I'm nowhere near good enough for you. I sure as hell don't deserve you, but I do love you, Deacon."

"That's what scares me," Deacon said. "I feel the same way, but things have a way of going sour for me."

"So ending things now—"

"It hurts, Steve, you have no idea how much, but better now than a year from now, when I've allowed my guard to drop only to discover you no longer like what you see staring back at you."

"Forever waiting for that other shoe to drop."

"I'm sorry. I know I'm a disappointment."

"We both have baggage, babe. I've lived half my adult life lying, and I realize that might give you pause for concern, Deacon. I still carry around that guilt, but you make me want for more. The more time I spend with you, the less desperate and isolated I feel. I thought, hoped at any rate, that perhaps I did the same for you."

"You do." Concern and self-doubt played out across Deacon's face. "Wanting more scares the hell out of me."

"I know, but you have to let me back in. If you care about me at all, you'll do that for me. You'll let me be that point of origin for you…your very own Northern Star…forever leading you safely back home."

Deacon sighed, his eyes welling up as he shook his head, trying to hold it all in.

Steve shifted on the sofa, facing Deacon.

"Please say you will, Deacon. I'll spend my forever trying to make you happy if you do. You'll never suffer regret at my hand, I can promise you that, with every fiber, I…"

He trailed off the instant the first tear ran down Deacon's cheek.

Steve knew he'd worked his way back in, and this time he was never letting go. He'd broken Deacon down from the inside out. Something they'd done to one another, truth be told. It started months ago, on a cold, lonely night in a hotel bar—when two strangers made love for the first time and recognized something in one another.

"Something familiar staring back at me through the darkness."

Deacon looked confused for a moment, then smiled, like he understood Steve had been working stuff out in his own head.

"I'm so damaged, Steve."

"We're all damaged, Deacon. Doesn't mean we're not worthy."

"You've helped me in so many ways. Each day with you has been a gift, but I was always prepared to see it end."

"You deserve some happiness, Deacon."

"But I'm not completely whole, you know that, right?"

"I do."

"What if I never get there?" Deacon asked.

"Then I'll have to learn how to cherish the good days and be content to hold your hand on the bad days. Isn't that what people do when they love each other?"

"You deserve better."

"What I deserve is a little more credit." Steve shrugged, taking Deacon by the back of the neck with his free hand, running his fingers through the soft, dark hair.

"I do love you."

Steve took a deep breath and then smiled. "I know."

"Desperately wanna be the thing you've been looking for, but—"

"I'm looking for wonderful, Deacon." Steve took the man into his arms and sighed, frustrated with the doubt written all over Deacon's face. "That would be you, dummy."

Deacon laughed.

"I'm damn lucky I found you." He gave Deacon a soft peck.

"Sad state of affairs when I'm what's considered lucky."

"Shut up, Deacon, won't have you disparaging the man I love." Steve said, kissing him and closing off any attempt at further contradiction.

They kissed, slowly and softly, Steve taking his time to truly savor the taste of Deacon. Slightly addicted to the way Deacon opened himself up to Steve's tongue, so willing and eager for more.

When the heat finally became too much to bear, Steve broke away. They each wanted the other, Steve could see how much so by the bulge in Deacon's shorts. He wasn't sure if this was the time for that.

It wasn't why he'd come here.

"Second thoughts already?" Deacon asked.

"I may take you over my knee later, young man."

Deacon laughed, biting his bottom lip like he might be pondering that scenario, and favorably so. "I am trying, you know, to not be so sad, but it's not always easy, and I find myself falling back into self-destructive patterns."

Steve smiled, shaking his head slightly as he stared deeply into Deacon's eyes. "That's how I know everything is going to be fine, what you just said."

"That I'm self-destructive?"

"That you're self-aware, babe. You fight to pull yourself out of it. That's all I need to hear. I don't expect to be all that you need. If you want or feel like it might help to talk to someone professionally, I would support you in that. Hell, it's likely something I should try myself."

Deacon kissed him again, sucking gently on Steve's bottom lip before finally letting go. "You taste so good."

"You like that, huh?" Steve asked.

Deacon laughed.

Steve knew Deacon enjoyed that cocky side of his personality.

"I do like it." He kissed him quick. "And I love you."

"That mean you'll be my one and only?"

Deacon chuckled over the cheese. "For as long as you'll have me."

Steve shook his head, not liking the negative connotation of that last statement. "You may consider yourself spoken for… indefinitely."

Deacon nodded. "Thank you."

"You're welcome," Steve kissed him quick this time. "Thank you right back."

* * * *

Deacon collapsed onto the twin bed next to Steve as they each struggled to catch their breath. They were practically on top of one another, arms and legs tangled as Steve scooted toward the edge, creating more room for Deacon.

He watched as Steve finished toweling the cum off his chest and stomach, and Deacon grinned, happy with the overall resolution to their afternoon.

"That was a whole lot easier than I thought it'd be," Steve said, holding onto the towel and looking around the tiny bedroom like he didn't know where the appropriate place to put it might be.

Deacon snatched the towel from his hand and tossed onto the floor next to the bed. "You calling me a slut?"

Steve appeared momentarily confused, and then he started to laugh. "No, sir, I wasn't referring to the sex." He rolled onto his side and then began running his palm slowly over Deacon's sweaty abs and chest.

Deacon watched intently as Steve kissed one of his nipples.

"The getting back together part," Steve finally clarified. "I was expecting more resistance."

Their gazes locked onto one another, and Deacon shrugged. "I don't want to argue anymore."

Steve's forehead crinkled up. "So I get you by default?"

"Don't twist my words, please. I was lonely. I missed you. I tried walking away, but I didn't want to, Steve. And you showing up here today, all pissed off and sexy? I don't possess the strength it would require to walk away a second time."

"I'm glad to hear it." Steve winked, kissing Deacon's chest once more.

"I'm not exactly sure I enjoy feeling so powerless. But even now, the thought of being away from you sends a shot of panic straight through me."

"Well, you're just gonna have to get the fuck over yourself." Steve nodded as if to punctuate the fact he didn't care about Deacon's discomfort. "You ever pull anything like that again, and I'll kick your butt clear into next week."

"Doe-mestic violence is not the answer, baby," Deacon said, utilizing his best hillbilly redneck imitation.

"You behave yourself, and it won't be an issue," Steve said, the big, cheesy smile on his face betraying the serious tone to his voice.

Deacon took his hand, squeezing it before holding it to his chest. "I am sorry, you know? I didn't know what else to do. Still don't, Steve. I'm not going to sit here and look you in the eye and pretend like I believe everything is going to be okay."

"That's understandable. All I ask is that you don't give up. It's one thing to try—to give it all you have and not have things work out. I could never fault either of us so long as we do that. But no more walking away because you're scared of the unknown."

Deacon nodded. "I shouldn't have done that, but I was terrified."

"I really hate hearing you talk like that," Steve said.

"He said it to me, a couple of days after overhearing that conversation with your mom, he reminded me of things I'd tried to forget, but—"

"Who?" Steve asked, interrupting. "Who reminded you?"

"Gale was here."

"And you're taking relationship advice from that piece of shit?"

"Things that he said…" Deacon took a deep breath. "They

weren't completely untrue, Steve."

"What things?" Steve asked.

Deacon shook his head. "I don't want you to hear them—can't be the one to say them to you. You'll look at me…"

"Differently?" Steve asked, propping himself up on his elbows when Deacon nodded, confirming that was his fear. "What could be so bad? I'm starting to think he did molest you, regardless of the denials from you."

"He couldn't have," Deacon said quietly. "I…loved him, Steve. Worshipped him, in fact. And he knew it all along. So you see? He couldn't have molested me because I would have been willing had he wanted me."

Deacon sat up, not able to look at Steve as the shame of that admission washed over him.

Steve quietly, caressed his back. "First of all, you were too young to truly understand what any of those feelings actually meant. Secondly, those feelings you had for him, Deacon, they were based upon a fantasy—one that Gale perpetuated in an attempt to get what he wanted from all of you. He lied to you, to your mom. He presented himself as one thing, purposely concealing the darker side of who he was."

"You don't find me repulsive?" Deacon asked, turning to look at Steve. "Because it makes me sick when I think about it."

"I think you're beautiful," Steve said. "I'm not sure I've ever met a sweeter soul. You're generosity comes without conditions. That your stepfather would twist that and abuse it in such distasteful and sickening manner pisses me off. You deserve so much more."

Deacon managed to calm himself down now that he understood the darkest part of him wasn't going to drive Steve away.

"Listen to me," Steve said, shaking him gently. "You were a kid, Deacon. Do not allow Gale to twist the fact that you loved him—the way any lonely child might have loved and looked up to him in the same situation—into something sick or evil."

"What does it say about me that I didn't see who he really was?"

"That you were a kid, desperate to be loved and looked after—for some sense of safety and security. You have nothing to feel guilty about. I can't say the same for that piece of shit, though. If I ever see him, I'll fucking kill him."

Deacon's eyes widened. "You'll do no such thing. You'd go to prison. Then where would I be?"

"Fine, I'll only threaten to kill him, then."

Deacon laughed under his breath. He took a moment to stare back at Steve who was watching him intently. "You really love me, huh?"

"Jesus Christ." Steve rolled his eyes. "How many times do I need to say it before you believe it?"

"I'm young and incredibly clueless it would seem."

"I'm…slightly older and much, *much* wiser," Steve said with a grimace that Deacon assumed came from sussing out a way to not refer to himself as old. "Stick with me and you'll go places, kid."

Deacon leaned back slightly so they could kiss. Steve groaned his approval, and they each started to laugh.

"You like that, huh?" Deacon asked.

Steve poked him in the side, making Deacon's entire body wriggle. "Shut up."

They stared at one another for what felt like an eternity. It was dead quiet apart from the chirpy bird in the tree on the other side of the bedroom window. The air conditioning clicked on, and the white noise of the fan forcing cool air into the room drowned out the sound of kids playing off in the distance.

Summer was nearing an end, and Deacon couldn't help but think a chapter in his life was ending right along with it. He'd follow Steve to ends of the Earth and back again if the man asked him to, and even though it frightened him, after the past couple of weeks without Steve, Deacon understood how horrible the alternative would be.

"I want you and Ashley to move in with me," Steve finally said, breaking the silence.

Deacon was stunned, and he turned away, hoping Steve wouldn't be able to see how much so. He'd mentioned this once before, but Deacon hadn't seriously considered it at the time. Even now it felt like an odd proposition. They'd just gotten back together.

Steve took him by the chin to pull his focus back. "Just hear me out."

Easier said than done. His mind was racing because the idea of living together didn't seem like a realistic option for them until after Ashley graduated from high school and went off to college. It was one of those off-in-the-future sort of ideas that he wasn't prepared to deal with just yet.

He'd lived with Seth, after all, and look how that turned out.

Living together was big.

Huge.

Monumental.

Not to mention something that could potentially change their relationship in ways Deacon wasn't sure either of them was ready for.

"Wow, you're really freaking out, aren't you?" Steve asked.

Deacon was irritated his boyfriend found this amusing, as evidenced by the smirk on his face.

"Look, aside from all the typical bullshit, like me loving you, you loving me and the selfish fact that I want to have sex with you all the time, there's the bigger issue."

Steve's forehead scrunched up, and Deacon could tell he was weighing the best way to say whatever had brought Steve to this conclusion.

Steve caressed his cheek, intently staring into Deacon's eyes. "I want to get you and your sister out of this house, Deacon. This place…it's poison for you both. Too much bad has occurred under this roof…for each of you. Don't you think the two of you would benefit from a fresh start?"

Of all the many wonderful things Steve had ever said or done for him, this was by far the sweetest and noblest. It made his chest ache in that soul-soaring, life-altering sort of way.

Deacon took him by the face and kissed him softly, doing his level best to say thank you without having to say the actual words—something he wanted to avoid as Deacon feared it would only bring about more tears.

He was done with crying.

When Steve finally pulled away, Deacon could see the man was anxious for an answer to his proposal.

"I'm not sure we can do that," Deacon said. "It's true, that I now have custody, but we still have the occasional visits from Social Services, and—"

"So we'll go to them first." Steve said, interrupting. "We'll do everything by the book, babe. We'll explain it to them, make them see how bad this environment is for both of you. I want to make this happen. Please let me do this for you. Let's not wait any longer."

"What if Ashley doesn't want to?" Deacon asked, still fretting over the thought on one hand, while the other yanked and pulled on his inner self, screaming for him to say yes.

"Then we'll wait, of course," Steve said. "Though I'll be honest and say that after some of the things she said to me earlier, I don't think she would say no."

"What did she say to you?" Deacon asked, hating that despite his best efforts, his sister was still experiencing trauma.

"It wasn't what she said, so much as the way she said it. She's still hurting deep down and so are you. I want to try and help, if you'll let me."

Deacon rubbed has palm over his face before brushing the hair off his forehead.

"Maybe."

"Seriously?" Steve asked, visibly holding himself in check like he feared he'd heard Deacon wrong.

"Yes, seriously," Deacon said. "As long as Ashley wants to."

"Shit, let's call her right now!" Steve bounced up off the bed, searching for his phone.

"Hold on, simmer down there, zippy." Deacon grabbed him by the wrist and yanked him back onto the bed. "I'd prefer to ask her alone if that's okay."

Steve frowned, revealing that he wasn't fond of this plan.

"She may not be as honest if you're there, and I don't want to put any pressure on her."

Steve nodded, laying back down and pulling Deacon with him. "You're right, that's the best way, but if she's open to it, I want to talk to her immediately. I won't have her thinking she's a concession for me—the thing I have to accept in order to get you."

"Okay, calm down, *sheesh*." Deacon patted his chest to let him know all would be okay. "You'll give yourself a heart attack, gramps."

"Oh, shut up, you little asshole."

Deacon laughed. "You like my little asshole."

"Fuck you."

"That's what you like doing to my little asshole," Deacon said, grinning evilly.

Steve shook his head, but he was forcing back a grin. "I'm ignoring your attempt to distract me with sex." He paused, momentarily staring at the wall. "So what do you think Ash'll say?"

"My God, if you keep on like this, she'll probably say yes." Deacon smacked Steve on the hip. "Then you can both stay up nights talking about your feelings and braiding each other's hair."

Steve's lip curled into a snarl. "Don't be a shit. I'm excited about the prospect of having you in my bed every night. Sue me."

"You've got me in bed now and don't seem to be taking advantage of the fact, so…"

"Jesus, I fucked you senseless like thirty minutes ago."

Deacon shrugged. "I'm insecure and require constant

reassurance from your cock."

Steve glanced down, watching Deacon massaging Steve's dick into action. "You are very naughty."

"Sounds like someone needs to teach me a lesson, then, huh?" he asked, getting Steve onto his back and straddling him.

Steve already had his hands on Deacon's ass, apparently no longer able to quite manage words at that point, settling for groans and grunts as Deacon leaned over and kissed him. The heat was instantaneous, skin on fire as hands roamed and Steve's fingertips dug into him. Deacon was addicted to that, the way Steve handled him, roughly but also cautiously. It was like the man knew just how far he could go before needing to pull back—the perfect mix of hard and soft.

Deacon was nearing delirium by the time Steve had him on his knees and pinned face first against the wall. He closed his eyes, begging Steve to go harder, faster, falling into a haze with each thrust edging him closer to bliss. Deacon's entire body was on fire, he was so close and while every fiber of his being was screaming for release, he secretly prayed they could go on like this together, forever.

* * * *

A violent shake woke Deacon, who could hear someone coughing. It took several moments before he realized it was himself. Steve too, who was standing across the room stark naked and kicking something at the bottom of the bedroom door, which was closed. The room was hot; Deacon was sweating, but he couldn't quite make sense of what was going on having been ripped right out of a R.E.M. cycle.

He wiped at his eyes, which were burning slightly, and finally noticed the dark smoke creeping slowly across the ceiling. Everything seemed to be moving in slow motion until a pair of jeans hit him in the face.

Steve was tying a T-shirt around his face, covering his nose and mouth, his screams for Deacon to get up were muted as a result. He continued to kick a blanket into the crack under the door, and all the pieces finally came together.

Fire.

Patty's house was on fire.

Springing up off the bed in one swift movement, he shoved both feet into the legs of his jeans. His eyes were watering, making it difficult to see, and the air was thick and hot. He found himself gasping for air only to cough and hack in response, which had him panicking over not being able to breathe.

Steve pushed past him, shoving Deacon to the floor as he carried the small, old tube-style television set, which he hurled through the bedroom window. The air in the room seemed to shift, and a hiss followed the crash of breaking glass.

Steve fell to his hands and knees beside him.

Deacon's eyes were burning, and the heat was stifling, he was afraid to even move. He could tell Steve was faltering, exhausted and also hacking and coughing. There was a dark spot forming on the white T-shirt where's Steve's mouth was sucking in air. He spotted a glow out of the corner of his eye and looking underneath the bed, could see the blanket Steve had kicked under the door had already caught fire.

Deacon knew they needed to get out quickly, otherwise they wouldn't be getting out at all. He blinked, forcing himself to focus as he grabbed the pair of pants Steve was clutching and took hold of the bedding with his free hand, yanking them off the mattress. He managed to get himself up off the floor and rushed to the window. Wrapping the pants around his hand, he quickly knocked the remaining jagged shards of glass free from the window frame. The bedding he tossed over the sill and turned to find Steve right behind him.

There were flames now licking up the bedroom door and ceiling.

In mere minutes, it had spread that far, and Deacon found himself slightly mesmerized by it.

Steve however, wasted no time, shoving on Deacon, forcing

him up and out the window. He pulled the T-shirt off his face, now gasping for air as he followed Deacon, who helped pull Steve outside. He could hear the sirens somewhere off in the distant dark of night as they hobbled away from the house. Deacon hissed in pain when he felt a small piece of glass cutting into his bare foot.

They both collapsed in the neighbor's front yard, unable to make it any farther as they each continued to cough, spitting up black saliva. Deacon felt hands on his arms, pulling him up as some of the people that lived across the street helped him and Steve up, getting them farther away from the inferno.

They got another yard over and to the sidewalk next to the parked cars before Deacon felt Steve grabbing for the pair of pants he hadn't even realized he'd still been clutching for dear life. The guy who had helped pull them to safety now held onto Steve, helping him pull the pair of pants on.

Deacon noticed the sweaty streaks of soot on Steve's back and torso and glanced down at himself, seeing how filthy he also was. They all covered their ears as the fire truck passed by, squinting from the flashing red lights cutting through the darkness as it screeched to halt in front of Patty's house.

Deacon turned to see the house now completely engulfed in flames.

It was a terrifying sight to behold, realizing they'd very likely barely made it out in time. He found himself unable to look away but fumbling blindly until he found Steve's hand. They both fell to their knees as an ambulance and several squad cars came screeching to a halt.

"Your sister?" one of the neighbors asked, after a firefighter came to check on them and see if anyone else might be trapped in the home.

Deacon could see the terror on his neighbor's face, like the man had just remembered Ashley and feared the worst.

Deacon shook his head.

"No one else is in the home?" the firefighter asked, clarifying one last time.

Deacon shook his head again, and the fireman took off as the paramedics rushed in.

The neighbor relaxed, nodding in reflex, like he was telling himself everything was going to be okay.

Deacon let go of Steve long enough to grab the guy's arm and give it a good squeeze. "Thank you," Deacon managed to get out in a husky whisper, which made his throat burn.

The lady who lived in the house they were now sitting in front of came out with blankets and bottles of water, but Steve and Deacon were both whisked away to the ambulance before being able to accept them. He and Steve looked on in stunned silence, sitting on the floor of the ambulance as the firefighters went about trying to put out the blaze.

The oxygen masks kept them from speaking, but every so often Deacon and Steve would turn to one another.

Sometimes words truly weren't necessary.

Steve tried to stand when he saw the firefighters pushing his car out of the way so they could get the hoses in the back of the house. They'd smashed out the driver's side window in order to put the car in neutral. He didn't have the strength to do much more than get up, and Deacon felt for him, knowing how much he loved that car. Even from where he now sat, Deacon could tell that the driver's side of the Mustang had been charred.

As they were each examined, Deacon watched the house burn while listening to the EMTs stating that neither had apparently suffered any burns—only scrapes, cuts and bruises. He barely even flinched when they dug the glass out of his foot.

The lady paramedic mentioned to her partner that they might be in shock. Deacon didn't think he was, but not being much of an expert, he reserved his own judgment. Instead, he concentrated on being thankful that Ashley hadn't been home and that he and Steve had made it out, each in one piece.

It was surreal, watching as the house sort of collapsed in on itself, crackling and popping, and he thought back to Christmas and the outlet that had sparked and popped. He'd never had anyone in to check that out. In truth, he'd never managed to save up enough money to hire an electrician.

That seemed foolish in retrospect.

It nearly cost him and Steve their lives.

When the second ambulance arrived, they tried taking Steve away. Deacon and Steve began to protest being taken away from one another, but the paramedic assured them they'd both be going to the same hospital.

That didn't settle Deacon down, but he was unfortunately in no condition to argue. He was terrified that something would happen, that he'd never see Steve again if they took him away. He tried to get up again, and the lady EMT got into his face.

She was calm and collected, able to see he was sincerely distressed, which made him begin coughing again.

"Hey, look at me, sir." She snapped her finger in his face until he did as she asked. "Everything's going to be fine, all right?"

His eyes flicked briefly toward the fire burning behind her, and she cringed slightly.

"You and your friend are both going to be okay, but you need to remain calm. You've inhaled a lot of smoke and fumes, and we need to get you to the hospital now."

He nodded, taking one last look at Steve who was being helped into the back of the second ambulance. Deacon acquiesced and followed suit. He climbed up and got onto the stretcher, where the paramedic helped him lie back, strapping him in. A second EMT was shooing a couple of cops away who were asking to interview Deacon, saying something about a witness seeing someone flee the scene just before the fire broke out.

The back doors closed, and moments later, the ambulance was on the move, sirens blaring. The lady kept telling him how lucky he was, but Deacon felt anything but. He had a sick feeling in the pit of his stomach as the cops' words continued to ramble around inside his head. Deacon found himself hoping it was a hate crime as opposed to the other option—that someone he knew had tried to kill him in his sleep. It was a short list, if that was the case, and only one glaringly obvious suspect.

Even that didn't seem like it could be real.

That Gale might hate him enough to do that?

He found himself clutching the woman's hand, holding it over his heart like that might shield him from any further pain or injury. She didn't appear to mind. Deacon shut his eyes and concentrated on breathing. It was the only thing he could control in that moment, and he realized that was going to have to be enough.

EPILOGUE ~ SEPTEMBER

Deacon walked into the house, wrestling the bags filled with groceries that he'd brought home from work. Thus far, it was all Steve had allowed him to pay for, which while much appreciated on some level, was quickly becoming a point of contention between them. Deacon wanted a partnership, not a free ride, but had decided not to go in with both guns blazing every time he didn't like something.

His new therapist pointed out that he had a tendency toward snap judgments and making unilateral decisions without consulting others—which he immediately decided was complete bullshit. It was somewhere during his inner-rant that immediately followed her insane observation, whilst deciding he'd simply have to find a new therapist, that it dawned on Deacon that she might be onto something.

He didn't particularly enjoy going to a head-shrinker. The idea of a total stranger shoveling her way through all the crap he'd spent his entire life attempting to bury? It didn't feel like a productive use of his time. Mrs. Garibaldi told him the fact that he didn't like it meant it was good for him.

It was in that precise moment that Deacon decided women were nuts.

Of course, the damage had now been done, no matter how hard he tried not to think about it, Deacon found himself looking back and examining his actions over the past eight years. Every single life-changing decision he'd made had been done quickly, with little or no thought to any possible consequences whatsoever.

The fight with his mother when Patty wished he was dead? That same night he'd packed his belongings and moved to Chicago.

Why Chicago? No clue.

He'd hopped into his crappy beat-up Ford Escort, which was falling apart at the seams at the time, filled up the gas tank and left town—never to return.

His relationship with Seth was another biggie. He recognized now that he'd never particularly cared for Seth as a person, so why go out with him, let alone move in with the bastard?

Was Seth good looking? Sure, but that wasn't the reason.

Was he good in the sack? Um, yeah…but again, still not the reason.

When Deacon really stopped and thought about all the events that had led up to him moving in with Seth, Deacon began to see it was yet another reactionary decision based on his fears of being alone due to that stint in the hospital with pneumonia—when not a single soul had come to visit him.

That had frightened him into action.

At the time, he'd convinced himself it was no big deal, but in reality, the experience had scared him far more than actual illness—he'd been so sick that he thought he might die for a couple of days there, and he wasn't alone. One of the nurses told him after the fact that it had been touch and go—even the doctors hadn't been sure he was going to make it.

Less than a month after getting out of the hospital, he'd met and moved in with Seth.

Picking up Steve in a bar after another horrible fight with his mother, not to mention getting viciously dumped by Seth? Another decision made with little to no thought.

His decision to move back here for Ashley? It had been the right thing to do, but Deacon was no longer sure if he'd truly thought about the consequences. He'd just sat in that hospital room looking at his unconscious monster of a mother and decided to do it.

The one thing he'd not run toward recklessly, despite the fact he'd wanted to, was calling Steve after moving back to Detroit. He'd had his business card. Deacon thought about calling every day, wanted to see Steve again—but something made him stop each time he went to pick up the phone.

Something had happened between them in that hotel room that first night.

Something more than just sex.

On some level, Deacon had been aware of that fact, and it spooked him.

Going out with Steve had been his one truly anti-reactionary decision. He wasn't convinced he'd have ever contacted Steve had they not run into one another by accident. That's how potent that first night together had been. Whether consciously or not, on some level, Deacon knew that Steve was going to be one of those life-altering experiences—the sort that had the potential to rip him into shreds should he try and fail. The couple of weeks they'd spent apart had been torturous—proof enough of that.

He finished putting the last of the groceries in the fridge and hung the recyclable bags onto the hook on the back of the laundry room door. The house was blissfully quiet, a rare thing as of late. Deacon strolled into the den and flopped down on the sofa. He needed to go for a run but was enjoying the serenity too much to leave it. He closed his eyes and smiled, sighing at the silence.

The insanity of the past weekend had taken its toll on Deacon's nerves, though Steve seemed to be thriving in the chaos. They had Kylie for the entire weekend for the first time. Clarissa was off for a romantic weekend with a new guy she'd started dating. On top of that, Deacon had made an insane error in judgment by telling Ashley that Mel could spend the night. Of course, that had been before he knew they would have Kylie—something Clarissa sprung on them last minute.

"Girls are soooo noisy," he mumbled to himself.

The X-box, Dance Party shenanigans from the night before accompanied a myriad squeals, screams and giggley-good fun had Deacon craving a Xanax. He'd never taken a Xanax, mind you, so he wasn't sure what benefits it might carry, but by the time he and Steve crawled into bed, they'd barely managed a peck on the lips before Deacon was out cold.

"Not even a little sucky-sucky," he muttered, rubbing at his crotch. "That's messed up."

His eyes popped open, hearing a car horn and screaming coming from somewhere off in the distance. It continued getting louder and louder, and Deacon faux-wept, positive that the destination of the incoming chaos was where he now sat.

"One more day," he said, getting up off the sofa and heading through the house toward the front door. "All that honking is going to piss off the neighbors."

He stepped out onto the porch as a red Mini-Cooper with a white top and white racing stripes along the hood turned into the drive. Deacon's mouth fell open, seeing Ashley behind the wheel with Kylie and Mel squealing like mad from the backseat. The car was barely in park before Ashley flew out of the driver's side and jumped into Deacon's arms, squeezing the fucking life out of him.

He was choking and laughing as Ashley said *thank you*, over and over again. Steve was laughing as he got out of the passenger seat and walked around the front of the car. The man practically oozed guilt, despite all the good cheer. The instant Ashley let go of Deacon, Steve grabbed hold of him and began mimicking Ashley's behavior, screaming Thanks yous in a high pitched girly voice. Deacon was trying to politely push him off as he was now completely embarrassed, but Steve was stronger than he was and the girls were all laughing hysterically.

Steve was cracking himself up, and hearing Kylie's belly-laughs from the backseat of the car was making Deacon chuckle.

Deacon smacked him in the gut when he finally did let go, and Steve gasped, his eyes going cross-eyed as he prat-fell onto the lawn like something out of The Three Stooges, pretending to be gasping for air.

"Steve gave it to me this afternoon," Ashley gushed, her cheeks flushed with pink from all of the excitement. "It's so pretty, Deacon, don't you just love it?"

He glanced down at Steve who winked up at him from the lawn where he still lay, puckering up like he was expecting the kiss of life to come at any moment. Deacon stepped right over his faux-corpse and walked over to the car to peek inside. Mel was crawling out of the back and getting into passenger side seat.

"We're gonna go get ice cream," Kylie announced with nearly

as much gusto as Ashley had gushing over the car.

"You want to come?" Ashley asked, all but forcing Deacon out of the way in order to get back behind the wheel.

"No, thank you," Deacon said, stepping aside to keep from being smacked by the door. "I need to have a little chat with Stevie."

He could hear Steve's rumbling laugh coming from somewhere behind him.

"Okay, we'll bring you back something," Mel called out as Ashley backed the car out of the drive, and they drove away, once again squealing and screaming at the top of their lungs.

Deacon turned to find Steve smiling sheepishly, still laughing as he climbed the steps to the porch and went inside.

You can run, asshole, but you can't hide.

* * * *

Deacon found Steve in the kitchen, rummaging through the cold cuts in the fridge. He was visibly pleased with himself and making no effort to pretend otherwise. That irked Deacon to no end.

"You bought her a new car?"

He sighed, tossing a rolled up piece of salami into his mouth while saying, "It was a trade-in, so technically not a new car, but I had the boys work it over. Car's in great shape, a little under forty thousand miles."

"I can't believe you'd do something like that without consulting me first."

"You would've said no," Steve pointed out, still grinning.

"Damn right," Deacon said. "It's too much."

"Says who, babe?" Steve asked, looking around the room at his invisible posse who apparently had his back on this one. "She's had a rough time of it lately. Hell, we all have. Damn it, Deacon, her father tried to kill us in our sleep. He burned down the only home she's ever known. Your mom's in jail—"

"Where she belongs," Deacon reminded him.

"All I'm saying is, I think she deserves to feel special, don't you?"

Deacon sighed, wiping his face with the palm of his hand, his mind racing over the events of the past month and a half. On the one hand, it was good that Gale had set the fire because it got Deacon off the hook, initially believing it had been his fault. But explaining it to Ashley hadn't been fun, even though she'd never had much of an actual relationship with her father, to know he'd burned down her home and nearly killed her brother wasn't the kind of news Deacon would've ever wished on his baby sister.

The police had arrested Gale a few days after the fire. Fortunately, one of the neighbors had been parked in a car on the street, making out with her boyfriend, coming home late after a long date. They'd each gotten a good look at Gale fleeing the scene only minutes before the fire broke out.

"This is her senior year of high school, Deacon, and we have the opportunity to make it an awesome year that she'll never forget. It's all you've ever said you wanted for her, remember?"

"Giving her a car isn't a requirement for that to happen, Steve."

"That's true, but I'm in a unique position to do this for her, so let me, *please*."

"Like I can say no at this point, you bastard."

"She's a good girl, and I just wanted to show her that life comes with the good, not just the bad, you know?"

"Why are you so damn good?" Deacon asked, shaking his head.

He shrugged. "I may have also used the car to bribe her into to giving therapy a shot, so not completely altruistic of me."

"That's horrible!"

Steve laughed, not appearing bothered in the least. "If she doesn't like it, so be it, but at least this way she'll have to try it before knocking it."

"I'm pretty sure it doesn't work like that." Deacon shook his head, a little disgusted.

"And FYI, my mother is now insisting we all come over for dinner next week," Steve said, licking his fingers and shaking his head when Deacon began to fidget. "She wants to apologize, that's all. It would be really nice if you'd stop stalling and allow her to do that."

"I can't believe you told her I eavesdropped on your conversation to begin with." Deacon was mortified. "But tell me where and when, and I'll be there."

They each stood there, staring at one another for a moment.

"That's really good salami," Steve said, laughing when Deacon rolled his eyes. "We've got a small window of time before the giggle-girls get back. Wanna fool around?"

Deacon started laughing as Steve wiggled his eyebrows and rubbed his crotch.

"Sure, why not," Deacon said.

"Don't strain anything by getting too excited over the prospect, *sheesh*. You sure know how to make a man swoon."

"A little preachy coming from Mister Wanna-fool-around."

Steve unbuttoned and unzipped his jeans. "Hey, that was a step up, baby, initially I was planning to go with 'wanna taste my salami?'"

"Mmm, always a crowd pleaser," Deacon said, watching as Steve pulled his dick out of pants, stroking it.

He was already licking his lips as he dropped to his knees. There wasn't a single fiber of his being that didn't believe that this was exactly where he belonged. Well, not exactly with regard to the down on his knees part, although he had zero doubts that he'd been put on the Earth to suck dick, as well.

But the being with Steve part, that was the one sure thing Deacon had going for him. Not that it was going to be all sunshine and roses, mind you. They were going to have a Come-to-Jesus or two along the way.

"Ah Jesus," Steve whispered as Deacon sucked him all the

way down to the root.

Deacon tried not to chuckle over the timing, which wasn't difficult with Steve's hard-on crammed down his throat.

He knew he loved Steve with his whole heart, body and soul, good habits and bad. Deacon had never been one of those 'find your other half' kinda guys. He'd always wanted to find love, to find a man who might be willing to return that love, but Deacon was fairly certain there hadn't ever been a time before when he truly believed it would happen for him.

"Suck my cock with that dirty little mouth," Steve muttered, taking Deacon by the back of his head and fucking his face.

What guy in his right mind wouldn't enjoy encouragement like that?

Deacon groaned his approval, and Steve's legs began to shake, a sure sign that he was getting close.

The explosion of cum in the back of Deacon's throat followed by Steve's body-twitching and screams of approval made Deacon feel as if he'd finally accomplished something productive with his day.

"Baby, that was hot," Steve said breathlessly while pulling Deacon up to his feet and planting a wet, hot kiss on his mouth. He was fumbling with Deacon's fly, trying to get to the goods. "Sorry I didn't ask you about the car," Steve said between kisses. "It was a shit move."

Deacon groaned his agreement, toes already curling as Steve fisted his erection.

"Shut the fuck up and blow me," Deacon said, pushing a now grinning Steve down to his knees.

Deacon's eyes rolled back into his head as Steve slowly and torturously apologized with his mouth and tongue… his sweet, full lips. That hot, wet mouth on his cock had Deacon believing he'd found Heaven right here on Earth.

"Fuck yeah," Deacon muttered, which had Steve picking up the pace.

As he raced toward an inevitable orgasm, Deacon allowed

everything else to fall away, concentrating fully on the sights, sounds and sensations around him. This was going to be his life from this point forward—fighting, fucking and maintaining a friendship with the man he loved. He might not know what else he wanted to do with the rest of his life, but Deacon knew he intended to spend it with Steve.

He called out, screaming Steve's name as he shot his load—vision blurring momentarily, his fingers digging into the very substantial muscles of Steve's shoulders.

"You taste so good," Steve said, finally standing back up after politely tucking Deacon's softening cock back inside his briefs and zipping his jeans back up.

They kissed again as Deacon struggled to get his wind back.

"I love sucking you off in the middle of the day," Steve muttered, his eyelids sort of fluttering dreamily as they finally separated. Deacon was rubbing Steve's chest and abs through the T-shirt, thinking he was ready for the full-monty and an intensely heated power-fucking.

"Later," Steve whispered, having apparently been able to read his exceedingly slutty thoughts. "After the girls have gone to bed, no matter how exhausted we are."

Deacon grinned. "That was pretty pathetic last night."

"Don't think I hadn't noticed either," Steve said, another soft kiss brushing over Deacon's lips. "We're supposed to still be in that honeymoon period, so passing out pre-sex is simply inexcusable."

"I was going to blame you and your old age, but I can't honestly recall who fell asleep first."

"You fell asleep first, shithead," Steve said, shaking his head as he went for the fridge and grabbed a bottle of water. "Next time, I'll fuck you anyway, unconscious or not."

Deacon laughed, readjusting himself in his jeans before snagging the water from Steve and taking a big gulp. "Something tells me I wouldn't have remained unconscious for long if you had, so I'll hold you to that."

They each stood there gazing at one another in silence until

Deacon finally said, "I love you."

Steve smiled, looking ever so sexy. "Right back at ya, gorgeous."

Deacon nudged his head toward the living room, and Steve followed him out to the couch where they both flopped down. Steve sighed, stretching until his back popped before relaxing into Deacon, who snuggled into the heat of Steve's body.

"You get your car back this week?"

Steve nodded, smiling at the thought. "The guys are finishing up the final touches over the weekend. I've really missed my baby."

Deacon laughed under his breath, then sighed his relief.

Steve's Mustang hadn't fared so well thanks to the fire. Deacon's Smart car had been parked in the detached garage and had remained unscathed, but the 'Stang had been parked outside right next to the house, and one whole side had been scorched as a result. Plus there had been damage to the body, some dents and scrapes received courtesy of the firemen during the process of putting out the blaze.

Deacon's stomach had dropped upon seeing it the first time, and Steve actually wept. Deacon had never felt worse; it was like Steve was mourning the loss of a limb.

Thankfully, there hadn't been any irreversible damage so once again, Deacon believed they had dodged another bullet. He was starting to believe that someone up there was finally watching over him, keeping those he loved safe from harm.

Steve took his hand and their fingers intertwined, leaning onto one another on the sofa and enjoying the quiet while it lasted. Deacon sighed, softly humming his happiness, content to stay just like this for however long he had left on this Earth. They weren't perfect by any means, both he and Steve still had a long way to go, but Deacon knew they were each committed to one another, so in truth, the only ones who could fuck things up were the two of them.

Deacon had found that thing he'd never realized he was actually even looking for—that safe harbor, his own personal

Northern Star, forever there shining brightly, showing him the way back home.

THE END

TRADEMARK ACKNOWLEDGEMENTS

The author acknowledges the trademark status and trademark owners of the following wordmarks mentioned in this work of fiction:

Academy Awards: Academy of Motion Picture Arts and Sciences

Band-Aid: Johnson & Johnson

Betty Crocker: General Mills

Brady Bunch: CBS Studios Inc.

Bud Light: Anheuser-Busch INBEV S.A.

Buick/Cadillac Series 60 Special/Corvette/Pontiac Firebird: General Motors LLC

Dance Party: Nintendo of America Inc.

Dancing with the Stars: The British Broadcasting Corporation

Disneyland: Disney Enterprises, Inc.

Encyclopedia Britannica: Encyclopedia Britannica, Inc.

Facebook: Facebook, Inc.

Formica: Formica Corporation

iTunes: Apple, Inc.

Jaguar XKE Series 1 Roadster: Jaguar Land Rover North America, LLC

JCPenney: J.C. Penney Corporation, Inc.

Jockeys: Jockey International, Inc.

Karmann Ghia: KGPR Inc.

Ken: Mattel, Inc.

Mini Cooper: BMW of North America LLC

Mustang/Escort: Ford Motor Company

Raiders of the Lost Ark: Lucasfilm Ltd.

Red Bull: RBNA Headquarters

Sapphire: Bacardi
Smart ForTwo: Mercedes-Benz USA, LLC
Solo: Solo Cup Company
Target: Target Brands, Inc.
TGIF: TGI Friday's Inc.
The Three Stooges: C3 Entertainment, Inc.
Toys R Us: Geoffrey, LLC
Twitter: Twitter, Inc.
Visa: Visa International Service Association
Xanax: The Upjohn Company
Xbox: Microsoft

ETHAN DAY

I am a gay man living in Missouri...I can hear the gasps already!! How very un-chic of me, yes I know. It was here I was born and here I have stayed. The youngest of four children and the only boy, I've always suffered from an extravagant fantasy life. When I played with my Star Wars action figures as a child, I liked to make up my own stories. Naturally, Luke Skywalker and Han Solo were totally meant for each other, and Princess Leia made a bitchin' wise-cracking Fag Hag.

I managed to survive high school living in a small, racist town in Southeast Missouri and emerged unscathed, realizing life was too short to pretend to be anything other than who I was. It was very Lifetime Movie Network meets After School Special, I assure you.

After several stints in college, I signed up for a Creative Writing course, choosing the class because there were no tests. For once my scholastic laziness paid off, and I found an outlet for all the fantasies running amuck inside my head. It was love at first write, and I've been doing it off and on ever since.

ALSO BY ETHAN DAY

Self Preservation
Dreaming of You
As You Are
At Piper's Point
Sno Ho
Life in Fusion
A Summit City Christmas
Anything for You
Second Time Lucky
A Token of Time
Love in La Terraza
To Catch a Fox
Zombie Boyz
Northern Star

CPSIA information can be obtained at www.ICGtesting.com
Printed in the USA
LVOW11s1546120914

403824LV00001B/20/P